"I STILL THINK it will not come here," a female voice said. "For weeks I've watched, and I've seen no sign of it. There isn't enough here to sate its hunger."

"There is enough just in the ranks of the staff," a male voice responded. "They've already called in a number of us. Who is to say there won't be more, and there may well be those in the student body who might be in danger still."

"But without magic . . . ," began the female voice.

"You know how hard we have tried to keep this place clean of it," he said. "But remember, we can't know about everything that is brought in as contraband. Who knows what attracts the Nothing to people? We have thrown some of our best mages at it, and at least three of them have paid for it with their lives. The Nothing is impervious to magic. What's more, it *feeds* on it. And the very worst of it is that I don't know how to guard against that."

WORLDWEAVERS

GIFT OF THE UNMAGE

·BOOK 1·

ALMA ALEXANDER

An Imprint of HarperCollinsPublishers

ACKNOWLEDGMENTS

My thanks to Jane Yolen—an inspiration even when her words are no more than a throwaway comment on a convention panel.

The usual thanks to the usual quarters—Jill, who made it happen; Ruth, who was the kind of editor writers dream of; the copyeditors who paid such close and detailed attention to the manuscript. And naturally, last but not least as always, to my first reader, strictest editor, and best friend who also happens to be my husband.

Eos is an imprint of HarperCollins Publishers.

Gift of the Unmage
Copyright © 2007 by Alma Alexander
All rights reserved. Printed in the United States of America.
No part of this book may be used or reproduced in any manner whatsoever without written permission except in the case of brief quotations embodied in critical articles and reviews. For information address HarperCollins Children's Books, a division of HarperCollins Publishers, 1350 Avenue of the Americas, New York, NY 10019.
www.harperteen.com

LIBRARY OF CONGRESS CATALOGING-IN-PUBLICATION DATA
Alexander, Alma. Gift of the Unmage / Alma Alexander.— 1st ed.
p. cm.— (Worldweavers ; 1)
Summary: As the seventh child born of the union of two seventh children, fourteen-year-old Thea has not fulfilled her parents' hope of having special magical powers, and they try a last, desperate measure before sending her to a school for those with no magical ability.
ISBN 978-0-06-083957-4
[1. Magic—Fiction. 2. Self-actualization (Psychology)—Fiction. 3. Fantasy.] I. Title.
PZ7.A3762Gif 2007   2006020123
[Fic]—dc22   CIP
                                                                              AC

Typography by Larissa Lawrynenko
❖
First paperback edition, 2008

The first book for Lea, the eldest

CONTENTS

WOLF MOON

1.

"YOU SMELL ANGRY," Aunt Zoë said as she walked in through the door, sniffing in Thea's direction like a hound dog scenting prey.

She was always coming up with things like that. Things like *The wind looks blue*. Or *That song was scratchier than a scouring pad!* Or telling someone that their purple dress was "loud," and meaning it quite literally. She heard things other people smelled, or saw things other people heard, or absorbed colors through the tips of her fingers.

Although she had been only three at the time, Thea vividly remembered the time that Zoë had said that the wind was blue. It might have been the first real, coherent memory that she could lay claim to. She had piped up with enthusiastic agreement, and had not failed to notice the immediate excitement her words had caused. What she had failed to understand at the time were the reasons behind that excitement, and had happily mimicked Aunt Zoë's strange ways on several occasions after that, seeking the approval that she had received the first time she had done it. But it had become all too obvious very quickly that she was merely saying the words, not experiencing them the way that Zoë did. The passing years had made Thea wiser. People had still been expecting great things of her when she was very young—anything she did, anything she said, might have a sign of the Double Seventh latency waking into its full potential. But it always fell flat, usually with someone sighing deeply, "Oh, *Thea.*" She'd been almost six years old before she realized that her full name was not, in fact, both those words.

"I'm just upset," Thea said to her aunt, kicking the edge of the couch with the heel of her free foot, the one she had not folded comfortably underneath her.

"Have they been at you again?"

Thea made a face. "They're *always* at me."

"What is it now?"

Thea gestured at the dining room table in the next room, where two objects rested amid an untidy heap of papers. One of them was a perfectly seamless metallic cube. The other was an irregularly shaped blob that may or may not have been made of the same material, and looked like something angular had tried and failed to hatch from a steel egg.

"What on earth is that?" Zoë said, fascinated.

"Ars Magica class assignment. We were supposed to turn the cube into the ball."

Zoë tore her eyes from the thing on the table and turned a sympathetic gaze on her niece. "Uh-oh. Did *you* do that?"

"You mean the blob? Nope. That was Frankie's effort. The cube . . . is mine."

The frustration and humiliation of an Ars Magica class were nothing new for Thea. The routine hardly ever varied—an assignment would be given, and then, at the end of the class, certain students would be invited to stay behind. Thea was invariably one of them; her brother Frankie, who was a year behind his peer group and known to be a klutz with anything magical, was another. But even Frankie could eventually do some part of the assignment, in however ham-fisted a way, while Thea could not even manage something that could be classified as a mistake. There would be others, whom Thea bitterly recognized as window dressing, who were there only to show that she was not singled out for anything—as though she could be fooled. The reactions of the others ranged from sympathy (from some who had to work harder at their own talents than the rest) to smoldering resentment for even being forced to sit in the same classroom as the two Winthrop siblings and being tainted by so much as being in their presence. Afterward in the cafeteria, one particularly vicious classmate had complained loudly about being forced to breathe the same air as Dunce and Idiot over there and how their ineptitudes were already eating at his own abilities.

"I can feel it," he had said in a mock-dolorous voice, his hand raised to his forehead in the manner of old television melodramas. "It's all fading, it's all going awaaaaaay. . . . This time tomorrow I'll be no more than a dumb 'dim, and my parents will disown me."

"Ah, I wouldn't worry," one of his henchmen said with a sly glance over at the other table where Thea sat by herself, with her hair hanging over her face to hide her flaming cheeks. "Their parents still love them, wouldn't you know. . . ."

It only became worse when Thea and Frankie brought their Ars Magica transformations back home that day. Thea had produced hers with a sinking heart, without raising her head to meet her father's eyes.

"What was it?" Thea's mother had asked.

"That," Thea muttered. "It was the cube."

"What was it supposed to *be*?" asked Anthony, the oldest brother. It was a Friday, he was home from college for the weekend and full of more than his usual smug self-importance.

Thea muttered something under her breath.

"What?" Anthony said.

"Oh, *Thea*," Frankie said. He produced his own effort, half cube, half shapeless blob. "It was supposed to be . . ."

"Well, not *that*," Anthony said with a chuckle.

"A ball," said Frankie defiantly. "It was supposed to be a ball."

"You mean like this one?" Anthony had picked up Thea's untransformed cube and had been turning it over in his fingers; now he passed his other hand over it, murmuring a single word, and he was suddenly holding a smooth metal sphere that sat on his palm like an accusation.

Thea grabbed for it. "Give it back! That was mine!"

"Oh," Anthony said, "okay." He passed his hand over it again before she had a chance to snatch it, and it was back in cube form.

"*Anthony,*" Paul murmured, in a halfhearted reproof.

"Show-off," Thea snarled, still avoiding looking at her father, her fingers curling around her cube as though she wanted to throw it. "When I get to University—"

"You won't," Anthony said. "Not at this rate."

"You wait! When I get to Amford—"

"You can't go to Amford," said Frankie. His words fell into the conversation like stones into a pond. Ripples of things that did not need to be said followed them into the silence. *You can't go to Amford, Thea. Amford is the University of Magic. You can never go to Amford, Thea. You can never . . .*

Not even Paul could gainsay that one.

Thea stared at her hand, willing her fingers to uncurl from around the unforgiving cube. Then she very carefully put it down on the dining room table and walked away.

She had meant to stalk off into her room and slam the door, but somehow she didn't have the energy to move any farther than the living room couch, where she sat and stared out of the window until her aunt came into the room.

Now Zoë was staring at the dining room table. "Frankie's supposed to finally graduate to the advanced class next year," she said thoughtfully. "They deal with living things there." She was looking at the mangled thing that Thea had called the blob, and it was clear that she was seeing some poor rat or lizard half-turned into a human ear by Thea's ham-fisted older brother. "Is he in trouble?"

"Not nearly as much as me," Thea muttered.

"Oh, *Thea.*"

Thea jumped up from the couch. "Don't you start! I've been hearing that all day. Even Frankie did the oh-Thea thing, and look at what *he* brought home." She rubbed at her nose with the back of her hand in a faintly reflective manner, as though she was using the gesture to help her think. "Maybe I was adopted."

"Don't be silly," Zoë said, and sniffed again.

"You're a miserable little thing today, aren't you? The very air in this room smells brown and shriveled, and it's all your fault. It's nice and crisp out—you want to go out for a walk? And tell me the rest of it? You'll feel much better if you get it off your chest, you know. Maybe I can help."

"Get what off my chest?" Thea said suspiciously.

"Thea, darling, you are prickly with secrets; I can feel them coming out of you like a porcupine's quills. You're upset about something that your parents haven't told you openly—you've been eavesdropping again. I can always tell, you know."

"I don't . . . ," Thea began indignantly, but just then a door closed loudly, and she threw a quick calculating glance that way and then nodded at Zoë with suspicious eagerness. "On second thought, I'd like that. A walk would be good."

"Just taking Thea out for a wander!" Zoë called out over her shoulder. "Grab your jacket and run," she whispered into Thea's ear, as she shepherded her niece out the door. "If they don't see you, they can't stop you."

Zoë was the kind of aunt who was less than

beloved by responsible parents. She was a con-
spirator with errant children, with a fine disre-
gard for rules and the charm to talk herself back
into everyone's good graces afterward. She was
perfectly aware of the crisis brewing in the
Winthrop household, centering—once again—
upon her fourteen-year-old niece, the child upon
whom so many hopes had been hung on the day
of her birth that Zoë sometimes wondered how
she had managed to grow up at all under the
weight of them.

The Double Seventh—the most magical of the
magical, the seventh child born of the union of
two seventh children.

The newborn Thea had made the newspapers
on the day that her mother, Zoë's older sister
Ysabeau, left the hospital. Then, it had all been
pure excitement—Zoë remembered the smell of
the air on that morning, sharp and bright like
electricity, the precious bundle cradled in her sister's arms. The baby—Galathea Georgiana, as
Ysabeau informed the waiting press with the air
of having named a crown princess—had resented
the hubbub that had greeted her arrival, and the
massive concerted flash of the photographers'
cameras had been too much. The front-page

photograph of the Double Seventh child had shown a bundle of dark blue baby blanket with stars on it wrapped around a small, tightly scrunched-up face that, at that moment, seemed to be mostly mouth.

"She has her father's gums," her paternal grandfather had commented irritably when the newspaper had found its way to him. "I suppose now that she's famous she'll grow up to be a little spoiled brat."

And for a while it looked like Thea might do just that.

The photograph and the accompanying front-page article had been placed in the Thea Book (all the Winthrop children had a scrapbook devoted to them)—Ysabeau had a fondness for the photo, even if only because she believed that it had been an unusually good likeness of herself. But Thea's scrapbook, started from the outset with a rush of hope and anticipation in a notebook much thicker than most of the ones devoted to her brothers, had remained disappointingly barren of material. Zoë had once told Ysabeau that she had never seen another single thing that smelled so much of despair.

Thea's thoughts were still mutinous as she and

Zoë made their way down the street, leaving their dark footprints in the thin layer of snow on the ground. She was not aware that she had been stomping ahead on her own, leaving her aunt behind, until Zoë's whistle brought her up sharply. She stopped, turned her head, and realized that her aunt was waiting a couple of hundred feet back.

"Over here," Zoë said. "We'll take the trail."

"But you usually can't get through there after it's snowed," Thea said.

"There are always ways," said Zoë mysteriously.

Thea, her hands jammed into the pockets of her anorak, trudged back to her aunt's side, her face thunderous. "Aunt Zoë, if you want me to practice any warming spells, you know what comes next. Anthony would give you a perfect spring day. Frankie would make it hot enough to grow bananas or else he'd turn you into a human icicle. Me, I am just going to do a whole lot of concentrating and then nothing will happen. As usual."

"You *do* have it bad," Zoë murmured. "Let me do the spells, hon. Just come this way. The road just smells too hard, I need earth beneath my feet."

They turned off the road, ducking into a

hardly discernible gap between bare-branched bushes that, in the summer, might have been a blackberry thicket. Beyond them the underbrush thinned as taller trees, cedars and Douglas firs, started to tower above the narrow path. There was snow on the ground, but less than Thea had thought there would be. Whether that was due to the heavy evergreens or because Zoë's warming spells were working, Thea didn't know, but it was quite pleasant to walk through the woods in the crisp cool January day. Thea fought to hold on to her funk, but the winter air worked its icy fingers into the snarls of her temper, loosening them until all she still carried was a kind of detached bleakness.

Zoë waited until she finally smelled the change of mood in Thea, and then turned her head fractionally to smile down at her niece.

"All right," she said. "Want to talk about it now?"

"Dad's eyes," Thea said.

This was the sort of shortcut verbal telepathy that Zoë could follow with the ease of one linked by blood kinship. She nodded.

"Yeah, I can see that. Was it when the Ars Magica blobs came in?"

"He's used to Frankie being a ham-fisted idiot," Thea burst out. "He's repeating this year of school, after all. When the . . . *blob* . . . came in, Daddy just sighed and rolled his eyes. But with me . . . with me . . . every time I fail . . ."

"He keeps believing in you," Zoë said gently.

"I don't know," Thea said. "I'm not sure if it isn't just that he wants to keep believing in me. And every time I muck something up, it's like I do it deliberately, just to hurt him. I saw his face when the last reports came in from school. It doesn't matter that I'm top of the class in math or in two different foreign languages. He turned straight to the Ars Magica report card and, well, you know what it said."

"No," said Zoë.

"What it usually says," Thea said, kicking a stone on the path with the toe of her boot. "That I'll never amount to anything. That I can't do the simplest thing that any toddler can do. That any *newborn* can do. I—can't—do—*anything*!" Thea punctuated the last sentence by sharp little blows of her fists against her legs. "And then, the sphere . . ."

"Tell me about the sphere."

"It was an exercise, as simple as that. We were

13

supposed to take the cube and turn it into that sphere, just as Anthony did it. Everyone else managed it, pretty much, although it took some of them half an hour to get it right. They kept me back when the class left—they always do it—'Keep trying,' they said, and just sat there and pretended not to watch me. . . . Aunt Zoë, it's like there's this *wall* and I can feel it right there in front of me and it's cold and tall and completely impossible to get around. And I'm on *this* side of it, and the cube is on *that* side, and that's all there is to it. I could have sat there until the middle of next week and it wouldn't have helped."

"I know it's upsetting," Zoë said, "but that isn't what's really bugging you. I'm guessing you brought the whole mess home and then went and listened at keyholes again, my dear child."

Thea threw her a defiant glance. "How else am I supposed to know?" she demanded. "Anthony would simply have used a spy spell. But I can't. I'm useless. I'm completely pathetic."

"You are most certainly not so. You—"

"In fact," Thea continued doggedly, as though Zoë hadn't spoken at all, "I'm so totally hopeless that they're sending me to the Last Ditch School for the Incurably Incompetent."

Zoë's head came up sharply. "What?"

"I heard them talking about it in the kitchen." Thea sniffed, her eyes full of sudden tears. "They said . . . th-they said they would let me finish out the year in my own class, and then they are sending me . . . sending me . . . somewhere, I didn't quite get that. Somewhere, in the summer, for someone to give me private lessons, or whip me into shape, or something. And if they can't—if I fail even at that—then I have to leave the school, and go to *that place.*"

"Which place?" Zoë asked, honestly confused.

Thea shrugged her shoulders with a violence that threatened to rip seams in her anorak. "You know. *That* place. The only school anywhere that has absolutely no Ars Magica in the curriculum."

"The Wandless Academy?" Zoë said, raising her eyebrows. "They're thinking about sending you there?"

"The Last Ditch School," Thea said stubbornly, clinging to her own definition.

"Thea, it's hardly that bad . . . ," Zoë began, in tones of sweetest reason, but Thea was not in the mood to be reasonable.

"Uh-huh," Thea grunted. "And then everyone can breathe a sigh of relief. It's the scrap heap of everything magical, Aunt Zoë. It's the place where they send those who will *never* amount to anything, just so that they can get enough of a mundane education to be able to do something for a living. And now I'm supposed to go there. And I'll have that stuck to me all my days. The one who failed. The one who sucked at things so badly that even her own parents washed their hands of her. And Anthony is going to sit there in his dorm room at Amford University, studying for his high thaumaturgy degree or whatever it is that he's doing these days, and he's going to *smirk* at me for the rest of my life."

"Do you have any idea as to who's supposed to be 'whipping you into shape'?" Zoë asked.

"I'm not sure," Thea said. "I just heard them talking. Why?"

"It might not be so bad, depending on whom they choose," Zoë said. "You've done such things before, you know. Like Madame Bellaria, for example, or last year, when—" She closed her mouth with a snap.

Thea looked up. "What?"

Zoë bit her lip. "Nothing."

"No, what?" Thea said, her blood thoroughly up. "Madame Bellaria taught me the violin, or at least tried to until they figured out I just didn't have the perfect pitch that was required, and last year . . . What do you mean?"

"Well . . . ," Zoë said unwillingly. She didn't want to lie, not baldly, and yet giving Thea any kind of hard-to-take truth right now wasn't going to help. "Let's just say that Bellaria is a Chanter Mage as well as a competent violinist, and that was the year you sang yourself to sleep every night, and they thought that music magic might be your path. And last year, when they sent you to stay with your Aunt Sarah . . . you know your Uncle Adam is a Class One mage, don't you? And he did spend a lot of time with you that summer."

Thea stared at her. "They never said anything to me," she said. "Although it makes sense now that Uncle Adam made me practice incantations every night before bedtime. He said it would help me . . . sleep." Her expression became thunderous again. "Nothing happened, of course," she said. "Maybe, if they'd told me what they were doing . . ."

"There are plenty of people out there who do

private lessons, as it were, and some of them are a lot of fun," said Zoë gently.

"Some fun," Thea said. She captured a stray strand of hair with the corner of her mouth and chewed on it furiously. "They tried it the cheating way and obviously it didn't work. Now they're going to make me go to slave camp. You know what it's going to be like. It's going to be a whole wretched summer of frying my brain trying to make cubes turn into spheres or levitate stones. And the cubes are going to stay cubes, and the stones are going to stay firmly on the ground, and then I'll come home from wherever it is that I've been, and Dad's eyes . . ."

"I'll talk to your folks," Zoë said. "I'll see what I can find out, okay? I'll come back and tell you. In the meantime . . ."

Thea shot her another mutinous look. "What?"

"It might be an idea to try extra hard for the rest of the school year," Zoë said. "If you manage to keep your Ars Magica teachers placated with just small things, they may let you . . ."

"No, Aunt Zoë," Thea said bleakly. "Mom and Dad won't let that happen. It was okay for Frankie to repeat a year—but not me. Never me.

They won't let them hold me back. Frankie merely sucks at it. With me . . . it's different. There's a point to prove. I can either do it big like I'm supposed to, or they'll make sure I don't do anything at all. It's all magic or no magic for me. I'm a Double Seventh; if I fail, I totally fail. I can't be a flicker—I must be a bonfire, or I must be out. . . ."

"Thea," Zoë began, a little alarmed, but Thea extracted a hand from her anorak pocket, pushed her wayward hair back behind her ears, and tossed her head. The gesture appeared almost angry, but when she looked up again her eyes were full of tears and there was so much misery on her face that Zoë bit her lip and simply gathered the girl into her arms. Thea clutched at her aunt's anorak collar with both hands and wept into her shoulder.

"Daddy's eyes," she sobbed. "I can't come home again and look into Daddy's eyes. . . . I swear, Aunt Zoë, I'd rather *die* than make him go in and have to tell everyone that he's finally given up all hope in his oh-so-special daughter. . . . I can't *help* it, I want to do well, I want to do well so badly. . . ."

"I know, hon. I know."

Zoë rocked Thea against her, letting her cry herself out.

2.

As it happened, Zoë knew exactly what Thea meant. There was something in Paul Winthrop's eyes when he looked at his youngest—there was hope and frustrated love and bitter disappointment he tried very hard to hide but sometimes didn't quite manage to tuck in behind his usual screen of calm acceptance. Zoë could remember that hope and a fierce pride that had burned in those eyes on the day that Thea had been born—one could even catch a glimpse of it in that famous front-page photograph that had started the Thea Book as he stood beside his wife and their squalling bundle of potential glory.

He had still been a Howler man then—a trained tamer of feral libraries gone wild in the wake of a carelessly uttered word or phrase. Grimoires were temperamental books, sometimes with a life of their own, unpredictable and often dangerous; they were usually kept well apart from the main part of any library, but even so accidents happened every so often and the consequences could be dire. An ill-chosen word, a set of syllables that somehow fit into some arcane spell, that was all it took—and it was almost impossible to keep a tight guard on one's tongue every moment of every day. Allowed to drop too close to a grimoire that had its "ears" tuned to that particular combination, such utterances would accidentally release ill-focused and sometimes downright malicious spells and cantrips into the world.

Zoë remembered the first time she had met Paul. She had been visiting the remnants of one such library as a sophomore in high school—her teacher had taken her whole Ars Magica class out to the warded building, under the protection of a Class Two mage, for the students to experience firsthand the repercussions of magic gone bad.

The first thing that greeted them, carefully pointed out by the teacher, was a gargoylelike face newly warped into what had been a perfectly ordinary door when the class had arrived at the library. It looked frozen in an expression of pure defiance, only its eyes mobile, following the class with a malevolent glare as they had filed past it—and that had been just the beginning.

There had been a lot of whispering and pointing as they crowded in. Most libraries had a back section carefully watched over by its own reference librarians, a place where books related to magic and spells were kept, and where the presence of neophytes or unsupervised students was frowned upon. Not many of the students in this particular class had even been allowed near those stacks. The rumors and weighty warnings that surrounded them like a miasma of peril were actually visible to someone like Zoë, a purple fog in which things rumbled and flashed dangerously like rolling lightning in a thundercloud. She had always had a healthy respect for that particular section in any library.

But now there was a patina of that purple, a ghostly echo of it, everywhere. The entire interior of the library was one bizarre thing after another: peacocks with human faces flitting in between the stacks, an odd sort of whimpering coming from the forbidden bookshelves in the back, a strange flickering in distant corners. The walls had been upholstered in striped wallpaper, and whole sections of vertical stripes had braided themselves into complicated designs, turned into leering faces with eyes that followed the visitors around the place with unnerving concentration, or had shredded themselves into smaller pieces that were trying hard to form themselves into writing. Zoë and one of her classmates had seen a particular wallpaper stripe detach from the rest, curl into a circle, extrude eight spindly legs, drop to the floor, and start scuttling down the carpet toward the girls' feet. The classmate had been unable to suppress a small scream; the shepherd mage had turned to deal with the problem, but before he could do anything a man simply stepped out of the wall and squashed the stripe-spider with his shoe.

"Not to worry," he said cheerfully. "They can't hurt you. Not anymore. The place is warded against mischief, and all that remains is to shut it all down. I'm working on it."

"I thought you were done, Paul," Zoë's teacher had said, a little sharply. "I wouldn't have brought the children if I'd known you were still working on it."

"Nearly done," Paul said, and actually winked at Zoë.

Her lips parted in a smile, and she dropped her eyes. She was fifteen years old, and he was dark-haired, bright-eyed, and devastatingly handsome.

"Just don't go into the back of the stacks," Paul said to the teacher, his manner brisk and businesslike again. "Anywhere else is fine. I left the elevators to the last, because they got rather creative. They're safe now, you might want to show the kids. I think they'd enjoy it."

Zoë's classmate, the one who had screamed, had looked up at Paul and simpered.

He merely caught Zoë's eye again, smiled, and waved a hand in the direction of the teacher. "Go ahead," he said. "I'll just be tying up a few loose ends in the back." Something scampered past the nearest set of shelves, and darted into the shadows. Paul whipped his head around. *"HEY!"* he bellowed. "Come back here!"

He loped off after the intruder, and Zoë's simpering classmate's smile broadened into simple adoration. "Isn't he something!" she said in a small breathless voice. "That's Paul Winthrop. My father was in the same class at Amford with his dad. We know the family—seven sons, he's the youngest—and they're all flat-out gorgeous. . . ."

"Don't you ever think about anything else?" Zoë had snapped.

Paul had been right about the elevators—the

class had spent a hilarious half hour riding up and down the chatty pair of elevator cars that had acquired the personalities of bickering four-year-olds. They'd snatch at passengers with a sulky "Mine!" and made people promise on a ride up that they wouldn't take the other elevator down, and then whimper in an injured manner if people broke their word. They could be effectively distracted by singing a nursery rhyme in the elevator car, or by any sentence that started with "Once upon a time." The shepherd mage opined that this was what came of having a children's section of the library opposite the elevators; and the Ars Magica class teacher had suggested archly that the situation might have been far worse. By the time the class left the area, the elevators had degenerated into telling each other knock-knock jokes on the top floor, and then falling down laughing all the way to the subbasement.

The second time Zoë had run into Paul Winthrop had been maybe a year later, when she'd tagged along with her older sister Ysabeau to an open lecture at Amford University. She had actually been pointing at him, telling Ysabeau about the occasion of the library visit, at precisely the moment that he'd turned around and happened to look at them. Scarlet with embarrassment, Zoë had wished that she could drop through the floor. But, incredibly, he had smiled, and then he'd come over, and somehow she wound up introducing her sister to the Howler man . . . and the next thing she knew she was carrying Ysabeau's flowers at her wedding, and everyone was talking about the marriage of the two seventh children and the glittering possibilities of their progeny.

Zoë wouldn't have wanted to swear to it, but despite the protestations on both sides that they'd simply fallen head over heels in love with one another both Ysabeau and Paul had decided to marry each other with a solid dose of clear-headed pragmatism.

The whole seventh-child thing was hardly a science. The purest combination of that would have meant the union of a seventh daughter and a seventh son and there would have been no eighth child (like Zoë) in either family to potentially mess up the bloodlines—this would have been practically guaranteed to produce a prodigy. But everyone felt it was close enough, and even this much was a rare event; while families with strong magical bloodlines produced the required seven children, the meeting and union of a seventh and a seventh didn't happen very often. So there was a lot of encouragement from both families when Paul and Ysabeau got together. The young couple's first child, a son, arrived less than a year after their marriage—and was doted on by everyone, as was only natural for a firstborn. But as the years passed and Ysabeau dutifully delivered son after son, it became increasingly obvious that it was something quite different that the pair were waiting for.

That something became flesh on the day that Galathea Georgiana was born. A child who should have been gifted beyond all dreams of power, as her weighty and sonorous name was meant to reflect. But somehow, over the years, the only magic that she had ever performed had been simply the transformation of her own person from the glittering Galathea so full of shimmering promise into the plain, solid, totally glitterless Thea. With not enough magic in her blood, apparently, to fill a thimble.

Thea had never been one to drown her troubles in an ocean of tears. She had given way in

the solitude of the woods, but then it was over—
and she extricated herself from Zoë's arms and
hunted in her pockets for a tissue.

Zoë produced one out of her own pocket,
keeping diplomatically quiet about its being no
more than pocket lint and thin air a moment
ago, and wiped her niece's nose in the businesslike manner a mother might use with a small
child.

"Aunt *Zoë*," Thea protested, grabbing at the
tissue and turning her head to get the nose out of
her aunt's way.

Zoë let go, smiling, and Thea blew her nose
and wadded up the tissue in her hand.

"I suppose we'd better go home," she said at
last.

"You sure? We can go down to the creek and
see what the falls are doing. . . ."

"I have to go home sometime," Thea said
pragmatically. "I live there. Besides, I forgot my
hat, and my ears are cold."

The instant they stepped into the house, they
heard Ysabeau's voice. "Zoë? Thea?"

At the summons Thea slipped out of her
anorak, leaving it in Zoë's hands, and sidled
down the corridor toward her room.

"You talk to them," she hissed back in Zoë's direction. "You *promised*."

Smiling a little crookedly, Zoë hung Thea's bright red anorak up beside her own forest-green one on the coat tree in the entrance hall, and followed the sound of her sister's voice.

"Hey," she said, strolling into the kitchen and opening the fridge door to peer inside. "Anything to eat around here? It's crisp out there and I've worked up an appetite."

"Where's Thea?" said Ysabeau, inclining her head toward the fridge. The door tugged itself out of Zoë's hand and shut with a small self-satisfied thud. "Supper is in an hour; you're welcome to stay if you want to, but I *wish* you wouldn't undermine us and just give in to all her whims."

"Me? Give in to Thea's whims? Thea has whims?" Zoë leaned against the fridge, crossing her arms. Her tone had been flippant, but her expression was very serious, and her next words confirmed that. "She's miserable, Ys. She's been listening at doors, probably, and hearing a lot of stuff she shouldn't have. She's drawing all kinds of conclusions, and feeling pretty awful about everything. She said you guys were planning on taking her out of school and transferring her to Wandless."

"We are," said Ysabeau shortly.

"What?" Zoë said. "I thought she had extrapolated that one. Are you serious? Has it really come down to that?"

"Zoë, what else are we to do?" Ysabeau turned her back on her sister, gripping the kitchen counter with both hands, her eyes suddenly brimming with tears. The bread dough that she had been rising with a quick incantation began to subside with a small sigh. "I can't bear to watch either of them anymore—Paul whenever the report cards come in, and Thea's face as she hands them to him. And we all know what they say. There's another exercise she hasn't completed or a transformation she hasn't done or a potion she's botched. We've done all we can. . . ."

"What's this about summer camp?"

"What summer camp?"

"She seems to be under the impression that she's going off somewhere to be mercilessly drilled in Ars Magica this summer," Zoë said.

"Not summer camp," Ysabeau said. "Paul called in a favor. We're trying something completely different. Maybe that will trigger whatever it is that's stuck."

"What?" Zoë asked.

"There's a letter," Ysabeau said, "in Paul's study. It's in the top drawer of his desk."

Zoë pushed off the fridge, took a step toward the kitchen door, and then appeared to change her mind about leaving. She reached out with her right hand instead, and a moment later a piece of handwritten parchment was in her palm.

"It wouldn't have killed you to have walked across the hall," Ysabeau said, staring at her dough in a meaningful fashion, but not unaware of what had just happened behind her back.

It had been a quick desperate rustle of shuffling feet outside the kitchen door that had decided Zoë against physically going to the study.

"Easier," Zoë said laconically, fingering the parchment. "I would have had to come back here and interrogate you about it anyway." She scanned the letter; it was only a handful of lines. *"Send her to me before Grass Moon wanes, else it will be too late to begin the work,"* she read. "Grass Moon? What is that? *When* is that? Who is this . . ." She skimmed down to the signature.

"Who is this Cheveyo guy anyway? Never heard of him."

"April, Paul says," Ysabeau said, slapping at the bread dough as though it had offended her. "Cheveyo is . . . It's complicated, Zoë. Paul hasn't told me everything. I do know that it isn't just a question of putting her on a plane to New Mexico—there's more to it than that. Paul says he'll have to take her himself. He didn't want me to know, but I saw an e-mail—he's been talking to the Thaumaturgy Agency about a Pass."

"A *Pass*?" Zoë echoed, staring at her sister. "Where is he taking her? To the . . . ?" She paused. "Ye Gods," she said finally.

Thea, she said fiercely in her mind, closely focused and aimed at her spying niece, *get back to your room right now. I promised to tell you, and I will, but I will not have you skulking out there and leaping to your own conclusions. I'm* serious, *Thea*.

There may have been no magic in Thea, but she could hear mindspeak, if the person talking to her was a member of her own immediate family. She had never really verbalized a reply in the same manner of communication, but she managed to respond well enough to convey her reaction to the mindspeaker's words. There was an echo of a grumble in reply to Zoë's rebuke, but Thea obeyed her aunt's instructions. Zoë sensed her withdrawing down the corridor and drew a deep breath.

"With all the troubles right now, with the Faele acting up and the Alphiri being all mysterious . . . ?" Ysabeau made a face at that, and Zoë raised her hands defensively, correcting herself. "Well, okay, more so than usual, for Alphiri, these days. Don't you read the papers? There's stuff going on on the borders right now that is certainly none of *our* doing, and there're rumors from the Senate about cutting back inter-polity trade, even. But that . . ."

"The longer we know the Alphiri, Paul says, the less we know about them," Ysabeau murmured.

"And thinking that, Paul is actually considering sending Thea to one of the other polities?" Zoë spoke in a low, intense voice. Thea might have pulled back from the keyhole but she still had perfectly good hearing and a better-than-usual facility for hearing her own name spoken.

"Don't think we haven't discussed it before," Ysabeau said, and Zoë's eyes widened in real shock. Ysabeau lifted her own eyes to meet Zoë's gaze levelly. "Think about it. She should have been born a mage, by all that's known of human magic. But nothing—not a spark, nothing at all. We tried the different kinds of known magic, hoping that she was simply specialized—but . . ."

"Bellaria and the violin lessons," Zoë murmured.

"And others," Ysabeau said with a heavy sigh. "When she was four or five we took her to Kitto out on the islands—we thought maybe colors, or painting . . . but she simply daubed a four-year-old's vision onto a blank page, and it was empty of magic. Then there was Bellaria, and the music; for a moment we thought there might have been something there, because she did seem to hear more things in the music than should have been there—but in the end, it didn't work out after all. We tried another handful of the specialized magics—Ilmo's water magic, an honest-to-goodness cauldron witch up in the mountains . . . even Sorcha and Seonaid."

"The Shapechangers?"

"They only had her for half a day—they liked her a lot, and they enjoyed having her around, but there was nothing in her that responded to that kind of transformation," Ysabeau said. "We're running out of options, Zoë."

"But—the Pass . . ."

"It isn't for any of the other polities," Ysabeau said. "From what we know of them, all that the Dwarrowim might be able to teach her is how to write stirring poetry. And there's always been enough trouble with the other two that I don't think even Paul is ready to turn his precious daughter over to the Faele, or the Alphiri—for all the interest the Alphiri have always shown in her. No, not the other polities."

"What, then? Who is this Cheveyo guy?"

Ysabeau tossed her head. "I'm not sure," she said at last, after a pause sharp enough that Zoë, with her own peculiar sensibilities, saw it shimmer into existence as a glowing neon-blue slash in the air between the two sisters. "Zoë, it isn't just a general travel visa. Paul doesn't need that anyway—he's got both the ability and the right contacts to cross polity borders, even to take others with him—a Pass is different. It's like having to get permission."

"Permission to do what?"

"I'm not sure, exactly. Permission to go . . . not where, but *when*. But he wouldn't tell even me the details of the whole thing—not everything."

"But you did some digging," Zoë said. She knew that defiant little twist to her sister's lip; it had been there since she was a child, every time she had gone against some grown-up's authority in pursuit of some purpose of her own.

"Some," Ysabeau said at last, almost unwillingly. "I have to say I am no longer sure who he's trying to save, his daughter or himself."

"*Who*, Ys?"

"I think it's a Time Pass," Ysabeau said slowly. "He's taking her *back,* Zoë. This Cheveyo . . . he's of a time long gone, a time when magic was much closer to the world, much stronger. I don't even know if Thea can handle that much primary magic—she's generations away from the rawness of it, the purity of it, and she's a *child*, Zoë. . . ." She paused, lifting one of her floured hands to push a strand of hair off her face in a gesture that suddenly twisted Zoë's heart because she had seen Thea make exactly the same gesture in the woods not an hour ago. Locking eyes with her sister, Ysabeau seemed unaware that her fingers had left a streak of flour on her temple and powdered her hair. There were many things in her gaze—uneasiness, frustration, real fear. "I can't be certain, but I think Cheveyo is of a people who have long been extinct in our world," she said. "He's Anasazi."

WHISPERING WIND MOON

1.

"WELL, THIS LOOKS like it, cookie," Paul Winthrop said as he brought the rented Chevrolet to a stop on the edge of an otherwise deserted road. The sun had barely gone down, but already the bright sunset was a memory and the sky was darkening into purple and an odd shade that was almost dark green.

Thea looked around, her arms crossed defiantly over her chest.

"There's nothing here," she said.

"Give it a moment," Paul said. He was edgy, ill at ease, both hands resting heavily on the steering wheel. One of them had fluttered as if wanting to reach out to his daughter, but then dropped back into place without completing the motion.

Thea felt an icy dagger of fear lodged in her heart. There was a time she would have run to her father for solace, but it was he who had brought her to this place. She felt an odd sense of betrayal. The little child in her wanted to clutch at his arm and ask why he didn't love her anymore. Her older self, however, was acutely aware that it had been love that had been behind the half-formed motion of his hand, love tempered by his need to protect her balanced against his frustration and disappointment about everything she almost was but had never quite managed to become. Her failings were somehow his failings, too, and he was desperate now, willing to try anything to awake her dormant gifts.

Zoë had kept her word and had briefed Thea on as much as she considered herself at liberty to tell her.

"I think that it might be a more exciting summer than you know," she had said, sitting on Thea's bed like a teenager, with her long jeans-clad legs crossed and silver rings glittering on every finger.

"I knew it. They're sending me to the Alphiri," Thea said.

"What? Where did you . . . ?"

"I *heard* it," Thea said stubbornly. "I heard Dad talking about the Alphiri, and a Gate—"

"Thea," Zoë interrupted sharply, "when will you ever learn that eavesdroppers hear no good of themselves? I *told* you to quit spying. They would tell you what you need to know."

"When?" Thea demanded.

"When you need to," Zoë said. She stared at Thea in a loving and helpless way; her heart was with her niece, but her loyalties were still, in matters of child rearing, with the adults in the family. "Don't worry, Thea. You *know* I've always been able to sense what you're thinking and feeling, even when you're far away. If I get any inkling that you're desperately unhappy or in trouble, I'll come and get you. Or make sure that somebody does. I promise."

But then January slipped into February, and things suddenly began to move far too fast. Something had happened, and almost overnight it was not summer being talked about anymore; only a handful of weeks after the episode with the untransformed cube, Thea found that everything was happening *right now*. With little warning, she was suddenly given a few tough exams at her school—as though she was being prepared for extra academic credits or being given a chance to make up work that she had missed . . . or would miss. Less than a week after she was done with those, Thea found her bag being packed. Her mother remained tight-lipped about her destination, but her simmering anxiety did not fail to register with Thea. By the time she and her father were finally alone together, they were in an airplane bound for Albuquerque, New Mexico, and her father seemed more inclined to treat her like a little girl and call her "cookie," a name he hadn't used since she was about four years old—and for some reason this sudden tenderness spooked Thea into silence.

Unable to broach the subject that scared her, she sank deeper into this fear of the unknown as Paul loaded her duffel bag into the back of the rented car and drove them into the back country. If she had not been so afraid of the immediate future, Thea was distantly aware that she would have found this place beautiful, particularly when the sun started going down and the rich golden light painted the hills and mesas improbable shades of orange and dark red. But she was too preoccupied to pay much attention, and then the sun was gone and darkness was falling.

Her father stopped the car. Thea remained inside as Paul got out and retrieved her duffel bag from the trunk. She felt helplessly mutinous, wondering what would happen if she threw a tantrum as she might have done back when she was truly her Daddy's "cookie," if she sat there and wailed that she wanted to go home. But Paul said nothing, did nothing, made no demands on her. He simply waited quietly beside the car, the duffel bag at his feet, as dusk faded into evening and the stars, bright and vivid in a night sky untainted by any artificial light, started winking into existence. To Thea, who was used to her father's forceful and direct presence, this patient stillness was doing nothing to calm her own fears.

He was barely more than a shadowy shape outside when she finally saw him stir, look at the sky, straighten up and gaze somewhere out into the horizon, and then pull something out of his jacket pocket with his right hand. With the left, he knocked gently on the window of the car.

"Come on, hon."

Thea reached over and opened the window a crack. "I'm not . . . ," she began, and then swallowed hard and peered outside, trying to read her father's face in the dark. "Where are we going?"

"Not far," he said. "Look."

He appeared to be pointing, and Thea squinted in the direction indicated by his out-stretched arm. At first she could see nothing, but then she noticed a distant shimmer out in the empty darkness, as if a handful of stars had fallen down to the earth and were huddling together on the ground. The shimmer grew larger, or maybe closer; Thea's mouth was suddenly dry.

"Daddy . . . ?" she said in a small voice.

"Come on, hon," he said again, this time reaching out and opening the door.

"Where are you taking me?" Thea said, sitting frozen in her seat.

"It'll be all right, I promise. I'm sorry I couldn't tell you more, but that was one of the conditions that he . . . Come on, cookie, I won't let anyone hurt you."

Thea swung her legs out of the car but did not stand up; she was staring, mouth open, at the shimmer that was now the size of a Newfoundland dog or a small pony.

"What is it?" she whispered.

Paul took one of her hands and folded it around the thing he had taken out of his pocket earlier. "Don't lose that," he said, "and come on. It's time."

Thea opened her hand reflexively and stared at what her father had given her. It appeared to be a medallion of some sort. She could not see much detail in the starlight, but her fingers told her that the surface was not smooth, that it had been worked into a symbol or writing. It was attached to a thin, strong chain that poured out between her fingers and hung from her hand, glinting gently.

"You'd better wear it," Paul said, "it's safer." He reached out, took the medallion from her hand, and looped it around her neck. It hung halfway down her chest, heavier than she had thought it would be.

The shimmer was coalescing, growing, coming closer, until Thea finally saw it shape itself into a glowing portal, a door opening from the starlit darkness into bright white light beyond.

And there was someone . . . or something . . . coming out of it.

Thea gasped.

"It's just the Guardian," Paul said. "He won't harm you."

Thea had filled in the blanks of the emerging Guardian with monster shapes, and it was with an odd sense of disappointment that she realized that the Guardian was an Alphiri, a race with whom she was familiar, whose language she studied at school. To be sure, this one was a little taller, a little larger—but he still had the tall, thin frame of the Alphiri, their knot of white hair piled up on the back of the head, and the golden eyes and long, pointed ears of all their kin. He wore the customary winged sandals that were the uniform of an Alphiri messenger.

It was an injection of the familiar, and Thea actually managed a small smile as she stood beside the car watching the Guardian approach.

"Greetings," the messenger said, inclining his head briefly to Paul Winthrop and favoring Thea with a small sharp glance. "You have the Pass?"

"She wears it," Paul said.

"Good. We will be collecting the fee as arranged. Galathea Winthrop, come with me."

Thea turned to Paul.

"Honey," he said, coming down on one knee beside her, "trust me on this. You're going to a friend."

"Aren't you coming with me?" Thea asked,

aware that she was sounding like a lost child but completely unable to stop herself from doing so.

"No, Thea," Paul said gently. "The Pass is for one. It will get you back through when you're done on the other side—don't lose it. Don't worry, it'll be all right. I'll be back for you soon. But he'll be there to meet you on the other side of the Portal."

"Who will . . . ? Who will meet me?"

"Come," the tall Alphiri said, his golden eyes glowing in the starlight. Thea tore her eyes off her father for an instant to look at him, and when she returned her gaze to where her father had been he was suddenly not there anymore—or, rather, he was small and distant, lost in the dark, and the bright light of the Portal was all around her as she stood beside the impassive Alphiri Guardian, her bag at her feet.

She screamed then, a thin, terrified scream; she would have run back to where the figure of her father was getting smaller and darker until he finally disappeared into the night. She would have run except for the weight of a hand on her shoulder, the heavy hand of the Guardian.

Thea knew about Portals—there was constant traffic between polities, for trade and tourism, it was a part of her everyday world. She hadn't known that it was Alphiri who Guarded them, but it made perfect sense, in context. They would have made it their business to get something out of the opportunity. The Portal Guardian had taken on a commission and he would deliver on it, according to the Trade Codex of his race. Full service for full payment. The Alphiri were all about trade and gain and making a profit.

It was like a recitation of something familiar, something she knew, something she could latch on to and pretend that she was still in a world that made sense. The rest of it was disintegrating around her, shattered into the Portal's splintered light—the Portal that was taking her from the known world to the unknown.

And her father had sent her here.

"I'm sorry," she sobbed out loud, unable to help herself. "I'm sorry I can't be what you want me to be. . . . I'm sorry. . . ."

2.

The sudden tears momentarily blinded her, and when she blinked them away it was to discover that everything had changed. The Portal light was gone. So was its Alphiri Guardian. It was still night, but the air was colder than the place she had just left, cold enough to make Thea shiver. Hanging large and heavy in the sky, shepherding the stars, was a waxing moon, nearly full and bone-white, flooding the empty country with a wash of ghostly light. Thea's bag lay at her feet, and she stared at it blankly, trying to remember what was in it and just why it had been thought necessary for her to have luggage. It wasn't as if she had been going on a holiday somewhere.

Thea wiped the tears from her eyes with the back of her hand and looked around. She appeared to be quite alone, except for a distant cry of what she supposed was a coyote.

"So," said a voice behind her. "You are here."

Thea whirled, stumbling over the bag and nearly falling backward. She flailed for a moment to regain her balance, feeling a flash of pure resentment at being blindsided like this, and then stared at the man who stood before her.

He was not tall, but managed to give an impression of looking down from a great height. His hand rested on a wooden staff, polished to a pale burnished shine. It wasn't a crutch or a cane; the thing was half again taller than he was, with two feathers—one black, one black-and-white—hanging from the tip on a leather thong. He somehow gave an impression of being ancient, but his hair was long, black, and so glossy it reflected the moonlight. His face was a strange mixture of chiseled and round, with high cheekbones and a hooked nose below a broad expanse of forehead and eyebrows that cast his eyes into shadow. He was wrapped in a cloak made from what appeared to be a mixture of fur and feathers, reaching almost down to his midcalf, but his feet were bare and thrust into a pair of sandals.

Thea clung to the resentment because it gave her courage.

"Who are you?" she demanded, in a voice that sounded much stronger and more self-confident than she actually felt.

"Cheveyo," said the man, as though that one word stood for everything. "You are Galathea." His accent gave her name an odd, unfamiliar lilt.

"Thea," she said stubbornly.

"No matter. Here you will have a different name; I will find out what it is in due time. Come, the Whispering Wind Moon is almost full. They sent you early. This is good."

He turned and began walking away, without looking back.

He simply assumed she would follow.

For an instant Thea contemplated sitting down on top of her duffel bag, and staying put. But this night, this place, made her feel utterly alone. Some part of her knew that her family, her friends, were no longer an easy plane ride away—that even Aunt Zoë's comforting promise of coming to get her if things got tough would prove to be impossible to fulfill. They were all lost to her here, in a different world. Here, she was all she had. Herself, and the man walking away from her, knowing she had no choice but to follow.

They had told her nothing, given her no clue as to what was supposed to be happening to her, other than the ongoing hints about "private lessons." And it seemed that this was it, that her instructor was that taciturn man in a feather cloak whose long stride was even now taking him farther and farther away from her.

The coyote howled again, somewhere in the distance, and Thea scrambled for her bag, stumbling in Cheveyo's wake. He made no effort to slacken his pace or adjust his stride for her, and she was almost running by the time she caught up to him.

"You might wait for me," she panted, trying to catch her breath, and only half aloud.

"I don't wait," Cheveyo said, without breaking stride.

Thea stumbled over an unseen obstacle in the dark. "Ow," she said plaintively. The muscles in her calves were burning; it felt like they were going slightly downhill and she was constantly braking, so as not to tumble down the slope. "Wait a minute. I think I have a stone in my shoe."

"You do not," Cheveyo said calmly.

"Just *wait* a minute!" Thea said. "I'm cold and I'm scared and I don't know where I am or why I'm here. . . . Well, I do know *that*, I'm being given a last chance to show some . . ."

"Here," Cheveyo said, "forget about what was. Here, you are not special. Stop thinking of yourself as set apart, as unlike any other. I will make no allowances for that."

"It isn't my fault. I was born 'special.' Everyone keeps telling me that," Thea said, limping after him. It really *did* feel like she had picked up a pebble in her sneaker. With every step, her right heel felt as though it was being sliced to ribbons.

Cheveyo turned his head fractionally to look at her, his eyes still mostly hidden in shadow but catching enough moonlight to show a tiny glint that might have been sardonic.

"Perhaps," he said dryly, "that is the problem."

"Hold *up*," Thea said crossly. "I'm limping, I'm cold, and I'm hungry. Where are we going?"

"Don't whine," he said. "Follow."

Thea walked in stubborn silence. *Whine*. She didn't whine. She had never whined.

In Aunt Zoë's manner of speaking, Cheveyo smelled just plain arrogant.

The terrain changed, at first subtly enough for Thea to barely notice, but it quickly became obvious that they were climbing and had been for some time. The ground turned into mostly coarse sand and loose scree, black as old bloodstains in the white moonlight. Thea tried to control her breathing, but she could not help the tears that came to her eyes, or the sob that escaped her, loud in the night. Cheveyo paid no attention to it. He climbed almost without slowing, using the staff to pole himself up a steeper slope when he needed to, leaving Thea to scramble behind.

Just as she was about to cry out that she could go no farther, he stopped in front of what seemed to be a solid rock face. Something sparked, and suddenly Cheveyo stood with a small tongue of flame apparently burning on the palm of his free hand. Its ruddy light softened the cliff before them into the lines of a dwelling carved from the living stone, and for the first time illuminated Cheveyo's face well enough for Thea to be able to take it in.

He appeared to be much older than she had taken him to be at first sight, back in the desert night—at least if the faint lines she now saw radiating from his eyes were any indication. There was something inexorably ancient, too, in the dark eyes that bent their direct gaze upon her. They were the eyes of a raptor, of an eagle, of a wild creature who has never known a chain or a cage. His thin-lipped mouth was stern, but Thea thought she could see a very faint smile curving the edges. But his voice, when he spoke, bore no trace of the kindness that ghost of a smile might have implied.

"There is a corner of the house to your right, behind the arras," he said. "That is where you will sleep. We will talk tomorrow."

He sent the flame from his palm and it floated expectantly in front of Thea. When she took a step toward it, it moved a step away, lighting her path. She stared at Cheveyo for a long moment, and then veiled her eyes with her lashes, tightened her grip on her bag, and followed the light into the house.

She was tired—far more tired than that walk through the night should have made her. It was partly an exhaustion of the mind, a reaction to all the fear and the uncertainty of the past few days. Still, she felt as if she had been physically put through a bone crusher. Every part of her ached—particularly, and most especially, her heart. She pushed aside the curtain that Cheveyo had been speaking of, the arras, without taking stock of the rest of the place; behind the arras there was a sleeping pallet covered with a single blanket. There was also something that looked like a lamp of sorts, a small, shallow dish made of rough pottery with a thin cord stuck wicklike into an oily substance. The guiding flame touched itself to the wick, lit it, and then winked out.

Thea threw her bag down beside the pallet and collapsed onto the blanket, the sputtering light of the small lamp casting wavering shadows on the wall behind her. The wall appeared to be solid rock. There was a rustle in her pocket as she curled her feet up toward her to take off her sneakers, and she stuck a hand into it to investigate, coming up with a half-empty bag of M&M's she had been eating on the plane. She was suddenly ravenous, and Cheveyo apparently didn't provide dinner; she stuffed a handful of the M&M's into her mouth with one hand while fumbling with her laces with the other.

Cheveyo had been right, there was no pebble in her shoe. Her feet felt bruised anyway, and she threw her sneakers into the far corner of her cubicle with furious defiance, feeling the tears come again. For a moment she allowed herself to wallow in the agony made up of equal parts resentment and self-pity, and then she heard his voice, as clear as if he were standing right beside her, whispering into her ear.

Don't whine.

She stripped down to her underwear and burrowed under what bedclothes had been provided. The pallet felt strange, hard and uncomfortable, and the blanket seemed pitifully inadequate for the bite she had felt in the air outside, but despite being utterly convinced that she would never go to sleep, missing her own warm bed and soft pillow, Thea was out almost as fast as she cradled her cheek in the hollow of her folded arm.

It was perhaps inevitable that the first person she met in her dreams was the Alphiri Guardian of the Portal.

The tall, white-haired Messenger kindred had been the first of the three polities to begin open trade relations with mankind, about forty years before Thea was born. They had been turning a tidy profit on the venture ever since, particularly in the early days of the relationship, before their human trading partners had gotten over their astonishment at finding that a race that looked so utterly ethereal, the embodiment of the noble Elves and everything that they stood for in human legend and imagination, were so completely pragmatic and shrewd in matters of business. It was hard to think of them in terms of trade, at least in the beginning, and it was twice as hard to have them constantly quoting what appeared to be the book that guided their civilization, a book they referred to as the Trade Codex and which provided numberless aphorisms with which Alphiri conversation was peppered. "Full payment for full service" was their favorite catchphrase, and one that they absolutely believed in.

"Full service for full payment," the Guardian of Thea's Portal said in her dream, turning the familiar phrase inside out, standing at the same Portal she had just passed through or one very much like it. As he uttered his words the Portal shimmered and disgorged a gaggle of simpering Faele, distant kin to the Alphiri but far less honorable a breed, full of trickery. Agreements with the Faele had to be carefully scrutinized because they had a habit of taking everything quite literally—and if something wasn't specifically described as unavailable in the agreement they would find a way to assume they were somehow entitled to it.

Faele were also prone to giving out what they called Blessings. They would cluster at a place where a child was being born, and unless they were bodily shooed away they would insist on bestowing "gifts" on the child, gifts in the guise of benedictions that had a habit of coming true in awkward and sometimes dangerous ways.

There must have been more than the usual

handful at Thea's own birth, unusual as it was—but it had never been spoken of, and whatever gifts they had bestowed had not been passed on to Thea herself. When she was younger, she had thought that they had simply been chased away before they could do any real damage. But here they were in her dream, some half dozen of them, sparrow-boned and narrow-faced and slant-eyed with their long fingers and straw-thatch hair. They hovered over a baby in a cradle, smiling their little sharp-toothed feral smiles and fiddling with the multitudes of tiny Faele-silver charms that were strung on silken cords around their necks.

The baby was a generic cherub with big blue eyes and a fine down of fair hair, but somehow Thea knew she was looking at herself.

"She will be a little princess," one of the Faele said, casting down a small crown.

"She will be pretty as a flower," said another, adding a tiny silver daisy.

"She will have everything that her heart desires," said a third, and a silver heart joined the pile of charms.

"But she will never know what her heart's desire is," said a fourth, throwing down something that looked remarkably like the cube Thea had been supposed to turn into a perfect sphere in Ars Magica class not too long ago.

"She will conquer nothing." The voice was still Faele, but it was darker, lower. There was a curious echo in the air, the words fading as though they had been uttered far away in space and time. *Conquer nothing . . . conquer nothing . . .*

The Alphiri Guardian smiled as the Portal closed, taking the Faele with it, and there was something in his smile, a knowing—but he was Alphiri, and the knowledge could be had only for a price. And all that the baby in the cradle had—and the baby was Thea herself in the dream—was a pile of charms that were Faele-silver and would melt away to nothing in the bright light of the noon sun. Baby-Thea in the crib gathered them in chubby hands anyway and offered them to the Alphiri, and Thea's own voice spoke from the baby's lips, "Tell me. *Tell* me!"

But the Portal's light was fading and so was its Guardian, with nothing left in the end except the memory of the knowledge in his smile.

Thea woke with a start and realized there was

a pale light filtering into her room around the edges of her arras. She blinked, rubbing her eyes, unsure for a moment where she was, and then it all came rushing back—the Portal, the starlit night, the man who called himself Cheveyo. She sat up with a gasp, looking around.

The rock wall behind her, against which her pallet had been laid, sloped up and above her head in an arch of living stone. The curve of it was so fine and smooth and regular that it looked like it had been hewed out of the cinnamon-colored cliff with a gigantic ice-cream scoop. Thea, momentarily distracted by her surroundings, found her mind playing with the possibilities of what might have happened to the round boulder that had been removed to create this space, indulging in a whimsical vision of a cinnamon rock sundae sprinkled with mint, but then she focused on something else, something far more important, and the whimsy was quickly replaced by wary caution.

Her duffel bag seemed to have disappeared. Her sneakers, too, were gone and in their place, laid neatly beside her bed, was a pair of sandals like the ones Cheveyo had worn. Beside them, instead of the jeans and sweatshirt she had taken off before going to bed the night before, was a plain tunic, and underneath that a cloak that looked like it had been made out of rabbit fur. She found herself gratefully thanking her lucky stars that she had kept her underwear on the night before—or that, too, might have been confiscated.

"Breakfast," said Cheveyo's voice from beyond the arras as Thea continued to sit on her pallet and stare at the items of clothing in blank astonishment.

Because she had no other choice, Thea finally scrambled out of her bed and put on the garments that had been laid out for her. In the absence of a comb, she ran her fingers through her hair and patted it down into some semblance of order, feeling grateful that the rock room boasted no mirror to show her the mess she was making of it. And then she emerged into the main room of the house feeling awkward and self-conscious, aware of the scrawny pale limbs that poked out from underneath the tunic and the oddness of her fair hair. She felt as if she had been forced to leave her personality, all that she was, behind somewhere in that moonlit desert last night. She was not, in some strange way, the

person she had been, and she was not yet someone else, caught in a moment of transition, and
she had a quick and quite unexpected flash of
empathy for Frankie's halfway-thing between
cube and sphere. The image made her wince.

"Can I have my own clothes, please?" she said
politely. Well, it was worth a try.

"You'll be more comfortable with those. You
will get used to their freedom very quickly."
Cheveyo was stirring the contents of a small pot
that stood over the cooking hearth as he spoke.
He took up a smaller pottery bowl and ladled
something out into it. He turned, holding the
bowl out to Thea. "Breakfast," he repeated.
"Come eat."

She almost asked what it was, feeling a vivid
yearning pang of longing for bacon and eggs or
pancakes dripping with maple syrup, but something stopped her and she quietly stepped up to
take the bowl from Cheveyo's hand. She even
remembered to murmur a thank-you, but he
didn't acknowledge it. He spooned some food
into a dish of his own and sat down cross-legged
next to the cooking hearth.

"Eat," he said. "You'll need your strength.
Today we go on a journey."

"Where?" Thea said. She didn't know what she was eating, but it tasted like corn, and it was warm, and it was good.

"Knowing which question to ask," Cheveyo said, "is having half the answer. You ask questions that will answer themselves. Patience. And wisdom. These are things that you need to learn, Catori."

Thea lifted her head. "What?"

"That is your name in this new world you have entered. Catori. Spirit. Learn it, and answer to it."

"My name is Thea," she said, her eyes snapping.

"Not here," he said. He had a maddening way of staying utterly unruffled by anything she said. It was so completely opposite to Thea's own quick tempers that she saw his calmness as a sort of personal challenge.

He sensed the brewing rebellion and looked up, his dark eyes inscrutable.

"I know why they sent me here," Thea said, putting her bowl down.

"Perhaps," Cheveyo said.

"You're supposed to make me find my magic."

Cheveyo's eyebrow lifted. "I am not supposed to *make* you do anything at all," he said.

"Just so you know," Thea said. "Nobody else has been able to teach me anything."

"You have a high opinion of yourself, Catori," he said tranquilly, putting away his bowl. "You stand alone, untouchable, unteachable. Is that your vision? I told you, you are nothing here except what you bring with you. You came into this world through your own *sipapu*, but that wasn't your own doing—don't let it make you think too highly of yourself."

Thea blinked. "What's a *sipapu*?"

"The navel of the world, the place where a people comes out of the womb and takes their place in the overworld." Cheveyo nodded. "That at least is a good question. It asks something you do not already know and that cannot be learned by doing."

Thea fingered the medallion that still hung around her neck. She had not taken it off the previous night as she went to sleep, and she spared a moment to be profoundly grateful for that— her father had said, "Don't lose this." The medallion might be her only way out of this place.

"You will leave this place," Cheveyo said, as though he could read her mind, "when I let you go. When I say you are ready. That which you wear is a Pass to let you cross the threshold back—but the only way to that threshold lies through me. Remember that."

"I'm not afraid of you," Thea said abruptly.

"Perhaps you should be," Cheveyo said. "Sometimes fear is a good thing. All sane people have a little bit of fear. The only people who are completely unafraid are gods or fools, people who cannot be hurt and people who will not believe that they can be hurt. The rest of us do well if we know when it is good to be afraid."

He got up and walked to where his feathered cloak hung on a rock protuberance on the wall, and flung the cloak around his shoulders without haste. His staff stood leaning on the same wall and he took it up with his left hand, turning his head fractionally to glance at Thea.

"Get your cloak," he said. "The day grows no younger, and we should begin."

"Begin what?" Thea said, and then pressed her lips together as Cheveyo's eyebrow rose fractionally. She was asking the wrong questions again. Without further words she stumped mutinously to where her own rabbit-fur cloak had been laid, and shrugged into it.

Cheveyo was waiting for her outside the cliff dwelling, his face lifted to the sky, as if he were scenting the wind. For some reason Thea's mind leaped to her aunt, to Zoë's strange juggling of senses. It seemed for a moment that Zoë and Cheveyo might have quite a bit in common.

But Cheveyo was not Zoë. There was nothing about him to suggest Zoë's affection and her bright spirit, and the resemblance quickly shredded away.

"Come," was all he said when she emerged, clutching the rabbit cloak about her.

There was a bite to the thin air, but the cold was dry and sharp, laced with smells totally alien to Thea; there was no rich aroma of fir forests, no smell of damp earth, nothing that she knew or was passingly familiar with. Her feet were bare except for the sandals, and the wind nipped at her ankles and at the exposed shins that stuck out below the rabbit-fur cloak. Thea curled her toes in the sandals and shivered once and then straightened her shoulders, lifting her eyes to Cheveyo's face in what was almost a challenge.

She thought she saw the ghost of a smile light

up the corners of his dark eyes, but he looked away before she could be sure she had seen anything, and strode off along the path snaking on the edge of the ridge leading away from his front door. Once again he had simply assumed she would follow. He had, after all, told her to come, and expected her to obey.

Thea smoldered inwardly. Always independent-minded and frequently indulged in her wishes, she did not take easily to being ordered around. But she was alone here, adrift, still unable to piece together the puzzle of who Cheveyo really was and why she was here in the first place. She didn't have the necessary information to make any logical decisions about anything, and she didn't have the power to do anything that did not involve obeying Cheveyo's instructions. So she smothered the resentment that nibbled at her with small sharp teeth and trotted off along the ridge in Cheveyo's wake.

He hummed as he walked. She could hear him as she began catching up with him, a low resonant hum in the back of his throat. There was a melody to it, but Thea took a while to recognize its existence—it was as if a collection of random sounds suddenly coalesced into something different, something bigger than themselves. She found the melody disturbingly familiar, as if she had known it before, many years ago, and was now struggling to remember it, patching it together from half-recognized fragments.

Caught up in that, it took her far longer than it should have to realize what *else* he was doing as he walked.

With his right hand wrapped firmly around his staff, he was taking long strides and almost poling himself along the uneven ground. His left swung free by his side as he walked, and there was a shimmer around the fingers that suddenly caught Thea's eye. Her mouth fell open as she realized what she was seeing—Cheveyo wove light as he walked, effortlessly making a complex skein with his fingers and then unraveling it with his thumb so that streamers of light flowed back from his wrist like strange ribbons until they faded and melted back into ordinary air, as though their magical presence had never been.

It felt like a habit, something so ordinary to him that he wasn't even aware that he was doing it, but it was beautiful. Thea stared, mesmerized, at the play of light in those long fingers, until she stumbled over a rock she should have seen but failed to notice in time. She staggered, tried to regain her balance, but it was too late, and her ankle twisted underneath her, depositing her on the ground.

She grunted.

Cheveyo stopped, midstep, without turning around. Fading half-woven strands of light still hung from the fingers of his stilled hand. He said nothing, merely waiting.

"I'm fine, thank you," Thea said, scrambling gracelessly to her feet and staring ruefully at the long scrape on her shin, which was starting to bead blood.

"That is good," Cheveyo said.

And he was off again. Striding, humming, folding light.

Thea limped after him in stubborn silence. She had gotten scrapes before. It wasn't going to stop her, wasn't going to let him show her up.

She forced herself to concentrate on his hand instead, to watch closely every small movement, every nuance of the woven light as it fell from his fingers.

"Very good," Cheveyo said suddenly, and Thea came to an abrupt stop, almost running him down. She blinked, surprised.

"What?" she said, staring around her, almost as though she had just woken up from a dream. "Where . . . Where are we? What is this place?"

The broken wilderness they had started out from was gone—they stood instead on what seemed to be a wide straight road, flat, solid. Above them the sky had turned milky with cloud, hiding the sun, giving the land an air of being lost and timeless.

"This is the Barefoot Road," Cheveyo said, his voice almost gentle. "You did well. You are here."

Thea glanced down at his feet, and then her own.

Cheveyo's were bare now, without even sandals to protect the soles of his feet from stones. Thea's own were still encased in the sandals she had put on that morning.

But so had he. He had been wearing sandals. She had *seen* them. She had been following those sandaled feet for . . . for how long? It felt like she had been walking for hours.

"But I am wearing shoes," she said instead, pointing out the obvious.

Cheveyo actually smiled.

"Yes," he said, "but standing on the Barefoot

Road is only the first step to walking it. You have done well to come this far."

"The song you hum," Thea said unexpectedly. "What is it?"

"You have heard it before."

"Yes. I think so."

Cheveyo nodded. "This is the kind of question you should think on. The answers are within you—the answers to all important questions are already within you. It is in learning how to ask the questions of our lives that those questions are answered, Catori. If we ask the right question in the right way, the answer lies hidden inside it, waiting to be discovered."

"You never give me a straight answer," Thea said.

"Did I not just tell you there is no such thing?" Cheveyo said with another unexpected smile. It had a strange effect on his face—it softened his cheekbones, allowed the habitual expression of stern dignity to dissolve into something that was almost joy.

"Why am I here?" Thea said after a silence.

"There is the Road," Cheveyo said.

"I am here because there is a road," Thea echoed blankly.

Cheveyo merely stood and looked at her, his eyes glittering, opaque with a black shimmer like obsidian.

Thea gave a huge theatrical shrug and flung a strand of escaped fair hair back with a flounce. "I have no idea what you are talking about."

"You will," Cheveyo said, and in his voice was a river of tranquility. "You will."

CROW MOON

1.

AFTERWARD, THAT rush of triumph, the sense of real achievement triggered by Cheveyo's sparse words of praise, became something of a bittersweet memory for Thea. It had seemed to her, just for a moment, that she stood on the brink of something—something that she had been blindly trying to get to all the years of her life. She had felt . . . She had searched for the right word for hours the night after she and Cheveyo returned from their first visit to the Barefoot Road. . . . She had felt *vindicated*. She had felt that there was a reason, after all, that she had been sent here to this wilderness and this strange closemouthed man whose every word created more mysteries than it explained.

But if that had been her first success, it was

also the last for quite some time. Cheveyo left Thea alone for a few days, except for drawing out gently but expertly some of the background that had brought her to him. Thea found herself telling him about her family, about her past, as they went about sweeping out the dwelling with a stiff broom made out of twigs and dry brush or getting water or preparing their meals. And then, without warning, Cheveyo gathered the two of them up again after breakfast one morning and set out once more to seek the Road. This time things did not go so well.

Thea could not remember their path being so strewn with rock and rubble on the first trip. She made no complaint and struggled gamely on for some hours, but it was a tough hike and she was panting and almost totally exhausted by the time Cheveyo abandoned that particular expedition with a thunderous scowl and turned them homeward—whereupon the trail seemed to magically clear up and they got back in half the time it had taken them to reach the point where Cheveyo had turned around.

After several similar attempts Thea eventually realized, with a familiar sinking feeling in the pit of her stomach, that she was waiting for the inevitable day that her teacher—she tried, without success, to think of him in terms other than that loaded word—would turn to her with that expression of disappointment that she had gotten so used to whenever magic was involved.

And she realized one more thing. She realized that she could not bear to see that expression on Cheveyo's face. There had been something in his eyes on that first day on the Barefoot Road that had made her heart leap. Somehow, for reasons she could not yet put a finger on, Cheveyo's approval mattered—more, perhaps, than anybody's approval had mattered before. Even—and this caught her entirely by surprise—her father's. On some very deep level Thea understood that Cheveyo was a different league of being from anyone she had ever met, that the "favor" Paul Winthrop had called in must have been greater than she knew.

There was a lot riding on this, apparently.

Thea found that she dreamed a lot in Cheveyo's home—far more than she had ever dreamed before, or perhaps she simply remembered her dreams in greater detail.

It started out as replays, with herself the infant in the crib, with the Faele raining their ethereal wish-gift blessings down upon her—mute like any infant would be, unable to ask questions, to demand explanations. She had never been told of their presence at her birth, so she had no way of knowing if this was a real memory dug out of some dark corner of her mind or if she was making it all up as she went along. Thea wished she could run out in the morning and ask her mother if the dream was a true one—or Aunt Zoë, who could be counted on to tell her the truth, even if her mother decided not to—but her family was far away in space and time.

And then the dreams changed, and she recognized them as real memories. They were very vague, distant, lost in the mists of early childhood, but these were things she did remember as having happened. Those memories, which came in her waking hours, were certainly not complete—she had been far too young when they had occurred. But enough had clung that Thea was able to actually recognize certain sequences of her dream as something already seen, already lived, already true. These were what the young Thea, at maybe four years of age, had once called the "Goobermint" years.

By the time the third Winthrop son, Charles,

was born, the bottom had largely fallen out of the feral library control market. Paul, good as he was at containment of wild magic, found himself in need of a new job to support his growing family. With his aristocratic family background—his was one of the oldest, most prominent mage families of the West Coast—his impeccable educational background (a summa cum laude undergraduate degree in Thaumaturgy followed by two specialist postgraduate qualifications from Amford University, the best graduate school of magic in the country) and a solid dollop of raw ambition, the choice was almost inevitable—politics. With two toddlers in tow, a babe in arms, and Ysabeau once again pregnant, the Winthrops moved from Washington State to Washington, D.C., and Paul joined the Federal Bureau of Magic.

The Double Seventh propaganda campaign moved into high gear. Charles was followed by Douglas, and then Edward, and then Francis. And then Ysabeau was pregnant again, and the TV cameras gathered around to watch and wait.

Media interest was not just confined to the American mainland. Journalists came from Britain, Sweden, Germany, Australia, Russia,

Brazil, India, and Japan, and as far afield as Lithuania, Iceland, and South Africa, hovering at the edges of the Winthrop family's lives, waiting to document Thea's first smile, first crawl, first word. Children sent poems for the Double Seventh, and a few of them had even made it into the Thea Book, carefully pasted in by Ysabeau.

But it seemed that interest in the affair had spread beyond just the human polity. The trading partners with whom Paul's office had dealings sent representatives to visit Ysabeau as she neared her time. Some had tried to bring gifts—but accepting gifts from the Faele was known to be more trouble than it was worth, even if one knew enough about that particular polity to make sure that their offerings were phrased with sufficient nonambiguity to ensure straight dealing. This was probably why Thea's original Faele dream was either pure imagination, or something deeply secret that her family had kept from the FBM pen-pushers, who would have heartily disapproved. But the Agency did allow a couple of short poems from the bards of the Dwarrowim to get into Ysabeau's hands—the Dwarrowim, at least, could be counted on to write poetry for the pure beauty and joy of it and expect nothing in return for it except appreciation.

The Alphiri had made discreet inquiries about possible franchise rights well before Ysabeau entered her fourth month of pregnancy. Thea knew about that, in theory, because the story was part of her family lore—she had always gotten a warm sense of being treasured and sheltered when her father's response to the Alphiri offer was mentioned.

"We don't sell our children," he had told the Alphiri delegation.

The Faele may or may not have been hanging around the infant Thea—she had been far too young to know. But it had, in fact, been the Alphiri who were Thea's own first real memory of encountering any of the nonhuman polity members.

She had been barely three. Drowsy with all the protection wards layered upon her, she had been taken along with her parents, her rather resentful older brothers left behind, on a national tour with the president following his reelection. The media had still been interested in her then, in a big way, and the flashing cameras that greeted the touring party as they climbed out of airplanes in a dozen American cities were equally divided in their focus between the lure of Paul's boss, the triumphant once-and-future president, and the smallest member of his entourage, carried in Ysabeau's arms and knuckling sleepy eyes at the press.

The Alphiri had come visiting in a Florida hotel. Thea's actual memory of the event involved herself wearing a particularly beloved outfit involving lots of yellow, walking around the air-conditioned hotel room. She remembered the three Alphiri for two reasons. One was their physical appearance, their tall angular frames, their odd pointed ears, and their long, long fingers. The other was their attempt to dress to human expectation, and the sight of Alphiri wearing bright Hawaiian-print shirts over red-checked golfing shorts with their strange feet thrust awkwardly into flip-flops had been enough to brand them into Thea's imagination. She didn't think she remembered the rest of it, until she returned in her dreams to that room and saw those Alphiri messengers again.

They had gathered around her, a trio of solemn faces on shoulders too sharply angled and legs too long to be human.

"We come," the first one said to Thea, "as traders."

"We offer knowledge," said the second.

"For a good price," said the third.

The Alphiri were always in the market for a good price.

It was entirely possible that these things had in fact been said to her parents and not to herself—but that wasn't a given. The Alphiri were known to go straight to the source, and they had never quite grasped the concept of human children other than as pint-size human adults. But whether they had spoken to Paul and Ysabeau or to Thea herself, Thea could not recall any response to what they had said. Whatever the reality had been, in the dream three-year-old Thea had been dumb, unable to do anything other than stare at them out of eyes as large and as cobalt blue as Florida's ocean. *What knowledge?* her dream-mind asked, but the Alphiri gave every appearance of not being able to understand, or not wishing to.

"We know you are seeking."

"We have maps."

"We have directions."

Where am I going?

In the real encounter, Thea would have been far too young to formulate such a question, and anything the Alphiri said would have seemed entirely unconnected. But now, in the dream, Thea realized that they did, in fact, reply to what she had asked.

"We can show you the roads."

"But we want something in return."

"We want exclusive rights."

Exclusive rights to what?

Again, the Alphiri in the dream seemed to respond directly to the questions she had asked.

"We will want a guarantee that we will have first claim."

"First claim on anything you do, on anything you find."

"We will pay well."

What am I supposed to be looking for?

One of the Alphiri had gone down awkwardly on one bony knee and had taken Thea's chin into his long-fingered hand, staring intently into her face.

"But we will want guarantees."

"We want to know if it is all true."

"We want to be sure."

And then, more ominously, and this was a part of the dream-memory Thea knew had never happened in the way she was dreaming it but somehow knew it to be a deeper truth, as though her dreams had made the Alphiri say out loud what they had been holding silent and close and wrapped in secrets.

"We will make sure."

"We will find the triggers."

"We will wake what needs to be woken."

Their eyes were huge and somehow cold and cruel as the three Alphiri leaned in closer to her, scouring her with that look, trying to see somewhere deep inside her.

Thea-the-child whimpered; Thea-the-dreamer cried out.

What do you want from me?

But that seemed to be the one question her dreams would not answer. And she would wake—none the wiser, sometimes so tangled in the remnants of her dreams that it would take her long minutes to wrestle with what was not reality and come back to herself and her real surroundings—frustrated, thwarted, and often just plain furious.

Cheveyo had asked her what the matter was on one morning when she emerged from a particularly fruitless Faele dream-chase.

"I ask and I ask and I never get any answers,"

she had muttered, as cryptic in her own way as he ever was. Part of her didn't want to share these dreams; another part reminded her that he was her teacher, and if there was any chance at understanding what she faced, he needed to know about these nightly battles of hers.

Cheveyo's eyebrow had lifted eloquently, and Thea had tossed her head at the expression on his face.

"I know," she said, "I *know*. I am asking the wrong questions again."

"Sometimes," Cheveyo said quietly, "I think it is more of a problem that you aren't listening for the answers. If you aren't told what you want to hear, you close your ears to the rest."

"But I want to *understand*," Thea said. "What's the point of hearing things that haven't a thing to do with what I want to know? The dreams . . ."

"Don't whine," he said.

He could be truly annoying. Thea ground her teeth in frustration at that gentle controlling tranquility.

"But what if they . . . ," she persisted, in the face of that admonition.

"The dreams will do what they need to do,"

Cheveyo said, sighing. "Patience. Patience and wisdom. When will you learn to sit still long enough for these to come to you?"

But it wasn't only the Faele and the Alphiri who haunted her dreams. There were other things that came to her, and, by some instinct that she didn't quite understand, Thea stayed silent on these dreams. They were woven around that melody that Cheveyo had hummed wordlessly on the first expedition to the Barefoot Road, the one she felt she was on the edge of recognizing if only she could keep hold of it long enough to figure it out. The one that Cheveyo had said was significant.

The melody came to Thea in her dreams as something high and ethereal, as though played on a flute or a soprano recorder, soaring effortlessly somewhere in the sky, hanging between the stars, looking down on the world it had made. Thea thought that it wasn't *quite* the same as Cheveyo's tune, that the reason she had thought she recognized his version was simply that it had reminded her of this one, the real one, the pure one, the one that she knew that she carried within herself all the time. In these dreams, she would find herself wandering alone in a place that was all clouds and billows of white mist—it swirled around her ankles so that she couldn't even see her feet, couldn't tell what it was that she walked on, or even if she walked at all or just drifted through this nothingness, a cloud herself. And then she would hear it start, the music, weaving in and out of the mists, shredding the clouds into streamers and then taking them away altogether, and she would see a patchwork landscape full of snatches of well-known things— something that would tease her senses although none of it belonged together in the same time or the same place. There would be the richly scented and magnificent fir forests of her home, and a glimpse of the paved straight streets of a city she recognized, and then it would all change and flow into the shapes of the hills that Cheveyo had started to make familiar to her with their tramps through the mesas sculpted from smooth rock and red sand.

And through it all the melody would run, the melody that spoke to her of age and of a new-born power all at once—*I am old and I am new and I was here before the world was born, I was the thing that the world was built on.* . . .

She still didn't know what it was, or what it

signified, and although she occasionally caught herself humming a snatch of it out loud she somehow never did so in Cheveyo's presence. It was as though this was her own mystery, something that she herself had been flung to try to solve and, whatever else Cheveyo was there to teach her, it was not how to make herself remember this tiny essential part of herself.

In some way she was aware that it was this— or something very close to this—that would allow her to return to the Barefoot Road, and this time to actually walk upon it, to feel through the soles of her bare feet the holy ground on which it had been made, as had been decreed in law and legend many generations before.

Cheveyo didn't stop the Barefoot Road expeditions just because they kept failing to reach their destination. On the contrary, he kept their walks in search of the Road a regular part of their routine, setting out almost every day. Several times they had managed to glimpse it, flat and mocking, beyond some expanse of tumbled stone—but they could not quite get to it, and Cheveyo's sandals stayed firmly on his feet, just like Thea's own.

Thea whimpered when she had seen the

mirage of the unattainable hanging before her, separated from her by a gulch she could not cross or a desert of thorns, close enough that if she threw a rock she would hit it, but too far away for her to dream of stepping upon it. But Cheveyo's response to that was a frown, too close for comfort to that expression of disapproval that Thea was so afraid of seeing on his face.

Driven in equal part by an insistent echo of her elusive piece of half-remembered music and a sudden stab of fear that the Road would remain forever out of her reach, Thea tried making a run for it on one occasion, when it shimmered particularly close to her, calling to her and yet forbidding her to come any closer. She launched herself toward the Road, heedless of the scratches that long thorns were leaving on her skin or the cuts that rough stones were gouging into her feet, bare within their flimsy sandals. For a moment, a breathless moment, she thought she could see the barriers melt out of her way—she stood on the edge of the Road itself, flat, level, straight as an arrow and pointing north, only a step away— and then Cheveyo's arm came out of nowhere and snatched her from it, whisking her away, and the Road receded as though it had been torn from her, reverted from a solid and tangible reality back to just a tantalizing image beyond an impassable ditch, and then disappeared altogether from Thea's sight.

"What did you do that for?" she wailed, struggling against the arm coiled around her waist. "I could have touched it—I could have stepped on it—I was *this* far away and you didn't let me try to . . ."

"Catori," he said, "the Road is not a thing to steal. It is a thing to win. It is something that you will find spilling from your feet when you are ready to take your first steps upon it. But you cannot force it, you cannot fool it, you cannot make it do your bidding. And if you try, you will pay the price. When someone stops you from doing foolish things, be grateful that they were there."

It hung unspoken in the air between them, his perennial directive: *Don't whine.*

Thea sniffed, shook herself free of his arm, and dusted imaginary fluff off her cloak.

"We will try again," Cheveyo said, and his voice was almost gentle, for him. "The Road does not hide from you. It merely tells you that you are not ready to know it."

"But when—," Thea began, and then bit off the rest of the sentence, turning away. Patience, he had said. She snatched at what scraps of it she possessed and wrapped them around her. If she had to, she could outwait him. She *could*. All she had to do was keep a guard on her tongue.

2.

After that, instead of constantly asking, she watched him. There were things that he did that seemed absurdly simple, a part of everyday life. But although she could reproduce the movements of his fingers when she watched him play with strands of light, she could never duplicate their effect. Cheveyo could weave whole ribbons of it—she watched him weave an entire intricate pattern that wore every bright hue of a particularly vivid sunset, and he did so without appearing to pay attention to what he was doing at all. His fingers seemed to move independently of his will, reaching for a touch of orange to blend with the thread of bright gold he already held ready, trailing ribbons of improbable scarlet and keeping in reserve the hues of the sky darkening into purples and deep blues on the far horizon. When

Thea tried to reproduce what she had seen him do, she grasped at nothing and watched empty air flow through her fingers. And when he clicked his thumb against his middle finger in a loud snap to summon the little flame with which he often lit their path if they stayed out after sunset, perching it atop his staff, where it shimmered brightly without burning the wood, it seemed a simple matter. But when Thea duplicated that snap, exactly and precisely and sometimes even more sharply than Cheveyo could, she summoned precisely nothing.

As the days wore on, it was beginning to seem depressingly familiar. There were tasks others did without thinking that Thea could not perform when she poured every ounce of her energy into them.

She had crept out of Cheveyo's house one evening and climbed to the top of the mesa, clambering behind rocks that hid the pueblo from sight, in time to watch the splendor of the sunset. She remembered Cheveyo's sunset, the one she had seen him weave into his pattern, and tried to reach for the light and color, to will it to come to her hand. Every fiber in her strained to do it, every last bit of passion and yearning she could muster was thrown into the task. But the sun sank inexorably behind the horizon, taking its colors with it, and Thea finally sighed, hanging her head, having failed to achieve her objective yet again.

Cheveyo's voice, when it came from behind her, startled her into nearly falling off the boulder she had been perched on.

"You need to be one with the sun," he remarked almost conversationally. "You're stalking the light instead."

Thea turned to face him, her eyes sparkling with frustration, impatience, defiance. "How long have you been standing there?"

"Long enough," he said, typically cryptic, no answer at all. He sighed, leaning a little more heavily against the staff from which he was rarely parted, and lifted his eyes to the sky where, in darkening amethyst, hung the pale golden orb of the almost full moon. "It might have been better if they had sent you here after Crow Moon waned. This is the moon of difficulties and obstacles and hard roads. It would have been better if you had come in Grass Moon instead, in the moon of calm and of belonging. . . ."

Thea had followed his glance, and now, after scrutinizing the moon in question, turned her own eyes back to his face.

"I know I ask too many questions," she said, "but tell me about the moons."

"Where you come from, they do not mean anything?" Cheveyo said, giving her a question-for-a-question answer, the kind she hated the most.

"Depends on who you talk to," Thea said, parrying, crossing her arms across her narrow chest and lifting her chin.

"Cay'ta, Canyan'ta, Tuani'ta, Mura'ta, Sui'ta, Taqu'ta, Chuqu'ta, Sunyi'ta, Senic'ta, Loviqu'ta, Matay'ta, Raqu'ta," Cheveyo said, almost chanting, speaking a language Thea did not understand. She stared at him, strangely taken by the music of his words, but completely mystified.

Cheveyo, seeing her expression, smiled. "Here," he said, "every full moon has a name, and the moon hangs in the sky in the name of something—it may be strength, it may be sorrow. You came here when Canyan'ta was in the sky, the Whispering Wind Moon—the moon that heightens sensitivity, opens eyes. Perhaps that is why you stood on the Barefoot Road so early, once, while that moon was still in the sky."

Thea's heart sank a little. "So if the wrong moon is in the sky, I'll never do it again?"

"There are moons when it is good to start on journeys, and moons when it is good to stay home," Cheveyo said. "There is a Hunters Moon that stands for seeking, and a Harvest Moon that stands for achievement and success. And then there's Tuani'ta. Crow Moon." He indicated the pale orb in the sky with an economical little tilt to his head. "The moon under which everything is a rock to be tripped over. And, alas, I do not think that you are finding this aspect of our lore to be anything less than truth in these days."

"You've been spying on me," Thea said accusingly.

"I've been watching you," Cheveyo said. "That is my duty. I may not know everything that you have tried to do, but I am aware of the attempts. No, I have not been spying on you— but I *have* been waiting for you to ask."

"Ask what?" Thea said. "You're always telling me I am asking too many questions."

"Not so," Cheveyo said. "If anything, you are not asking enough questions. What I have chided you about is that you ask the wrong sort of questions."

"But that's going backward," Thea said.

Cheveyo raised an eyebrow at her in lieu of spoken word.

"I have to keep backpedaling," Thea said. "In order to figure out what to ask, I have to figure out how to phrase the question first."

"So what is the problem with that?" Cheveyo asked calmly, without giving the least impression that he was bothered by mention of pedals and the incongruity of the concept in his own world.

"The problem is that if I knew precisely how to phrase the question so that it satisfies you, I'd pretty much know the answer to it already," Thea said.

"Yes?" Cheveyo said, his voice rising at the end, making the single word an eloquent question. *So what is the problem with that?*

"I . . . ," Thea began, and then uncrossed her arms and flung them out in a gesture of pure frustration. "I don't know how to say anything anymore!"

"That is a temporary condition," Cheveyo said. "You can blame the Crow Moon for that, if you like. It will pass, and when it does you will find that you have an entirely new clarity of expression."

"And I can answer all my own questions," Thea said.

"Perhaps," Cheveyo said.

"Then I can go home," Thea said, her voice breaking on the last word, just a little.

"Perhaps," Cheveyo said, but there had been a pause before he had spoken, a barely noticeable one, but it had been there. Thea had heard it. She narrowed her eyes to stare at him, trying to read his expression, but as usual he was giving nothing away. Instead of making any further direct response, Cheveyo snapped his fingers, summoning his flame. "And perhaps we had better turn in. There are others in these hills after moonrise, and you have not learned their language."

As if in response to his brooding words, somewhere in the tumbled hills—far enough away for it not to be immediately threatening but close enough to make Thea shiver—a coyote sent a mournful echoing howl into the night.

"Supper," Cheveyo said, as if an afterthought, "is waiting."

He turned and began walking away, his guiding flame hovering on top of his staff as usual, making the customary assumption that Thea would follow.

She hesitated for a moment, dividing a long speculative glance between the pale orb he called Crow Moon and the retreating flicker of the magic flame.

"Someday," she whispered, squaring her shoulders.

A faint echo of the melody, *her* melody, came drifting out of the hills in the wake of the coyote's call, as if in response to her words.

Cheveyo gave her something the next day, a strange-looking contraption that Thea stared at in pure confusion.

"What is it?" she asked, and then, after a moment's thought, qualified her question. "What does it do? What am I supposed to make it do?"

Cheveyo allowed himself a small smile of approval before he responded. "Weaving," he said. "Perhaps you should try it with a skein of real thread before you reach out for the sun. For some things, it is best if you go back to the beginning."

"Is this how you learned it?" Thea said, curling her fingers around the thing he had given her. It was a short wooden cylinder, hollow in the middle, with four wooden pegs driven into the rim at one end. She inspected it, trying to figure out where the thread would go.

"No," Cheveyo said, with his usual annoying serenity. "Weaving is women's work."

Thea's eyes snapped up to his face. Her expression was made up of equal doses of outrage and incomprehension. "It's a girl thing?" she said, the cliché taken straight from a background of being the only girl in a brood of brothers, of sometimes being excluded from their world simply and solely because of that fact.

"Catori," Cheveyo said patiently, "my mother and my sisters had those in their hands all the time. No, my fingers did not learn to weave. My mind did, watching their fingers fly with the skeins. But I cannot teach you like that, because I never learned to do it. You cannot watch me weave—not the earthly weave, not the weave that will give you the knowledge of how the thing works. So it is needful that you learn it with your hands first. For what it is worth . . ."

"What?" Thea said when he paused.

"For what it is worth, female child, for you it is not going to end here, as it did for my sisters," Cheveyo said. "It is rare enough for my people to teach such things as you are eager to learn to a girl-child. My sisters, who share my blood, who could have shared my knowledge, were never considered for it after they learned to weave a simple ribbon on their spool. For them, it was the end of the road. For you, it is perhaps the first step toward the Road—the Barefoot Road, which maybe only a handful of my people's women have walked in their time."

Thea stared at him. "Have you had . . . pupils . . . before?" she asked carefully.

"Some," Cheveyo said, an admission that admitted nothing. And then he broke his habit, and answered her question precisely and completely, even the parts of it she had not quite asked out loud. "But you are the first who is not of my kindred, and you are the first who was born a daughter instead of a son."

Thea did not demand more answers, and for that received a small nod of acknowledgment and respect. She went away instead, with the weaving spool and the handful of different-colored threads that had accompanied it, and tried to puzzle out the way things were supposed to fit together. The operation was reasonably complex in the sense that she had never seen anything like this before, and details of its operation had to be fully thought out before the thing would work properly—but once she had the basic idea of it the rest came easily and quickly. It was a question of looping the threads over the four pegs and then lifting the previous loop over the new one, creating a "stitch" in the ribbon. It took her longer to figure out how to change the colors in the skein, because simple knots didn't appear to work that well. If tied too loosely they would break when she was some way into her ribbon, and unravel everything above it as soon as the loose thread end was pulled. If tied too tight they would play havoc with the tension of the ribbon, making it come out stiff as a piece of wood, or twisted to one side, or part of the pattern would vanish into the background because the thread would be stretched too thin to leave a color mark or it would snap somewhere in the middle and then the whole thing would unravel. But Thea stubbornly worked at the spool until the tips of her fingers were red and tender and her eyes watered with concentration.

The first ribbon that she completed with which she was remotely pleased she kept to herself, tucked underneath the pallet she slept on.

The second one, more practiced, she handed to Cheveyo with quiet triumph when she emerged for breakfast one day. He accepted it gravely, inspected it, and then lifted his eyes in a speculative glance up at the heavens through the low stone roof of his pueblo room.

"Tuani'ta is waning," he said, nodding to himself. "The things that were obstacles are resolving, perhaps. Maybe in the next day or two, when the Crow Moon is almost gone, you and I will try and seek the Barefoot Road again, Catori."

As he spoke, he tucked the completed ribbon into a waist pouch that he wore, and Thea could not help a small smile. "You can have that one if you like," she said.

But her heart had leaped at the mention of the Road. They had not gone in search of it for more than a week, not since Cheveyo had caught her trying and failing to weave the sunset, not since the day he had put the weaving spool into her hands. It was as if he had been waiting for her to achieve something with that—with the thing that was rooted in the real world—before he would try again with the big things that shaped lives, the tasks the achievement of which would matter.

She had taken the weaving spool with her on impulse, when they had set out on the Road search the very next morning. She had got used to scrambling up and down the hills of Cheveyo's country by now and did not need both arms stuck out for balance—she now recalled her early treks and was amused by the image of herself as a dizzy long-legged heron who couldn't walk upright except if both wings were stuck out in ludicrous poses to lean on the wind. But now her feet were sure, even in the sandals that she had found so strange and unsteady in the early days. Her hands were busy with the spool as she walked that morning, her fingers now happy with their task, nimble on the pegs, evolving shortcuts to tasks even as she wove, a long and perfect ribbon emerging from the bottom of the spool as she walked in Cheveyo's wake as usual.

She had not been paying much attention to her surroundings this time, other than her immediate environment, instinctively feeling where to seek solid footing and keep up the steady pace Cheveyo set. Somehow the pattern of this walk had found its way into her mind, into the pattern of her ribbon, and she was not even aware of it when things changed very subtly, and she began to hum her mysterious tune as she walked—the first time she had ever done so in Cheveyo's presence. Thea hummed and walked and wove, and it was a moment of pure startled awakening when she suddenly became aware of Cheveyo's gentle hand on her shoulder, bringing her to a stop.

Her eyes flew up to his face in a startled, questioning glance, but his fingers merely tightened a little as he urged her, with a small motion of his head that required no words, to look down again to her hands.

She did, and gasped in pure astonishment.

Her left hand held the weaving spool very loosely—and her right, frozen in the instant of Cheveyo's intervention, had been in the process of lifting a loop of color over the stitch already on the peg. Except that the loop in Thea's fingers was not cotton thread but a ribbon of pale air, the same color as the washed-out blue sky above them. Beneath the spool, the ribbon she had been weaving shimmered with that color, and also with the white of a cloud, with the gold of a ray of pale sunlight, with the charcoal-gray darkness plucked from a shadow underneath a mesa.

Even as she watched, the thing shredded and disappeared, and the solid, more physical part of her ribbon—the one she had started weaving as they had set out—fell to the ground at her feet, its edges rough and unraveling, not attached anymore to the pegs, which had held nothing but light for some time. Thea stared at the thing that she had made, so imperfect in itself now that half of it was gone, so perfect in its memory of the promise it had held.

In the hills—and she honestly did not know in that moment whether it was real or just echoing in her mind—she could hear the spill of the flute music that had wrought this miracle in her hands.

And, looking down at her feet, she suddenly realized one more thing.

She and Cheveyo no longer stood in the tumbled wilderness of the thorn-covered hills. Her feet were bare, as were his own; they stood on a flat firm surface, on a road—on the Road—on which now her incomplete ribbon lay like an offering.

"You brought us here, Catori," Cheveyo said.

Thea lifted her eyes to his face. She had not known just how full of tears they were, but her vision was blurred and Cheveyo's features were hard to determine until she blinked sharply several times and a tear spilled from the corner of her eye and ran unheeded down her cheek.

"What did I do . . . ?" Thea whispered.

For a moment the haggling Alphiri of her dream appeared in her mind—*We can show you the road. . . . We have directions. . . . We have a price.* What had the price been? Had she paid it?

Was it over? Was she no longer the One Who Couldn't?

"Take a step," Cheveyo said. "And do not be disappointed, whatever happens. What you have done today is a great thing, and anything further is a gift; there is more waiting for you, but you do not have to, you cannot, claim it all today. Take a step."

Thea lifted one foot, narrow and pale, blue veins snaking around the ankle; she seemed to have difficulty doing so, as though the Road was covered in glue and the glue was holding her toes attached to it, unwilling to let go. But then the resistance ended, quite suddenly, and the foot came off the ground quickly, released.

Before Thea could bring it down again, the Road had vanished, and her foot returned to the earth in the tumbled hills she had come to know so well. She thought she could see the Road still, for a long moment—there and yet not there, shimmering underneath everything as if glimpsed through a window into another reality. And then it was all gone, and only the unfinished ribbon remained, still there at her feet.

That, and the music, echo in the hills. *I am the beginning, I am the first step, I am what created your first and your favorite world. I am the first vision. I am what you remember from the dawn of time. I am. I am. . . .*

"Where did it go?" Thea whispered, staring at her feet, planted firmly in the usual scrub and scree, with the Road as though it had never been. She was suddenly tired, bone tired, shivering with exhaustion. Cheveyo's hand, still on her shoulder, tightened its grip, and then it vanished momentarily just as Thea's eyes closed and she felt herself perfectly ready to fall into a deep and—this time—utterly dreamless sleep. But then she felt herself being picked up, one of Cheveyo's arms around her shoulder and the other underneath her knees as he lifted her up and began walking.

Thea's eyelids flickered open momentarily, and she caught a glimpse over his shoulder of a staff planted in the ground amongst the rocks—

a familiar staff with two feathers fluttering from the tip of it, the staff that Cheveyo was never parted from.

"You left . . . ," she murmured incoherently into the curve where the muscles of his shoulder knitted into the base of his neck. She struggled to put what she wanted to say into words, but it wouldn't come. "You left . . . your . . ."

"How else would we find this place again, if I had not?" Cheveyo said softly in response. "This is the place, this is the Road, and here we will return."

GRASS MOON

1.

UTTERLY SPENT, THEA slept deeply the night she returned from the Barefoot Road. When Cheveyo finally woke her up on the following day, it was to the bright almost shadowless light of high noon.

"Are we going back to the Road?" Thea asked sleepily, rubbing her eyes, still lying on her pallet.

"You have stood on it," Cheveyo said, "and therefore you will do it again. Once you have stepped onto the Road, you always find your way back—it accepted you once, and now your feet know how to return there. But not yet. Not yet. Before you do . . . perhaps it is time."

"Time for what?" Thea had said. She propped herself half upright on her elbow, her chin in the palm of her hand. Her mouth curled into a little grimace when Cheveyo's own lips twisted into a slight smile. She knew that smile of his; she knew what it meant. She could almost hear him say it. *Questions, again. With you, Catori, it is always questions.*

"Well, but who knew you'd be a true weaver," Cheveyo murmured, apparently in response to her words, giving her nothing, as usual, until she proved willing to unwrap the kernel of information that she wanted from the layers of words in which it was veiled. "Perhaps this is as good a time as any for you to meet her. Perhaps I should let you rest up for a day or so; there will be another moon in the sky tonight, it might be worth waiting for the Grass Moon to come into its own to begin this. But no, I think you already feel its gifts in your blood. This is the moon of belonging, and I think you are starting to sense what that might mean."

"Who must I meet?" Thea persisted.

But he had said no more than that before they had taken to the desert trails, giving Thea barely enough time to eat a hurried meal and make sure her sandals were securely fastened around her ankles.

They walked for hours. Although her body

had ostensibly spent almost twelve hours recuperating in deep slumber, Thea started out tired, stumbling frequently and stifling several large yawns, but then she got her second wind and fell into the rhythm of Cheveyo's walking, so lulled by it that she almost walked straight into him when he abruptly stopped right in front of her.

Ignoring her stumble, he merely pointed to what looked like a vertical cliff rearing squarely in their path and said, "Climb."

"Climb? That? How?" Thea gasped after a moment of stunned silence, craning her neck to where the edge of the towering mesa seemed to split the sky. "I can't crawl up sheer rock walls like a spider!"

Cheveyo seemed to find something about that remark amusing, because there was a flash of a smile in his dark eyes. But he chose not to respond directly. Instead, he merely pointed to what seemed to be no more than a small indentation in the rock. Taking a closer look, Thea suddenly saw something she had failed to notice before. What she had thought of as a tiny hole in the rock had another just like it a little way above it. And then another.

It was a toehold. This was a ladder.

Thea looked up at the cliff face again. "Oh, my stars," she said in a small voice.

She glanced at Cheveyo, but he, other than folding his arms across his chest in a manner that suggested that he'd wait as long as necessary, merely inclined his head at her.

"Did your people make this?" she asked.

"And climbed it," he said tranquilly, "with water gourds on their heads when it was the dry season. You carry nothing except yourself. Climb."

Thea drew a deep breath and tucked her sandaled toe into the first indentation, feeling for the matching handhold above her. It was lower than she thought it would be; she knew a moment of panic as her fingernails scrabbled on bare rock, but then they slipped into their niche. Thea hung her weight from her fingers, lifted her other foot, found a toehold, and inched upward with exquisite care. She was so focused on this that she was almost twice her own height up the cliff before she felt an emptiness at her back and below her. Clinging to the rock face with all four limbs, she risked throwing a precarious glance down to the solid earth she had just left.

Cheveyo was still standing at the foot of the

cliff, his face turned up to her, watching.

Thea blew a strand of irritating hair from where it had worked loose from the braid she usually wore and hung over her mouth and nose. "Aren't you coming with me?" she said, and her voice sounded loud in the silence of the wilderness.

"No," he said economically.

It made sense—anytime he wished to accompany Thea somewhere he was generally striding in the lead. She should have known, she told herself, that he wasn't coming when he told *her* to climb and made no movement to perform that action himself.

All the same, she felt oddly abandoned.

"But . . . ," she began, her fingers tightening in the handholds.

"I will be waiting," Cheveyo said, "when you come down."

"But what am I . . . ?"

"There is a tree at the top of the mesa," he said. "Wait there until you are summoned."

Thea shifted her grip a little. "But how will I know who . . . ? When is . . . ?"

Cheveyo heaved a deep sigh. "Catori," he said, "if there is one thing you should have learned by now, it's that your questions almost always answer themselves. Go up, find your tree, sit. Wait." And then added cryptically, "Kill nothing up there."

She had little choice. She squared her jaw, straightened her body, lifted her eyes, sought the next handhold. She did not look down again until she was pulling herself up, breathing hard, over the edge of the mesa.

Cheveyo had gone.

Alone, she took stock of her perch. The mesa was smaller than she had thought it would be, and far from flat—it had a rugged, uneven surface that had a definite downward slant in the direction facing away from the ladder. There had been a ruin halfway up the cliff—something that might have once been a dwelling, now just a single wall jutting out from living rock with a narrow window still picked out in a kind of ancient, crumbling adobe brickwork—but up here, there was nothing except a few scraggly juniper bushes and a solitary gnarled pine tree that crouched squarely in the middle of the mesa.

The sun had set. It was the instant before moonrise, and there would be a full moon. And it was no longer Crow Moon, Tuani'ta, the moon of hardship and trouble. When the pale round disk broke into the sky, it would mean the rising of the Grass Moon. Cheveyo had called it Mura'ta, the moon of belonging, of peace of mind, of heart's ease. And in the days after achieving the Barefoot Road, Thea had started at last to understand what that might mean to her.

Clifftop junipers blazed white gold with the reflected light from the disk that had not yet broken Thea's horizon. She waited where Cheveyo had bid her, sitting cross-legged with her back against the twisted mesa-top pine, for whatever it was that she was here for. A moment before she had been uneasy and shivery and full of an odd sort of dark dread, but the distant promise of moonlight distracted her, pulling her mind away from dark thoughts and into the white glow.

Thea amused herself by weaving a tiny ribbon of the reds and golds of the fading sunset, a feat that until only a few weeks ago would have seemed nothing short of miraculous to her but that was now something oddly familiar, something that brought comfort and peace to her. But then it began to grow dark with unsettling speed, shadows spreading like a cloak across the land.

Thea was left with nothing but a ribbon of woven sunlight to warm her. She usually allowed her handiwork to dissipate as the light that gave it birth faded from around her, but this time she held on to it, cupping it in her hands, willing it to stay together. As the sky brightened with moonrise, she even reached out for a strand of distant silver and began working it into the edges of the evanescent thread of light that she held.

Who knew you'd be a true weaver.

Cheveyo's cryptic words echoed in her mind. She tried to weave the words into her ribbon, puzzling out their meaning, and then felt a sudden tickle as something scampered across her bare shin. She loosened one hand from her lightweaving, raised it to swat at whatever had climbed up onto her, and then froze mid-motion as Cheveyo's voice echoed in her mind:

Kill nothing up there.

Her skin crawling at the touch of insect legs, Thea clenched her teeth and allowed her hand to fall gently back into her lap.

"Look at the ground at your feet," a tiny but imperious voice instructed Thea.

She did and realized that there was a darker shadow there, a hole in the ground, something she could have sworn had not been there moments before.

"Welcome," the tiny voice said. "Please, come into my house."

Thea involuntarily glanced upward, but the mesa was just as empty as it had been a moment ago—except for that disembodied voice, and the small hole by the toe of her sandal.

"Where are you?" she asked.

"In the palm of your hand," the small voice said.

In the midst of Thea's sunset weave that had been edged with moonrise sat a spider, its legs sunken into the light.

"Come into my house," the spider said.

"But how can I?" Thea said helplessly.

"Follow me," the spider said. It disengaged itself from the weave, and almost instantly disappeared into the gathering shadows. But the light clung to its feet like droplets of water, and it left a delicate trail of splintered light where it walked—off Thea's hand, over her knee, onto the ground, into the hole.

"But I cannot come through this entrance," Thea whispered, watching the spider track vanish into the darkness.

"Stand," she was told, the spider's voice coming from within the hole.

She obeyed, and as she did so the darkness swirled inside the hole, and the hole somehow grew bigger, but without apparently taking up any more of the space of the mesa-top than it had done before. Or the mesa-top had grown larger with it, to accommodate it. Or else Thea had shrunk down to the size of a spider. . . .

Her mind spinning, she fell forward into the hole . . .

. . . and found herself standing upright, on her own two feet, in a cavern lit by a pair of torches and a large fire on a central hearth. Beside the hearth, on a comfortable nest made from animal skins, sat an old woman.

Or maybe a young woman with an old woman's white hair bobbed just at the jawline, swinging forward as she reached out to prod the fire. It was hard to tell—as she looked up at Thea with a smile hovering around her eyes, her face was a young woman's face with smooth unlined bronze skin.

"As old as time, as young as eternity," the woman said, apparently in response to Thea's unspoken thoughts.

"Cheveyo sent me," Thea said, and then felt like an utter idiot. It was as though she were offering a password to someone who had not asked for one. Instead, she had been invited into this woman's house. In Thea's world, visitors brought offerings—flowers, chocolates, sometimes a contribution of food, depending on the occasion. Here, she was the visitor, someone who had barged in without a gift, without a thought for simple courtesy.

She had nothing to give, nothing except . . .

She glanced down into her hand. The light weaving still shimmered there, dulled now in the brightness of the cavern, but still holding on to its own glow. It was the longest Thea had ever had a light weaving hang together; a part of her wanted to know *how*, *why*—what had she done that this should be so? In that sense the thing was precious, the only remnant of a magic she had somehow worked, and without it she had no way of knowing how she had worked it.

But it was hers. Hers to give.

She stepped forward, extending her hand with the light patch resting in the middle of her palm.

"This is for you," she said.

The woman inclined her head, nodded graciously, and took the weaving in both hands, examining it.

"A true weaver," she said at length, after a few moments of silence. "This is a precious guest gift, more than you know. Will you sit at my fire?"

Thea folded herself with as much grace as she could muster onto a separate pile of furs apparently laid aside for a visitor, without taking her eyes off her hostess's face. It was an odd face, a young face under hair glowing white with old age—but it was more than that. It seemed to shift and flow; even the skin changed hue subtly as Thea watched, shading from a pale blue-white to a warm glow of something resembling polished mahogany, and back to a creamy ivory. Her eyes reflected the flames of the hearth as though tiny little fires burned behind each bright surface.

For a moment, Thea thought she caught the features shaping themselves fleetingly into a more feminine version of Cheveyo's own chiseled face.

And she had used his words. His exact words.

"Who are you?" Thea said at last, very quietly.

The woman chuckled to herself. "Many

names are mine," she said. "You may call me Grandmother Spider."

In a world of strange things, that almost failed to seem odd to Thea. She could have queried the name and what it meant, but under the circumstances there were other questions that seemed more urgent. "Has he sent me here to test me?" she asked. Her voice trembled, just a little, despite her best efforts to control it.

"Perhaps," Grandmother Spider said. "That entirely depends on what you mean by being tested. My guess is that he saw a true weaver and sent her to the center of the web. You are a seeker, I think—you ask questions, and Cheveyo my son is not one to give answers freely. . . ."

"He is your *son*?" Thea said, unable to stop herself.

"As all men are my sons," the woman said, "and as you are my granddaughter, and as life sprang from my music and my thought and my flesh and my bone."

"I think I have read about you," Thea said, choosing her words carefully. "Are you one of the old gods?"

"There are no old gods," Grandmother Spider said serenely. "They are, or they are not. The things people believe in are born anew every morning in their souls, like the sun rises new at every dawn. I go everywhere and I know all things. I know whence you came and where you are going. If such things make one a god, then perhaps I am one. But I am what I am—I was a beginning. One of many. Or maybe there is only one beginning and some of us are merely echoes of that first primeval light of being."

Thea, aware that her mouth was hanging open in a most unseemly fashion, shut it with a snap. At least Cheveyo was relatively practical; if he summoned flame in magical ways out of the thin air around him, it was practical magic, applied to a practical purpose—lighting his way in the night. Grandmother Spider seemed more like she had stepped out of a fairy tale. . . .

"Teaching tale," Grandmother Spider said as though Thea had spoken her thoughts out loud. "And old Grandmother Spider is as practical as practical gets. If giving mankind corn that sprang from the bones of my avatar, whom I told them to bury in a particular field when she died, is not practical enough, just look around you."

Thea swept her gaze over the cavern's walls but could see nothing there except a handful of what, in her own world, found its way into gift shops under the name of "dreamcatchers." Grandmother Spider's were impossibly delicate, webs spun so thin that they trembled in every breath of air that brushed them, strung within a frame of something fragile and transparent, like long slivers of glass.

It did not look very practical to Thea.

"And yet," Grandmother Spider said, "these catch real dreams. When the Alphiri came for them, I sold them only the design, not the magic. Some of it clings, sure, because the purpose for which a thing is made is part of its magic. But no real magic, not for a dreamcatcher. The Alphiri would have asked too high a price for those, if they had got their hands on them."

"The *Alphiri*?"

That was all Thea could manage to utter. The words contained everything—astonishment, fury, even a little fear. In the back of her mind the vision of her dream returned, vividly: the three Hawaiian-shirted Alphiri traders bending over Thea the child in that long-ago hotel room.

Grandmother Spider turned serene eyes on Thea. "The Alphiri," she repeated firmly. "The World-eaters. They've been to many worlds searching for the one thing they cannot find. They came but recently to your own world, a young world, ready and eager to trade its dreams even before the dreams knew their own nature. You yourself know this. They were at your door with a copy of the Trade Codex before you could talk—but it was the wrong world, and things never got past the beginning. . . ."

"I remember the Alphiri," Thea murmured. "They came when I was young. They wanted something from me."

"They still do. They keep an eye on things from which they might make a profit."

"You know," Thea said, jogged into an unexpected memory, "my father sometimes brought home some of the weirder things he found lurking in the feral libraries after he cleaned up the backwash of the wild magic. There was a time he brought back a whole bunch of things that had somehow become actual living creatures. I remember, there was a peeve, and a chuckle, and a murmur, and a glance, and a chortle. . . ."

"A chortle? What sort of creature would a chortle be?" asked Grandmother Spider with an almost impish grin.

"It was a bird, round and fat, much like a

robin," Thea said. "A peeve was, well, more or less a piglet. A murmur was something with a lot of fur, but it was always asleep with its snout buried into its paws, I never did see its face. A glance was something that looked like a cat with wings, with these huge dark-lashed dark eyes. And the chuckle . . . I wanted to keep the chuckle as a pet."

"Show me," said Grandmother Spider unexpectedly.

Thea threw her a startled look. "How?"

"One of those," Grandmother Spider said, with a nod toward the dreamcatchers on the wall. "Oh, you know how."

Thea bit back a denial, and instead stared at the nearest dreamcatcher. The shape of the chuckle formed in her mind, the sweet little squirrel-like creature, auburn-furred, with bright black eyes like two round buttons and a high chittering voice that sounded like human laughter. The dreamcatcher shimmered once, and then its web flowed into an even mirrorlike sheen. The image of the chuckle took shape in the mirror, a reflection of the one in Thea's mind.

She allowed herself a small gasp. The image shivered once, but held.

"Very cute," Grandmother Spider said. "So

what happened to the chuckle?"

The red-furred chuckle in the image chittered a little, and then a child's hand came into the image, finger outstretched, to tickle the beast at the top of its head. For a moment it seemed to enjoy the attention, closing its eyes and making its tail shiver with pleasure. Then it turned with startling suddenness and sank its tiny rodent teeth into the caressing finger.

The image popped like a balloon, and the dreamcatcher web was back.

"Ow," said Grandmother Spider sympathetically. "That had to have hurt."

"Well, Dad took it back the next day," Thea said. "Mom insisted that I get a tetanus shot although Dad scoffed at that—how could such a creature possibly have tetanus?"

"How old were you?"

"I don't know . . . four, maybe . . . five . . . something like that."

"So what made you think of the chuckle right now?"

Thea thought for a moment. "I don't know," she said. "Except . . . except that there was something like that in the way that the Alphiri looked at *me*."

"And how was it that they looked at you?" asked Grandmother Spider, crossing her arms in a manner that made Thea think that she was annoyed. But it wasn't Thea that she was annoyed at; it was those long-ago Alphiri that had drawn her ire. She *disapproved*, and every line of her body said so.

"Like . . . like they wanted to keep me," Thea said.

Grandmother Spider snorted in a most inelegant manner. "Offer, counteroffer, trade," she muttered. "There's nothing that can't be bought and sold in their world."

"You said . . . ," Thea began after a moment, hesitating.

"I said, 'the wrong world,'" Grandmother Spider said, smiling. "I know all about worlds, my child. I have created many—but most of my children only get to live in one, the right one if they are lucky. If they choose the wrong world, they waste a life. Sometimes that is inevitable."

"You can't choose where you are born," Thea said.

"Ah, but you can—and there are many reasons. And sometimes you get tricked into doing it. And sometimes it's even a good thing. For you—if you had been able to do all that they expected of you back in the world you chose for yourself, the Alphiri would have probably had you signed, sealed, and delivered by now. To perform whatever tricks brought them the largest profits. But you obstinately didn't do magic in that world. . . ."

"Couldn't," Thea corrected with a grimace.

"Didn't," Grandmother Spider repeated gently but firmly. "You knew the dangers, it seemed, even when they were unknowable to you."

"But I could never do anything!" Thea said. "My entire family did, every day! Even Frankie, the ham-fisted little twerp, can do some. My father traps impossible things like chuckles and peeves into cages. My Aunt Zoë can see the color of the wind. My mother makes dough rise by saying words over it. My brothers do class transformations with a wave of their hand—well, except Frankie, but then he always was weird . . . and then there's me . . ."

"And do you really think that your world is the same as your father's? Frankie's?" Grandmother Spider smiled. "Your Aunt Zoë's? Cheveyo's for that matter?"

Thea blinked. "I don't understand."

"Sometimes we share worlds," Grandmother

Spider said. "Not always the best ones for our-selves, but it is a world we share with people we love or respect or need to be near. And there is a price to be paid for that." She frowned delicately, her face pale and thin-lipped, her eyes slanted and narrow. "I hate to say it, but sometimes I think the Alphiri do have something in that wretched Trade Codex of theirs."

Grandmother Spider looked up again, lifting lashes that were now pale auburn and framing eyes of a startling emerald green. Thea sat in the midst of her shattered worlds, keeping as much of her dignity about her as she could, but there was a tremble to her lower lip that she could not quite control.

"Oh, sweet child," Grandmother Spider mur-mured, reaching out to touch Thea's cheek lightly.

"Then I don't belong back there? Back with my family?"

"I didn't say that," said Grandmother Spider carefully. "I just said . . . that your world is not quite the same as any of theirs. You know how you throw two pebbles into deep water, and they both make circles, and there are places where the circles intersect?"

"Yes," said Thea, keeping her words short, aware that she felt like nothing so much as bursting into tears.

"Well," said Grandmother Spider, "it's like . . . you're in those intersections right now. You're at the edges of their world. I didn't say you didn't belong there, it's just that the center of your own world is not where you thought it would be, and it's certainly not where your mother and father—or the Alphiri for that matter—think it is. It is my belief that you haven't found that center yet."

"But I still can't do any magic in that world. *Their* world. Where it's important."

"It may be important for all the wrong reasons," Grandmother Spider said. She smoothed Thea's unruly hair away, tucking the usual stray strands that had escaped confinement back behind Thea's ears. "Yellow, like corn silk," she murmured, her own hair turning that color very briefly, as though in homage, before shading back into brilliant silver-white. The thought that accompanied the gesture was unspoken, but it was there, in the gleam of a loving eye. *Beautiful*.

Thea sat up, her eyes quite wide.

Grandmother Spider laughed, but it was a kind

laugh, full of affection. "Well," she said, "when you're done looking like a startled owlet . . . I have you for a little while. We can speak of all of this, and more—there is time enough, when you are at the beginning of time. In the meantime . . ." She rose to her feet, a graceful, fluid motion, and waited as Thea scrambled to her own in response. "Are you ready?"

Thea wriggled her toes in their woven sandals. "Where are we going?"

"Out of the *sipapu* again," said Grandmother Spider, "although it may not open into the same world as the one through which you entered."

Thea blinked.

Grandmother Spider laughed again—she laughed easily, for sheer joy. "Don't worry, my granddaughter. I will be with you. Hold out your hand to me."

Thea obeyed, extending her hand palm up. In the moment her attention was focused on her motion, Grandmother Spider the woman had winked out of existence and, instead, a small brown spider sat in the palm of Thea's hand.

"I know all paths," the spider said, its voice the same high sweet trill that had invited Thea into this strange house in the first place. "I have made myself small; I will sit behind your left ear and tell you what to do. Now go, let us walk under the First World's bright stars together."

2.

And it was done, as though the words had conjured away the glow of the firelight and the shimmering dreamcatchers on cavern walls. Thea was out in the open, a wide flat plain; the sky was dark except for the stars, but the stars were huge and bright, and under their light alone it was possible to see quite clearly. The air smelled of sagebrush and of freshly fallen rain.

"Is this your world?" Thea asked, her voice a mere whisper. "It is beautiful."

"Not entirely," the voice in her ear said. "We all carry our own worlds within us. Some of this is you. For instance . . ."

Thea suddenly caught a whiff of something, a faint scent, evanescent, as though it came from far away; it was gone almost before she had had a chance to understand it. But it was a scent so comforting, so familiar, and so unexpected in the present setting, that she froze where she stood, her nostrils wide to the night air, trying to retrieve it.

The scent of wet firs after the rain. The woods of her home.

"Not here," the spider said. "Memory. Although you could bring them, if you so chose. And we might still go there this night, you and I, because I would like to see this thing that you love so much. There is something wonderful about seeing a magic-wielder's own world as wrought by their magic. But not yet. Think of it as ice cream. You can't have it before dinner or you'll spoil your appetite."

There seemed nothing unusual at all in the way this strange creature knew all about ice cream and one of Thea's mother's favorite admonitions. Instead, Thea sighed and picked up on the larger thing.

"But it's *that* world, and you just said I can't do magic there. . . ."

"I said you chose not to, for a reason," the spider said, a gentle admonishment. "We'll figure it out. If we have to go to your sacred places to do it, we will. But first, we will go to mine. To those, I know the way, and I know the safest passage. That way—aim between those two mesas there."

"Which?" Thea said, narrowing her eyes. In

the shimmer of starlight everything looked alike, distant hills' shapes blurring into one another; Thea had the uncomfortable feeling that she could walk in circles for days in this country and not even know it.

"Those. Where you're looking. Perhaps following the *rim* of the canyon is wise. . . ."

This last was an amused warning, because Thea had apparently been quite unaware that a few paces in front of her the ground dropped away into deep shadow, opening into a maze of canyons whose far edge seemed impossibly distant and speckled with stars.

"Sorry," Thea said, backing up a couple of careful steps.

But the far side held her attention; it seemed to her that it was from there that the smell of green firs had come wafting over to her, and she could not seem to tear a gaze full of longing away from the far side of the chasm that opened at her feet.

"On the other hand . . . ," murmured the spider thoughtfully.

"Can you hear that?" Thea said suddenly, tilting her head to the side.

It was the music again, *her* melody, and it seemed to her that it was coming to her from across the rift. From where the memory of the fir trees stirred in the shadows.

"Oh, yes." The spider sighed. "Rushing winds and flowing water. We made a world to that once, the god of light and I."

"Cheveyo hums it when he walks . . . or something like it, not quite the same. I hear him and I think I recognize the melody—but I don't, it merely reminds me of this, of the real one, the one I know. . . ."

"They are all real," the spider said, "and they are all just echoes of the First Song. But it's a path into a world—light and sound and life— you already held the light in your hands, child, and bent it to your will. Can you do that with the song of your spirit?"

Thea's fingers curled, hooked a bit of starlit shadow, let it slide between her fingertips like silk. "Weave the song? Like I do this?"

"Weave the song," the spider said, "*into* that. Weave what you hear into what you see. Let us see where the bridge that you make will take us."

The stars sang to Thea as she reached into the shadows of the chasm, and something began to take shape underneath her fingers. Not a bridge—not a structure that arched out into the nothingness at her feet and spanned her side of it with the far rim. Instead, what chose to form was a doorway—built from its shining keystone, set into thin air as high above Thea's head as she could reach, and then flowing downward toward the ground. All of her life Thea had heard her aunt speak of "hearing" colors or "seeing" birdsong—once, even, she had piped up her wholehearted agreement to one of her aunt's weird sense-shifting pronouncements—but she realized that she had never really known what Zoë had meant by it until this moment. Because suddenly she was inside that mystery, and the stars felt sharp under her hand like broken glass, and they smelled of silver and of forest green, and they sounded like a melody drawn gently from a flute. She could even taste the melody as it came pouring from the reeds of the instruments at a set of disembodied lips, and it tasted bittersweet, like dark chocolate. And she could see all this, because it was she who gave it form and substance, who molded this strange raw material into something that was darker than darkness and yet crowned with a star at the top, like a jewel.

"It's a door," Thea said, her voice full of wonder, as her hands made the final few motions and then stilled—and her creation hung before her, shimmering like a dream, solid and a little cool to the touch. "It's a door. . . ."

She suddenly collapsed onto her knees, one hand resting gently on her creation as though she could not bear to let go, as though only that gentle touch kept it real, kept it there. It was a dream come to life, a glory full of light and music, something she could not believe she had wrought with her own mind, her own hands.

And yet she had done it. The evidence refused to go away. In the face of her own awed disbelief in its existence, her doorway stood there, glimmering, a promise fulfilled, a potential met. . . .

"A true weaver," the spider said. "Now open it, and let us see where you have led us."

Thea stroked the edge of her doorway with a gesture that spoke of both frustration and regret. "I don't think I can."

"Why do you say that?"

"Look at it," Thea whispered, her voice full of tears.

It was a doorway, and it held a door, but the door had no handle or keyhole or hinges. It was a door that could not be opened.

"I think . . . ," Thea began, her fingers still gently caressing the starlight trapped in her creation, and then faltered. "I think it would take me . . ."

"What is it, child?" murmured the spider gently.

"I think just knowing how to open it would lead me to one of the true sacred places," Thea whispered. She gave the Portal she had created a long, longing look, her gaze blurred with sudden tears. "I just wish that I could show this to . . ."

Grandmother Spider, who had taken her human form again to watch Thea build her doorway, inclined her head a fraction. "Your brothers," she said, "are not your equals. Even if you were in competition with them, which you are not—or at least you do not have to be. The fact that they have not seen your gate does not erase the fact that you wove it."

"But they will never see it," Thea said. "And I'll go back home and Frankie will *still* be better than me—because he can do magic, even if it is bad magic."

"The Alphiri," said Grandmother Spider, "did not come to bargain for him, though, did they?" She suddenly bent down and picked up something from the ground. Two somethings. She appeared to weigh two things against each other in her closed hands. "Think of it this way," she said. "On the one hand we have obsidian." She opened her left hand, and in it gleamed a perfect obsidian flake, black and sharp-edged, polished into a gleam. "On the other, flint." The other hand opened to show a flake of flint, dull in the starlight but sturdy, edged, lethal. "This is easy," Grandmother Spider said, lifting the obsidian knife. "It's easier to make. It flakes into blades as though it had been made for that purpose and no other. It polishes to a mirror gleam and it looks fine and valuable and even precious. But one mistake . . ." She brought down the obsidian knife blade she held, hard, and it struck a nearby boulder and shattered, shards falling from her fingers. "This, on the other hand, is tough. It takes a long time to make. And when you make it well . . ." The flint blade did not shatter as she brought it down in a glancing blow on another rock. Instead, it struck off a spark; the spark arced off the flint edge, and passed squarely through the middle of Thea's Portal, vanishing instantly.

"Somewhere," Thea said, "that might have been a thunderbolt."

Grandmother Spider took her hand and closed it around the flint blade. "So, then," she said. "Let us go and see if we can find the tree split by that lightning."

MILK MOON AND THE MOON OF THIRSTY GROUND

1.

SILENCE COULD BE as eloquent as any words, Thea discovered, the night she walked the starlit wilderness of the First World. The stars, big and brilliant, could not seem to make themselves stay still in the heavens. Some shimmered between near-fade to almost too bright to look upon, giving the impression of vivid restlessness, of just waiting for an opportunity to dive out of the sky and take off on some daring adventure. Others, apparently more confident, had already taken that leap—the sky was full of them, shooting stars tearing across the heavens like tiny comets, leaving trails of light. It was an odd and sometimes rather disturbing sky-scape, but Grandmother Spider did not describe, did not explain. She merely offered the occasional whispered word of direction, crouched behind Thea's ear in her spider form.

She made just a single apparently extracurricular comment, and that seemed directed more at herself than at Thea.

"The Trade Codex," she muttered at one point, her tiny spider's voice heavy with disapproval for the book by which the Alphiri measured their own world, and every other world they set foot into. "They'd offer a living star money for its soul. . . ."

But that one opening was enough for Thea. Cheveyo would have wept at the alacrity with which she leaped onto those words.

Questions. Always questions with you, Catori . . .

"Their *soul*? The stars are alive?" Thea said, her eyes raised to the heavens in wonder.

"Of course," said Grandmother Spider serenely. "Would you like to meet one?"

Thea's eyes were round as an owlet's again. "*Meet* one? You mean, meet a star?"

The laugh came again, a high sweet giggle from the spider in Thea's hair, the only comment Grandmother Spider had to make.

"I guess," Thea said hesitantly, trying to imagine such an encounter, and spectacularly failing to wrap her mind around it.

Grandmother Spider laughed again, the laugh filled with the sheer joy of that moment. "Put me down, please," she said. "Over there, on that rock."

She changed back into her woman form and stood bathed in the starlight, both hands raised to the sky, her head flung back and her throat arched, humming a strange melody.

As though replying to her, the sky got very busy for a moment. Dozens of stars streaked across it chaotically, leaving random sparkles where two wakes crossed. It looked like a particularly spectacular fireworks display, stretching across the entire vault of the heavens, and then not one but two separate streaks of light changed direction and came directly to the spot where Thea and Grandmother Spider were waiting.

Grandmother Spider was suddenly bathed in a liquid glow of twin spills of sharp light, one shading into gold, the other a brilliant white. Two shadows, limned in different colors, stretched out behind her as the two stars touched down on the ground before her, gently, weightlessly. One of them, a burnished orange-gold, resolved into a vaguely elongated humanoid shape, looking like something a cartoonist might have drawn to indicate the effect of a speed blur on a human body. He stood, tapping one of his very long feet, crossing and recrossing his arms in front of his chest in a manner that seemed to indicate annoyance. It looked as though his arms might brush the ground if he untangled them. The other, the white one, transformed from a diamond-bright shaft of light into a beautiful woman with hair that was spun starlight and eyes that were dark with the velvet blackness of the night sky and as full of shimmering starlight as that night would have been.

"Why do you summon us?" demanded the starman. His voice, in a way that Thea knew her aunt would have understood instantly and perfectly, was pure light; it was not so much heard as seen, the words taking shape in the air like fireflies.

"To meet a guest," Grandmother Spider said. She gestured for Thea to step forward, and Thea, her eyes glowing with wonder and pleasure, obeyed.

"Who are you?" said the starman crustily.

"I'm . . . Thea," Thea said, at a loss.

"I am Maia," said the starwoman. "You might know me as one of the Seven Sisters. What your people—at least I *think* I know your people—have named the Pleiades. I am happy to make your acquaintance, child of earth." She glanced at her companion. "He is Aldebaran," she added, with a degree of impishness, as though that explained everything. "He follows. Where I or my sisters go, he follows."

Aldebaran chose to ignore this, and instead looked Thea up and down. She felt an urgent need to curtsy; he had such an air of an old-world king demanding absolute obedience from his subject. The impression that he managed to convey was that she had transgressed by simply having raised her eyes to look at him.

"You're just a snip of a girl," he said. "And you aren't of the First World. I'd know, there would be a light about you. What's she doing here, Old Grandmother?"

"Learning," said Grandmother Spider.

"She *does* have the light," Maia said, reaching out a hand that almost but not quite touched Thea on the cheek. Thea felt the warmth of it, the pure sweet heat, as it passed close to her face. "And I know whose light it is. Why did you not call him, Old One? He was always your own companion."

"Who?" Thea said, unable to hold back the word.

Grandmother Spider shot her a look that was almost reproach, but Aldebaran gave a sharp bark of a laugh, scattering light motes everywhere, and the starwoman smiled again.

"Tawaha, of course," Maia said. "The one whom you might better know as the Sun—your Sun, the star whose light is in you, in your world. With whose light this Old One created all the worlds in which your kind draw breath."

The words were simple, on the surface, but there was something underneath them. Thea's mind reached in and unraveled the images hidden in Maia's deceptive simplicity: *Are there other worlds? Where other kinds of folk live?*

And then she blinked. Of course there were. She knew that. There were worlds of the Faele and of the Alphiri and of the Dwarrowim and of who knew how many other different races whose paths had never passed into the human realm. Perhaps never even could. Thea suddenly had a vision of world upon world peeling away from a central kernel of primeval light, like skins off an onion, each full of its own wonders.

Aldebaran chose to break the moment. Unable to leave without at least a modicum of graciousness as befitted a great lord dealing with his lowly subjects, he unfurled his long arms until they hung by his sides, almost touching the ground, and gave Thea a shallow courteous bow from the waist. He cleared his throat portentously. "Brightness to you, child," he said. He spun on his heel, turning himself into a small tornado of warm golden light, and then the tornado detached itself from the ground and hurled itself back up into the heavens. It diminished fast, and very soon it became impossible to tell it apart from any other shooting stars still careening madly across the black sky.

"She should meet Tawaha," Maia murmured, still smiling at Thea. "After all, he *is* her father."

Thea shot a look of what was almost panic in Grandmother Spider's direction, and Maia laughed.

"In a manner of speaking," she amended.

Grandmother Spider's mouth curled into a small answering smile. She gave Thea a reassuring nod.

Maia raised one of her elegant hands in a

wave of farewell, and then her hair brightened into a brilliance that quickly became too dazzling to look on directly, and she vanished into a scintillating light sphere hovering a little way above the ground. After a moment she, too, was gone, the bright sphere only a flicker, one star among many. Here, in the chaotic sky of the First World, the constellations had yet to be formed into the shapes that hung in her own sky. Back home, maybe, Thea could look for the Pleiades, and find them, and perhaps even pick out the individual star who was the beautiful woman with fiery hair. Not here, though. Not yet.

Besides, she had far more important questions.

"Tawaha?" she said. "The Sun? *Our* Sun?"

"Yes, you would know him as such."

"But what did she mean, exactly . . . ?"

"Later, maybe," said Grandmother Spider, almost primly. She motioned for Thea to hold out her hand, and was once more the small spider, nestling in Thea's cupped palm, almost invisible in the diffuse light; Thea lifted her up to her customary perch, and felt the tiny spider feet on her skin for a moment as the spider climbed up to nestle in her hair. "Go on. That way."

"But I don't understand," Thea said, beginning to walk again, obeying the spider's whispered directions. "Why would a star want to send itself out . . . to send a part of itself out . . . why would they want to walk a world?"

"Many of the worlds they walk, they have created," Grandmother Spider said, sounding solemn and pensive, as though she spoke of sacred things. "These worlds, and the beings upon them—and there are thousands upon thousands of such worlds—they have spun out of the outer darkness, with the breath of those stars to give them life, with the stars singing the song that made the seeds wake and the plants grow and the beasts run, and the people laugh and dream and tell legends of how it all came to be."

"Like Tawaha," Thea said. "And you."

"Yes," Grandmother Spider said. "It was long ago, the dawn of our time. But there is still love between us, no matter how many mountains are lifted from the earth and ground back down again into the sands of the centuries." She sighed, a tiny spider sigh, almost inaudible except for a slight gasp at the end of the last word.

"When did you last see Tawaha?" Thea asked.

"Perhaps," Grandmother Spider said, "too

long ago. Or was it just yesterday . . . ?" Thea felt the spider feet tickle her ear as the spider climbed up to a better position. "Time is so different here, child."

Overhead, in this particular world's sky, a waxing moon hung overhead, nearly full. It looked almost the same as the one that Thea had used to weave into her ribbon of sunset light, but there was something marginally strange about it, as though time had moved . . . backward . . . as though the moon had yet to reach that bright-orb fullness that had been Mura'ta, the Grass Moon, under which she had entered Grandmother Spider's house. The moon that Cheveyo had told her meant calm, serenity, a sense of belonging—all of which she had felt, all of which had been real—but now it was different, it was as though her blood was roused again, as though the whole conflict of her magicless existence in her home world had been turned on its head.

It still made no sense at all to Thea, but something had suddenly become very obvious. Galathea Georgiana Winthrop, Double Seventh, the most magical of the magical, apparently did no magic in her world not because she could not do so—but because she chose not to do so.

And Thea had no inkling as to the reasons why.

The air was humming with warnings and a vague but pervasive unease. The moon was wrong. The worlds of her father, of Cheveyo, Grandmother Spider's First World—all had collided somehow and she was in the center of it all: she, Thea, the Double Seventh who never was . . .

"The moon is different," was all she said out loud.

"Yes," Grandmother Spider said, lifting her eyes to it. "That is Sui'ta, the Milk Moon, and I can see it stirring your blood."

"But that would mean I've been here nearly a month," Thea said in a small voice.

"Time," Grandmother Spider said, "does what it needs to do. You have woken to many disquieting things, and it was no longer the proper time for Mura'ta to be in the sky. She was there when she needed to be, the Grass Moon, because she led you into my house and you knew you belonged there. Sui'ta takes you on. And soon, soon, that will be past, too, and the Moon of Thirsty Ground will light your way. And you will gain strength from it."

"But that would mean . . . ," Thea began, and then stopped.

"Yes?" Grandmother Spider said gently, reaching out to smooth Thea's hair away from her face.

"It seems that here . . . you call the moon, the right moon, to come when it needs to be there. . . ."

"Yes," Grandmother Spider said again.

"In my world, the moon is fixed," Thea said obstinately. "It waxes and it wanes and there is a pattern and you can build calendars on it. . . . When you call a full moon Mura'ta, and call that the time of belonging, where I come from you come into that time and then out of it and in time it will come again, but the time is fixed and unyielding—you can't have a Grass Moon one day and a Milk Moon the next, any more than you can walk into a place and feel you belong there and call whatever moon there is in the sky by the name of Mura'ta. . . ."

"And why not?" said Grandmother Spider, smiling. "Sometimes your world comes with too many rules."

"But . . ."

"Hush," said Grandmother Spider. "Let it

151

pass. You will understand, when the Moon of Thirsty Ground comes for you."

2.

The sky was brightening in the east as the shooting stars began to fade away into the gray pearly light of morning. It seemed to Thea that she had spent the whole night walking, sometimes with Grandmother Spider beside her in human form and sometimes as the small spider hidden in the hair tucked behind Thea's ear. She remembered far too many things from this the night that was not bound by normal laws of space and time; she thought she remembered sleeping briefly, as though she had spent an hour or two outside herself watching her sleeping form stretched out in the starlight. But even that was a memory she could not quite trust—it was so unreal, so dreamlike, that she could not be certain that she had actually slept and not just thought about the possibility of sleeping. In some ways it felt like she was being filled with information, like a computer would be back in her own world—information that waited to be organized into files and folders and given passwords so that the material could be easily accessed later, at her convenience when she needed it.

Her mind did not feel tired, though. It was full of images, visions, ideas . . . and, inevitably, questions. Grandmother Spider didn't seem to mind those as much as Cheveyo, and would answer willingly, but almost always cryptically.

It might have been just another question to add to the rest, but oddly enough, it was with a sense of closing a circle, of almost a semblance of enlightenment, that Thea realized they had returned to the Portal she had woven out of song and starlight at the beginning of her visit to Grandmother Spider's world.

In the cold light of early dawn, the thing looked at once far more solid and yet a lot more otherworldly than Thea remembered from the moment of its creation under the First World stars. It was also . . . different. Under the moon and the stars, the space defined by the outer boundaries of the Portal had looked solid, dark, an impassable barrier that even light could not penetrate—the illusion of a thick oaken door with iron bolts that might have been at home in a medieval dungeon. As dawn washed over it, however, Thea realized it was nothing of the sort.

It was still opaque, but it was dark blue, almost black. And it was not opaque like that oak dungeon door that she had envisioned. Rather, it was the impenetrability of very deep water, the ocean-trench depths where the sea turned black beneath the hulls of tiny boats, black with fathom upon fathom of lightless mystery leading to the heart of the world.

"I should be afraid," Thea murmured, staring at the doorway.

"Why?" Grandmother Spider, back in her human form, said reasonably. "You made it."

"Yes, but . . ."

"Touch it," Grandmother Spider suggested. "Gently. Carefully. Just brush it with your fingers."

There was knowledge in those words, as well as curiosity, and Thea thought she knew what lay behind them. Grandmother Spider had called the door a bridge, a gateway, a place where worlds touched and the fabric between them was thin and porous. But, as with most magic, no two things were ever exactly alike.

This was a gate wrought from First World light and music, something created from almost the exact same raw materials that Grandmother

Spider herself had used when she had first set out to spin her worlds. And it was while Thea was under Grandmother Spider's wing, in *her* realm, that Thea had done this thing. That alone would have made it different from any other similar gate anywhere. Thea could understand perfectly that Grandmother Spider wanted to see what Thea had done with the building blocks, where this particular door led, what kind of link Thea had made between her own worlds.

Thea reached out a hesitant hand and then snatched it back, as if burned, at the unexpected sound of a small diffident cough that came from the right of the two women. They were no longer alone.

"What are you doing here?" Grandmother Spider demanded, even as Thea spun to face the newcomer.

A shape peeled itself away from the still-dark, knife-edged shadow cast by a nearby boulder in the sharp, fresh light of early morning. The visitor was a young man, his shock of dark hair with a curious pale streak down the side framing a smooth, sharp-chinned, bronze-skinned face and eyes of pale gold.

He inclined his head in the direction of the

two women and smiled. His teeth were white, and perhaps, just perhaps, a little sharper than human teeth could have been.

There was something about him that tugged at Thea's memory.

"Do I know you?" she murmured.

"I meet most folks, sooner or later, from time to time," he said, stepping forward. "You think you recognize me?"

"Maybe," Thea said guardedly.

He laughed, a sharp bark of a laugh. "Maybe, then," he said. "Call me Corey."

Grandmother Spider snorted. "Pretty name, this time around," she said. "I ask again, what are you doing here?"

"I come bringing warning," Corey said.

"You? Warning?" Grandmother Spider sounded skeptical, her wonderful eyes now dark and wary, measuring Corey from the top of his tousled head to the tips of the snakeskin cowboy boots, and eloquently finding him wanting.

"Even I," Corey said with a small, mockingly courtly bow, "have sometimes been known to do . . . good."

"Only by accident," Grandmother Spider said, a touch acidly. "You've been more trouble than I care to remember for more years than I want to think about. So, warn."

"You left your dreamcatchers," Corey said enigmatically.

Grandmother Spider blinked. "Yes. I have been known to do that from time to time."

"Ah, but you always leave a part of yourself to guard them," Corey murmured, veiling his eyes with his long dark lashes.

"And so I have this time . . . *shards*!" Grandmother Spider straightened sharply, her eyes going distant, her vision focused somewhere very far away.

"I thought so," Corey said, lacing his fingers together. "You had a fascinating visitor. Even you get distracted sometimes. And the Alphiri know you've been double-dealing, and haven't sold them the whole secret. They've been far from happy about it."

"I know that," Grandmother Spider snapped. "But the dreamcatchers don't need guarding from the Alphiri. Whatever else you can say about them, they buy. They do not steal."

"But the Faele do," Corey said. "The Faele will steal anything, and leave a changed thing in its place. Give them the ghost of a chance, and they will do it—sometimes for no better reason than because they can, or because they are bored, or because a thing is pretty and sparkling and they simply want it."

"You would know," Grandmother Spider said with a deceptively limpid smile. "You and the Faele, you're cut from the same cloth. Mischief for the sake of it."

The Alphiri . . .

"Trade Codex," Thea whispered. "I remember. *We buy from whoever sells.*" Her voice took on an almost pedantic tone, as though she were standing up in a classroom being examined on recent history of the trade polities for a grade. "The Alphiri assume that the person offering a thing for sale has ownership of it, and any further disputes do not concern them—if there is doubt and strife, it's between the original seller and whoever he might have got the thing from. As far as the Alphiri are concerned, once they pay for a thing it is theirs, and they do not care how it was obtained before that."

"They merely let it be known that they want something," Corey said. He had progressed from looking a little startled, as Thea had launched into her catechism, through a moment of smirking cynicism and then into practical agreement. Now he nodded, managing to imply by that economical little motion that he thought Thea talked too much but also acknowledging what she was saying as the truth. "Somehow, it is procured—and the Alphiri ask no questions. They just pay the agreed price."

For some reason, those words made Thea flinch. They seemed to apply uncomfortably closely to her own situation.

"*Shards,*" said Grandmother Spider again, this time far more emphatically, obviously thinking of something entirely different. "Shards and shattered webs. I'd better get back there. Thea, wait here. I'll be back as fast as I can. You, come with me." The last was addressed to Corey, whose hooded gaze had never left Thea.

"Oh, but you don't plan on leaving the child all alone out here?" he said with a commendable attempt at guilelessness. "There is danger, and she could need protection. . . ."

Grandmother Spider laughed, and there was an edge to the laughter that made Thea's spine stiffen with suspicion. "You? Leave you with her? I would sooner trust the Faele with my dreamcatchers. You cared enough to come all the way out here to lure me back home. Fine, you're coming with me, to face whatever waits there." She held out an imperious hand. "To me!"

Corey crept forward, a whipped dog, managing to give the impression of having his tail tucked between his legs and his large ears laid flat back in canine submission. As he reached Grandmother Spider's outstretched hand and touched his fingers to hers, Grandmother Spider folded her long fingers around Corey's hand. "Wait for me here!" she instructed Thea, and then she and Corey simply winked out, one moment standing there by Thea's fantastic Portal still shimmering with captured starlight, the next moment utterly vanished.

Thea sank down onto the ground beside her gate, leaning her back against a large rock, taking care not to touch any part of the Portal. The urge to finger the strange deep-water darkness within the Portal had disappeared, replaced by a kind of confused dread, a feeling that touching it with bare skin would somehow be *wrong*, be ill-advised. The mention of the Alphiri had done that. Their name had become a dark talisman for Thea, and now it was indirectly their fault that she was left here alone in the cradle where all worlds were born.

3.

Once again she might have dozed off, because when she swam back into conscious awareness of her surroundings things were quite different. The sun's light was flat and harsh, and the sky was high and blue and blazing with heat. Thea swatted ineffectually at a deerfly that buzzed around her face and sat up, blinking; she was sitting in full sun, and her skin felt as though it might blister any minute. She dragged herself into the rapidly shrinking shadow from which Corey had emerged earlier. Already, in the northeastern horizon, billows of white clouds had begun to build, harbingers of an afternoon thunderstorm.

Summer thunderstorm

Summer.

Thea let out a small whimper. It seemed that a day in the First World allowed whole seasons to go by elsewhere. She remembered coming to Cheveyo's world in what had been early spring in her own; it definitely wasn't spring anymore. Not here, anyway—wherever *here* was. Her mind told her that she should have been at least two months older than when she had come to Cheveyo. Her body insisted only a night had passed since she had left him at the foot of that tall mesa he had told her to climb.

"And so it goes," a familiar voice murmured.

"Grandmother Spider? You're back?"

"Yes," said Grandmother Spider, in woman-form beside Thea in the shadow, looking cool and serene. Her eyes were the color of golden agates.

"Is everything all right?"

"Yes," Grandmother Spider murmured. "False alarm. Now . . . where were we before we were interrupted?"

"We . . ." Thea glanced across at the Portal, still shimmering with the illusion of dark water. "You wanted me to touch it."

"Have you?"

"No, you weren't here and I was . . ."

"Yes?" prompted Grandmother Spider when Thea trailed off.

"I was afraid," Thea whispered.

"You do know that it could take you home?" Grandmother Spider said softly.

The word brought her own world crashing back into Thea's memory. Not Cheveyo's desert—*her* world, the smell of wet trees, of damp ground; the sense of being inside a cloud, with drifts of mist clinging to fir-covered slopes. She almost gasped with the sheer pain of its absence.

"You do want to go home, don't you?"

As if hypnotized, Thea got up and walked slowly toward the Portal. She stopped with her face inches away from its surface and stared at the thing she had wrought. And then she bent forward, very slightly, and allowed her forehead to rest against the dark surface.

Except that it didn't. Her face sank into the darkness, and for a moment it was as if she breathed the essence of Pacific Northwest, the consistency of liquid honey, condensed into a single long breath. As through a translucent veil, she saw things beyond the Portal—the green-colored light filtered into conifer woods through thousands of dark needles, a familiar house, someone (her aunt?) just coming out the front door, a deer making its graceful wary way along the back porch with its ears turned forward to catch every breath of potential danger. . . .

And then, as poised as that deer, she noticed the shadows waiting in the wood, hooded in dark green. She saw the edges of cloaks held together by elongated fingers that looked as though they had too many joints.

One of the figures turned toward her, very slightly, as though scenting her presence. Thea glimpsed the sharp features and the bright glittering eyes, even the shape of one long, pointed ear.

They were waiting, at the end of this road. The Alphiri were waiting for her.

She was the prize, not the valuables left unguarded in Grandmother Spider's house. Thea herself was the dreamcatcher, the prize that the Alphiri were hoping to win.

She shivered, and then pulled back as slowly as she had leaned in. The hot sun from the high mesas spilled on her shoulders again, heavy, like a cloak of heat and light. If she had reached behind her, she could have woven it. . . .

"I can't," she said.

"Sure you can," Grandmother Spider said coaxingly, her voice bright and encouraging. "You just did. I saw you do it."

Bright. Encouraging. Almost pushing for it.

Before, she had urged care, gentleness, caution.

And there was something missing in her face, in her voice. Something that Thea knew ought to have been there. There was no trace of the pure and all-enveloping love and acceptance that she felt every time that Grandmother Spider had looked at her.

"I was asleep," she said slowly.

"Indeed," Grandmother Spider said. "You were tired. It has been a long night."

"I was asleep, in the sun."

"Yes, child."

There was a trace of impatience, of anticipation, in her voice. Thea turned her head and met the eyes of Grandmother Spider . . . who was certainly not the Grandmother Spider that she knew.

"And you left me sleeping in the sun?" she queried softly.

"You needed your rest." The voice seemed to be just a little strained now.

"You're Corey," Thea said with certainty.

"Grandmother Spider" sighed, blurred, and reformed into the handsome bright-eyed young man Thea had seen that morning.

"You got me," he said, shrugging his shoulders.

"Where is she? What have you done with her?"

"Me? Absolutely nothing—do you really think that folks such as me can do anything to her ilk?"

"But you came here to take her from this place," Thea said.

Corey shrugged. "Trickery is what I do. Not even *she* is immune to that . . . some of the time."

"So what was it that you want with me?" Thea said, a shade defensively.

"Me? Absolutely nothing," he said again. Same words, different context.

Thea began to have an idea of what was beginning to take shape around her. She was, somehow, improbably, prey—or not prey, exactly, not in the way the Alphiri thought of it. She was the bargain.

And bargains were the Trickster's stock in trade. He had been promised something, if he could deliver Thea to where the Alphiri wanted her to be. The Trade Codex clearly stated that the transaction was with whoever currently held the goods—and if the Trickster delivered them, then the Trickster would be the one to be paid.

It was an irresistible game to someone like Corey.

"Just as a matter of interest, how did you

know?" he said, interrupting her thoughts, sounding just a touch aggrieved. "I thought I did a pretty good job."

"You did," Thea said. "But you don't love me."

His eyebrows shot up. "Oh? Child, you're wrong—I absolutely adore you. . . ."

"The idea of me," Thea said, "the things that I could mean for you. I don't know what those are. But she, *she* . . . she looked at me with love in her eyes, and all you could manage was . . . well . . . *interest*. Not the kind of interest that meant you cared what happened to me, but the kind of interest that I was something only valuable because you could trade me for something else. She would never have left me asleep in the sun."

"Curious," said Corey, sounding a little chagrined. "I clearly need to work on my technique. I am apparently terribly rusty."

"What is your real shape?" Thea said suddenly.

He glanced up, startled. "What real shape? They're all real. Unless you mean this . . ."

He blurred again, flowed into a smaller shape, lower to the ground. And there he was, the dog that Thea had sensed in him, except that this time he was not cowed and his tail stood high, a plume of reddish fur that blended into the rust-colored rock behind him. His ears stood forward alertly, and a pink tongue lolled out between white canines from which the lips had been drawn back ever so slightly in an approximation of a snarl.

Or a clown's grin.

Thea suddenly smiled, and Corey flipped back into his human shape, scowling.

"Your kind is supposed to be afraid of wolves," he said, annoyed.

"Wolves, yes," Thea said. "You didn't turn into a wolf. Exactly. You looked . . ."

"What?" he snapped.

"Well . . . cute."

"Oh, swell," Corey said, leaning back against his boulder.

"What *did* you do with Grandmother Spider?" Thea said conversationally, changing the subject.

"She'll be back all too soon," Corey said. "Won't you just go through that door? Don't you *want* to go home?"

"I don't know if it leads home," Thea lied

glibly. "Besides, don't you want to know where you went wrong?"

"You already told me that," Corey said. "I didn't love you."

"That, and . . ."

"And what?"

"Well, there's always the little things."

"What?" he said, interested in spite of himself.

"The way she walks. The way she carries herself. The way she turns her head. The way she speaks."

"I got *all* of that wrong?" Corey said, sounding honestly appalled.

Thea could not help laughing. The Trickster sounded so wretched, so defeated.

"All I can tell you is that there was something . . . different," she said. "It's hard to explain. If you could turn, for instance, into *me*, then I could tell you exactly how good your illusions are. But then, you probably couldn't."

"You think I can't change into your form?" Corey demanded. "Whatever makes you think that? You're almost too easy!"

He blinked again and when he resolidified, Thea saw herself, standing a touch awkwardly in the shadow of the boulder, her hair blowing about her shoulders.

"Do I really slouch like that?" she said, caught by surprise.

"Oh, yes," Corey said, sounding smug. "And you're always doing this. . . ."

He blew a stray strand of hair off his face . . . *her* face . . . and then reached to tuck it behind an ear. The gesture was warmly familiar, and it tugged at Thea's heart. It was odd to be looking at her own likeness, and not in a mirror—a double that moved and talked and looked like her, but independently of her.

She cleared her throat. "Well, for a start, you got that wrong."

Corey smirked, the expression strangely disturbing when nestled on her own features. "You think so? You've never watched yourself, then."

"That would be kind of hard to do," Thea said.

"But I know there are people in your own world who can," Corey said. "Folks who can send out their spirits and see the world and themselves in the world—"

"Then you also know that I was never one of those people," Thea said abruptly, feeling the ache of an old hurt.

But her response was instinctive and no longer

quite true. Even as she flung up her old defenses, Thea was aware that Corey's words didn't sting as they might have done only a very short while ago. Thea was still struggling with the reasons behind I *won't* rather than I *can't* when it came to her doing magic, but the difference was clear, and it was one of choice. It was hard to feel quite as inadequate as she used to.

Corey turned back into his young-man form. "It's hot here," he said, drawing a hand over his brow to wipe away a film of perspiration.

"Yes," Thea agreed. The sun was an almost solid presence now, beating down with the relentless white heat of the desert summer day.

"You could be home, you know, through that door. In minutes. In seconds. Instantaneously. *Really*. You could."

"How do you know that?"

He looked coy. "I know many things."

"Well, but I'd rather wait until she comes back," Thea said.

"But then it will be too . . ." Corey caught himself, and a new and different curiosity came into his eyes. "So, then," he asked, as if he couldn't help himself. "What *did* you see?"

"What do you mean?"

"When you looked into it, just now," Corey said. "What did you see?"

"Nothing," Thea said. "Mist."

"But even I can smell—" He shut up abruptly, looking down at where he was scuffing the dry earth with the toe of his boot, raising a small cloud of dust.

"You don't believe me?" Thea said. "Go look for yourself, then."

"Are you serious?"

Thea shrugged. "You don't need my permission. It's an open gate."

"A-*ha*!" Corey pounced on her words. "If it's an open gate, then it must lead somewhere."

"I'm sure it must," Thea agreed placidly.

"And I definitely smell something strange," he said, his nose twitching, glancing at the gate with raw curiosity.

"So look," she said.

"It won't hurt me?"

"How should I know? I told you, I didn't see anything."

"Well . . ." Corey approached the gate warily, again giving himself away. It looked as if every sense he possessed was now concentrated in the quivering questing nose of a dog sniffing for danger. He lay a careful hand on the side of the door and turned in Thea's direction again. "You sure?"

"As sure as I can be," Thea said sturdily, no less than the truth.

Corey sniffed once more and then stood up against the Portal as Thea had done, and allowed his face to sink into it.

The effect was curious, looking at it from the side. The doorway was just a frame, from nothing into nothing, only the shimmering veil of darkness in the middle giving an indication of something otherworldly. Had he chosen to, Corey could have walked right around the door and still remained in this world. It was almost wholly two-dimensional, its depth a handspan, measured in inches. If it had been a normal door, by the time Corey's ears entered the doorway, his nose should have been emerging on the far side.

But that was not what happened. He leaned into the Portal and buried his head and neck almost up to his shoulders into the veil, but nothing came out from beyond the door on the other side. The rather eerie effect was that the doorway was swallowing him whole.

Corey sucked his head back into the same

dimension as the rest of his body, and turned to Thea, blinking.

"Are you certain you see nothing?" he said. "I could swear I see things . . . trees . . . mountains . . . a house . . ."

"Really?" Thea said, making her eyes go round and wide. "Are *you* sure? What kind of house?"

Corey made a series of sketchy gestures with both hands, shaping a house in the air before him. "Just a house. With a dark front door, I think. And so much damp." He wrinkled his delicate desert-bred nose.

"You're obviously better at this than I am," Thea said. Apparently oblivious of her flattery, Corey preened just a little.

"I've been at it longer than you can dream," he said.

"Could you see it clearly?" Thea said, sounding wistful, almost plaintive. "If you could describe it, I can tell you if you're looking at my house. But maybe . . . maybe you could . . ."

"What?" Corey said.

"Well," Thea said slowly, "if you looked at it . . . as . . . well . . . as *me* . . . you know, through my eyes, maybe you'd know instantly, just as I would know—and if you can tell me that's where it leads . . ." Thea sighed. "I *do* want to go home. . . ."

"You raise a good point," Corey said. "It's your gate, and it's attuned to you. Which does make me wonder why you can't see . . ."

There were real tears in Thea's eyes when she looked back at Corey. She had never been very good at guile, but perhaps it was just that this time she wasn't wholly pretending; the fake self-pity that filled her gaze was leavened by genuine pathos and pain. "Tell me!" she said, and her voice broke on the words. "Tell me if you can see my home!"

Corey hesitated for a moment, and then shrugged. "It can't hurt," he said.

He changed into Thea again and stepped back up to the Portal, letting his face—*her* face—sink back into the veil.

Thea crossed the space between them in two long strides and pushed as hard as she could with the palms of both hands flat between his shoulder blades, propelling him forward into the Portal. She thought she heard a startled yelp as though from a very long way away, as he stumbled forward, and the Portal took all of him, took him *somewhere else.*

175

Her heart thumped painfully, Thea waited a span of long minutes and then carefully, very carefully, allowed her own face to sink back into the veil just enough for her to see through it.

It was home, that was for certain. There was a commotion in the trees as something struggled there, and the door of the house in her vision opened to reveal her father, peering out in a puzzled manner. Then Thea saw the knot of shapes in the trees fall apart, resolve into three tall Alphiri looking up helplessly as a large black bird—a raven—flapped with graceless speed away from them and escaped, flying through the trees. Thea could hear its angry, raucous screech as it wheeled once above the treetops and then disappeared into the distance.

The Alphiri were left empty-handed in the woods. Thea thought she heard an angry hiss, could even make out a few words if she strained—*It was he, it was the one we seek. . . .*

Then one of the Alphiri looked over his shoulder, his gaze pointed inexorably in Thea's direction. The expression on his face was one of cold fury.

Thea pulled back quickly, stumbling back a couple of steps into the safety of the dry desert heat, gasping for air and shaking her head to clear the vision of those angry eyes.

"Well done, child," said a familiar voice. "You tricked the Trickster."

Grandmother Spider—the *real* Grandmother Spider—stood a few steps away, and the love that Thea remembered was in her eyes. Grandmother Spider opened her arms, and Thea ran into the safety and comfort of that embrace, her narrow shoulders suddenly heaving with sobs.

"But I did want to go home," she managed to get out. "I wanted to go back so badly. . . ."

"But not on someone else's terms," Grandmother Spider murmured. "You have enough wisdom to know that your road back does not lie through that gate, wondrous as your achievement was. The Alphiri would have counted the price of passage not paid, and would have taken you instead. You have to walk back. The long way."

Thea rubbed her eyes with the heel of her hand, wiping her tears away.

"The Barefoot Road?" she asked quietly.

"Not even that, although learning to control it is important," Grandmother Spider said gently.

"No, you have to go back the way you came. You have to keep the bargain."

"But it was through an *Alphiri* Portal that I—"

"I know, and it is through one that you must return," Grandmother Spider said. "Or the deal is broken. The Trade Codex is quite clear on these matters."

"Are your dreamcatchers . . . ?" Thea gasped, lifting her head.

"Oh, they are quite safe, although the Faele would have grabbed them if they could," Grandmother Spider said reassuringly. "It was to deal with those little thieves that I stayed away for so long. I didn't know he would come straight back for you—I am so sorry. I should never have left you alone."

"But who said," a new voice interrupted, "that she was alone?"

The voice was warm and pure, like liquid gold, like . . . like sunshine. Like that vivid presence of the sunlight that had been with Thea for hours out here in the desert.

Thea raised her head, the tears drying on her cheeks. She caught a glimpse of Grandmother Spider's face, and if there had been love there before it had been the love of a mother for her child, gentle and rich and nurturing. The expression that she wore now was full of a different kind of love, the kind given and received from heart to heart between two equals, between chosen soul mates.

"Hello, Tawaha," Grandmother Spider said, and there was glory in her voice.

THUNDER MOON

1.

As she turned, Thea saw what she first took to be a lion-headed man. A closer look revealed that this first impression was an illusion. Tawaha's face, with its strong, chiseled features and great amber-colored eyes, was framed by a cloud, a mane of bright burnished hair that seemed to lift and float about his head as though alive. He was barefoot and wore nothing more than a simple loincloth made out of some tawny beast's hide. His body was stockily muscular, solidly built in a manner that suggested raw strength, and possessed of a catlike grace that filled every movement.

He reached out a hand and brushed Grandmother Spider's cheek very gently, as though in passing; the movement continued almost uninterrupted until the extended hand stopped to hover barely above Thea's shoulder. His fingers did not touch her, but even through her clothes she could feel the heat of his presence, her skin crisping into the redness of sunburn.

"You're right, my touch would burn you, my child, my far-kin, one born to my people so long after I first shared the sky of the First World with them," Tawaha said. He was answering what had been mere feelings, barely formulated into thoughts—as though in his bright presence there were no shadows in Thea's mind where he could not see if he chose.

Tawaha, the Sun, the first light of the First World. Her many-times-removed ancestor, who set his hand and heart to a dream shared by Grandmother Spider when they sang the worlds into existence.

"You couldn't hurt me," Thea said, raising her eyes to Tawaha's face.

He withdrew his hand, but only slowly with every appearance of reluctance. "I could," he said, smiling, "but never would I want to." He flicked his eyes back to Grandmother Spider. "Maia told me that now would be a good time for me to be here," he said, and Thea had to think quickly before she remembered with almost a jolt that Maia had been the starwoman whom Grandmother Spider had summoned down from the sky. "Why did you not call me?"

"Because I knew you would come," Grandmother Spider said.

Thea suddenly felt like an uninvited guest, a child who had blundered into a grown-up party. She stared, rapt, aware that she was watching something the likes of which she would probably never see again. The first love story ever, before worlds were spun to hold the love that these two beings shared long ago, shared still, would share forever. For all time.

Grandmother Spider gave Thea's shoulders one last squeeze and let her go.

"Do you think," she asked gently, "that you are ready to go back to Cheveyo now?"

"Yes," said Thea. Her voice was a cry of yearning to stay here instead, to be a part of whatever it was that these two shared.

But she was not a part of it, except as a ghost from a distant future, a descendant many times removed from the glorious world shared by these, her sacred ancestors. She had been here for a reason, for a purpose. That was achieved—she had proved something here, something important. The gateway that stood and still shimmered behind Thea on the edge of the great canyon was a testament to that. Now it was time for her to go.

"I wish I could stay," Thea said, raising her eyes to meet Tawaha's again. "But I am very happy to have had the chance to meet you, Father Tawaha."

The form of address was instinctive, born of something greater and older than herself. Tawaha inclined his head in acknowledgment.

"Only remember this, my child," he said. "Where you are and where light is, I will always be at your side."

"And so will I, in spirit and in thought," Grandmother Spider said, taking Thea's hand again, her eyes again brimming with that love that Thea had missed in Corey's impersonation of her. "We may meet again, somewhere, perhaps in the web of a dreamcatcher. In fact, I am sure we will. But for now, it's time to say goodbye."

She turned Thea around, her arm slipping around Thea's shoulders, until they faced the

Portal again. "Through that is Cheveyo's mesa," Grandmother Spider said. "It's only a step away."

Thea balked. "But I *know* that it goes to . . . I've looked inside and I've seen . . ."

"Thea," said Grandmother Spider, "look at me."

Thea turned to her companion.

"You made that gate," Grandmother Spider said. "But we are in the First World still, and here my word matters. When you are here by yourself, it may be that there is only one other place that this gate will lead you to, or that in the moment that you looked into the gate there was only one place where you wanted to be. But right now, in this moment, with me holding your hand, it will take you to where I command."

"I believe you," Thea whispered, but then shivered despite herself. "But I remember seeing my father coming out of the door of my own home. I *remember*. It was clear and it was real and it was there. . . ."

"Sweet child of my spirit," Grandmother Spider said, "remember, there are many worlds, and it was I who led the first people born of my spirit as they crossed from one realm to another,

I who opened the gateways of *sipapu* for them as they slipped from the world of darkness to the world of twilight to the world of light. This gate will not take you home, but it will take you to a place that you might have already started to think of as another home, a home for your spirit. Cheveyo is waiting for you."

"All right," Thea said. The serenity of pure trust filled her. She squared her shoulders and lifted her chin even as Grandmother Spider reached for her hand.

"Come, then," Grandmother Spider said.

On the threshold of the gateway, Grandmother Spider released Thea's fingers gently. Thea paused for a moment, turned; Grandmother Spider had stepped back and now stood beside Tawaha, her hair wheat-gold and her eyes the color of honey amber as though in an instinctive response to his own bright bronzed skin and tawny hair. Grandmother Spider raised a hand as though in farewell, and Thea lifted her own in response—and then, just as she stepped through the Portal, she reached out and hooked just one strand of the living light that hung in Tawaha's presence and pulled it after her.

She thought she heard an echo of laughter

behind her, a delighted, indulgent laughter which suddenly and painfully reminded her of the way her father once laughed with her, when she was much, much younger and her flaws were still hidden, swept aside with the convenient excuse that she was still too young.

A part of her had thought that she would return to the high mesa from which she gained Grandmother Spider's house for the first time, that she would have to clamber down that steep and terrifying cliff—indeed, Cheveyo had left her at the foot of the mesa with the admonishment that he would be waiting when she returned. But obviously he had been doing his waiting somewhere else, because Grandmother Spider had set Thea down only a few steps from Cheveyo's own house. She could clearly see the entrance from where she stood, clutching a thin ribbon of light that was starting to feel painfully warm, as if she had stuck her hand into a fire.

As Thea watched, Cheveyo ducked out of his doorway and stood for a moment looking at her with his glittering obsidian eyes.

"Your turn to make breakfast," he said. "I will be back in an hour."

"But how . . . ?"

He raised a single eloquent eyebrow, shifted his grip on his staff, and then turned his head very slightly, his nostrils flaring as he tasted the air.

"You brought change with you," he commented conversationally. "I smell thunder. It is Chuqu'ta, the Thunder Moon; there will be rain today." He nodded in the direction of the entrance to his home. "Breakfast. One hour."

With no further word, he turned and strode off along the path that snaked behind the mesa, using his feathered staff to anchor his steps.

But didn't he leave that back at the Barefoot Road? Thea thought, confused, as she watched him disappear behind the boulders. She shrugged philosophically and ducked into the house. There was little point in trying to second-guess Cheveyo.

She rummaged, one-handed, in the storage niches in the back room. One of the first things that Cheveyo had taught her was how to make flat unleavened bread from ground cornmeal and bake it in the embers, and Thea supposed that was what he meant that he wanted for breakfast. Her other hand still clung to the thin ribbon of First World light, so bright that it illuminated the whole of the inside of the house, its incandescent fire wound painfully about her fingers. She had noticed that the fire on the cooking hearth was banked, almost out. Muttering to herself, she thrust the ribbon of Tawaha's light into the ashes.

The light writhed for a moment like a living thing, coiling like a serpent, and then the almost-dead fire burst into golden-red tongues of flame. It looked, perhaps, like any other hearth fire—but Thea stared, fascinated, caught up in the play of colors as the fire danced and flickered. The earthenware pot of cornmeal was forgotten on the ground near her foot as she crouched beside the hearthstones. She had called something extraordinary from the First World to take up residence on this hearth, used for such everyday purposes as baking flatbread or roasting ears of corn.

Thea could see the sunlight in this fire—but not just the molten heat of the desert summer. There was also the high cold white sun of the far north, frozen light cuttingly sharp in the brittle sky; there was the scintillating sunlight sparkling off the surface of the sea or caught at play in the tumble of a waterfall; there was the filtered green sunlight so familiar to Thea, drifting through the firs in the green-gold haze of summer. Touched by Tawaha, the little fire blazed and danced in first morning of the month of the Thunder Moon. . . .

Cheveyo had explained the moons to her. Now Thea reached back into her memory, sorting her thoughts, retrieving the information. Thunder Moon, Chuqu'ta, carried within it the dangers of overoptimism, even hubris, but also the gift of reason by which such rash impulses could be checked. If caught in time.

A dry chuckle behind her startled Thea to her feet. She kicked the cornmeal pot at her heel and overturned it, scattering meal on the ground.

Cheveyo stood watching her with amusement crinkling the corners of his dark eyes.

"Do you realize," Cheveyo said, tilting his chin in the direction of the fire, "what you have done?"

"I was trying to make flatbread," Thea said lamely, dropping her eyes to the scattered cornmeal.

"With sacred fire?" Cheveyo said.

"I didn't mean to—"

"I know," Cheveyo said. "That's why I brought these."

He handed her a bag he wore over his shoulder, and Thea took it, looking at him quizzically.

"Breakfast," he said. "Berries. And then we can talk."

"Grandmother Spider said you still had many things to tell me," Thea said. "She also said that time was running short. Why did they *really* send me here, Cheveyo?"

"I would have thought you got a lot of answers to questions like those in the time you spent in the First World," Cheveyo said.

"In the First World, I can make gates between worlds," Thea said. "Here, I can weave a ribbon of light. Back home, I can't do anything. You still haven't taught me to do anything that I can take with me when I—"

Cheveyo's eyes snapped, a spark of black fire. "I expected more of you than that," he said curtly. "Haven't you been listening to a word I've said to you since you've been with me, Catori? I haven't spent a single moment teaching you how to *do*. I've been teaching you how to *be*."

"That's not true!" Thea said. "You've been trying to get me to walk on the Barefoot Road— and that's doing. What of the weaving?"

"None of that matters," Cheveyo said calmly.

His serenity had regenerated, as though someone had thrown a stone at the still surface of the deep pool that was his spirit, and the surface stilled again after the ripples died away, giving no indication that it had ever been disturbed. "None of that matters, because every action you have taken has been based on a change in yourself, in the spirit you brought here to me to be healed of what it believed were its faults. But now you know better, don't you?"

"I may know," Thea said, "but I don't understand."

Cheveyo nodded. "Very good," he said. "That is an important distinction. What makes you think you lack understanding?"

"I know the *where*," Thea said. "I know it's something to do with the world of my home, and the way that world and I affect one another. I know the *when*—it's been going on all my life. But I knew all of that long before I came here."

Cheveyo waited in silence. Thea's eyes were sparkling with frustrated fury, with a glint of tears.

"I even know *who*," she said. "It's the Faele and the gifts they gave me at birth, and the Alphiri who seem to think that these gifts are valuable, and the family who wants so much from me, and all the people who waited while I grew up and failed to do what everyone expected. Most of all it's me and some strange choice that I made when I was born, before I was born. What I don't know . . ."

"Yes," murmured Cheveyo, "the last two questions."

"I don't know the *how*, and I don't know the *why*," Thea said. "And I'm supposed to be going home, with no more than that. I come back and the situation remains exactly the same, doesn't it? I'll still be me, and I'll still be bound by my choices."

"But not by your world," Cheveyo said.

"What does *that* mean?" Thea said. "When I go back home, I go back to the same world that I left to come here. Don't I?"

"If you say so," Cheveyo said, annoyingly calm, reaching out for another handful of berries.

"Well, I do say so," Thea said. "It's all very well to know that I don't do magic back home because I have for some reason chosen not to. But *why*, Cheveyo? Why did I choose not to? And just when exactly was it that I chose that—

I can't remember making that choice. I can't imagine making that choice—not with my family, not with what I was born as! They expect so much . . . and all I know is that I have somehow deliberately turned my back on those expectations. What do I tell them, when I go home? That I am still Thea, the One Who Can't? What do I tell my father?"

"The one thing that you can take back from this place," Cheveyo said, "is the sure knowledge that, when there is a battle to be fought, it is you who can choose the place of the battlefield. I cannot tell you why you chose what you chose, but you are going back to your home with weapons with which you can break the bonds those choices have forced upon you. The answers you have gained—the answers to your *who* and *when* and *where*—you may have had all the pieces before, but you had no idea how they fit together. It's like that spilled cornmeal. Now, after the time you have spent here, you know it belongs in a pottery jar."

"Thanks," Thea said, unable to stop a wry grin. "Can I take the jar back home with me when I leave so I can stuff all my troubles in it?"

"If you think that it would hold them,"

Cheveyo said. "But you are your own jar, Catori. You hold all your questions, all your answers. This place has been a way station, not a destination—you were never sent here to become one of my people or to be adopted into my tribe. You were not meant to live out your days in the mesas and the red sand, however beautifully they reflect the light. Tell me, have you ever paid conscious attention to the patterns into which you weave your light?"

"I think I . . ." Thea shot Cheveyo a look full of astonishment. "I thought I did," she said, correcting herself. "And yet, now that you ask, I can't seem to remember a single pattern I ever did—it's as if they just come by themselves and decide what needs to be woven."

"It is no different with the things that you weave to shape your life," Cheveyo said. "Do you believe your light weaves have meaning?"

"Of course they do!" Thea said, so emphatically that she stopped, startling herself into a reflective pause. "But if I didn't know the pattern," she murmured, "how do I know it is significant?"

"Because in another context, seen from a different angle or a different point of view or simply distanced from you by time and experience, many patterns that seem formless and without meaning suddenly become something that shapes your very existence. What you have woven here in the desert with me—what you have woven back in the First World with the Old Ones who breathe life and spirit into us all—all of this is now in the pattern of your life. All of this will mean very different things to you when you return to your home."

"My answers?" Thea said, her voice almost plaintive.

"To more questions," Cheveyo said gravely, "than even you can think to ask. But I think you need to prove something to yourself first, before you leave my home to return to yours."

"What's that?"

"Come," he said, rising. "We will walk."

"We're going back to the Road, aren't we?" Thea said, scrambling to her feet, wiping berry juice off her chin.

"You are going back," he said. "You will lead me."

"But the last time," Thea said, "your staff—"

"Yes," he said, and held out his staff to her. "This will show you the way."

"But it's . . . but that is . . . I can't take that!"

"No, you couldn't, not if I were unwilling," Cheveyo agreed, his usual faintly aggravating self-possession back in full force. "But you are not *taking* it, you are borrowing it with my blessing. That is a very different thing. Now come, this is Chuqu'ta. If we do not do this before the clouds bring the rains this afternoon, we may have to run for cover. These are the male rains, the summer storms—they do not last very long, but they are violent, and even I respect their power. They and I try not to argue too often because I am not certain that I win enough times to make it worth the fight. Take it. Let us go."

Thea reached out hesitantly for the staff. For a moment both their hands rested on it, side by side, Cheveyo's large, calloused fingers and ridged nails and skin tanned almost into leather from years of exposure, a stark contrast to Thea's, smooth, pale, long-fingered, full of a feminine grace even given the grime underneath her nails and the red welt across the fingers that had held the ribbon of Tawaha's fire. And yet there was something very alike between them, too. They were kin from afar, separated by their different worlds, different times, but linked in the bond of power, of that fundamental magical sense that Thea had for so long bitterly reproached herself for lacking.

She had it. She *had* it. All she had ever needed to learn is why she had never tapped into it.

"Well?" Cheveyo murmured.

Without another word, Thea turned, gripping Cheveyo's staff firmly, and began walking.

2.

Thea had not forgotten the early treks that Cheveyo had taken her on when she had first come to his house. Sometimes they had caught the barest glimpse of the Road as it stretched out into the horizon, insubstantial, teasing the edges of vision like a hallucination. Sometimes she could see the Road taunting her from just beyond some impassable hedge of thorns or a wilderness of sharp stones, solid and real and as far away as if it had been on another planet. Sometimes, many times, they had failed to find it at all and spent fruitless hours walking in the heat, searching for what seemed to be no more than a fevered dream.

And yet she had stood on it once, stood firmly on the level hard ground, finally feeling the power of it through the soles of her bare feet.

The day she had been carried from it when her spirit had quailed at the power of what she had done.

This time it did not take very long at all. It was as though the Road was no longer a wild thing hiding from Thea, playing games with her mind. She had been allowed to step upon it, had stood on it, had been invited to return. By every sacred law, it was hers now, a part of her, something she could claim as her own.

Even so, she hesitated for a long moment as she came to a sudden unexpected stop at the wall of unshaped stone that bordered the Barefoot Road here, which had apparently decided that it would choose to exist less than an hour's easy walk from Cheveyo's front door. The Road stretched as far as Thea could see, absolutely and precisely straight from horizon to horizon, some thirty feet wide, its surface smooth and bare of stray blades of grass, as even and flat and hard as any paved highway of Thea's own world. It looked as though it had been slapped into shape and kept clear by a thousand years of passage, by many thousands of reverently bare feet set upon it.

"Where does it go?" Thea finally asked quietly, her eyes resting on where the Road met the horizon.

"To where it needs to take you," Cheveyo said. "You can give me back the staff now. You don't need it anymore."

As once before, when he had taken her to the mesa from which she had stepped into the First World, his voice came from behind her. Thea turned her head, realized that she had somehow taken that step onto the Road or it had stretched to enclose her, that she stood with her feet bare upon it and Cheveyo's staff resting lightly on the ground by her toes. She glanced down, curled her feet against the Road, felt its solidity beneath her soles, and then looked up at Cheveyo again.

"You aren't coming, are you," she said.

"The Road takes no two people to the same place," Cheveyo said. "It was my task to bring you here. Where you choose to let the Road take you now, I cannot follow."

"Can it take me home?" Thea asked a little wistfully.

"It can take you anywhere," Cheveyo said, "although it may choose its own manner of achieving that destination. Give me the staff."

"Is this good-bye?" Thea said, hesitating, clinging to the staff for another moment, her eyes unexpectedly bright. At the moment of parting, she suddenly knew that she would miss Cheveyo—his dry humor, his brusque good mornings followed by precise orders of what the day's activities would be, his apparent inability to give quarter in anything he asked her to do, and his quiet pride when she did succeed in her tasks, even the aggravating quiet serenity that was his shield against the trials of the world. He had taught her everything without seeming to teach her anything at all.

Thinking back, she was astonished and a little ashamed at how she had wronged him when she had first arrived. He had not been the ending of anything at all—he had, in fact, been the beginning of everything. . . .

For some reason Thea's mind latched fleetingly on the duffel bag she had brought with her when she had stepped out of the Alphiri Portal into Cheveyo's world—the duffel bag that was still pretty much packed exactly as it had been when she had carried it into Cheveyo's house and left it slumped against the wall behind the curtain that divided her space from his in the single room. How little she had needed its contents. How lightly she abandoned them, as she set her face toward home.

Cheveyo allowed her the moment of reflection. When she looked up again, it was with a sense of something powerful and new within her—an echo of Cheveyo's own serenity, perhaps.

She held out the staff. "Thank you," she said. There was nothing more she wanted to say, nothing less. She didn't feel the need to ask a single question.

Cheveyo took the staff, bowed his head in acknowledgment.

"I will never forget you," Thea said, lifting her hand in a gesture that was farewell, taking a single step away from the edge of the Road, ready to start walking.

"I know," Cheveyo said, "because I have something for you. Wait."

He unfastened the two feathers that had always been tied to the head of his staff with a leather thong, the black feather and the black-and-white. Then he took something from around his neck, threading the two feathers onto a new thong that had been his necklace and already had something hanging upon it. When he was done, he held his handiwork out to Thea.

"These two you know," he said, nodding at the two feathers he had just taken from the staff. "You have seen them every day, for as long as you have lived in my house. For once, I am giving you an answer to a question you never asked—what they mean. The black-and-white feather is an eagle's; the black one is from a raven. They were given to me by my own teacher, many, many years ago, and now I pass them on to you because they are symbols of things you already have, of things you brought here with you—the eagle's feather for courage, the raven's feather for wisdom. The third feather is a gift from me to you, one I have carried with me for many weeks in the knowledge that this day would come."

Thea stared at the third feather, her vision a little blurred with tears. It was a long one, barred gray and white, and one she could not identify. "Whose is the third feather?" she whispered.

"My people take animals as totems of our faults and virtues," Cheveyo said. "One of them is the wild turkey, and it is from a turkey's wing that this third feather on your necklace comes. It will serve, I hope, to remind you of one of the most important lessons you have learned while in my care."

Thea felt the beginnings of laughter bubbling within her. "And what is that?" she said.

"Patience, Catori," Cheveyo said with one of his rare smiles. "Patience."

Thea ducked her head to let him place it around her neck, and then, after another long moment, they stepped away from each other, Thea farther onto the Road, Cheveyo into the desert scrub at his back, the stone wall between road and desert suddenly a solid barrier between them. He lifted a hand in blessing and farewell.

"Go well," he said gravely. "Perhaps it may come that we shall cross paths again, for the Road goes everywhere. And now, I think I shall go back and see if this time I cannot prevail upon the gods of the summer storms. I am in the mood for a challenge."

Thea said nothing, not trusting her own voice, merely raising her right hand in a gesture that was an echo of Cheveyo's own; her left was curled with protective pride around the three feathers that he had given her, the three virtues with which he had blessed her. Then she turned and began walking away without looking back.

Somewhere far behind her she could hear the distant sound of thunder, as if in answer to Cheveyo's defiant words.

The mesas rising to the side of the Road were beginning to reflect back the orange-gold light of a sun sinking toward sunset before Thea stopped walking, as though waking from a dream. The parting with Cheveyo had left her feeling wretched, but she had not felt *lonely*, not until this moment, not until she realized that the sun was going down. With the liquid sunlight of summer pouring down all around her, she had almost unconsciously been remembering Tawaha's words: *Where you are and where light is, I will always be with you.* However irrational it might have seemed, that litany had made her feel safe from harm.

Now, suddenly, she felt the first flutter of panic. The sun was going down, the swift desert twilight would be upon her very soon, and after that, night. And she had no real idea of what to do next, other than to keep walking. The way back, she had been told, lay through an Alphiri Portal—which was fine, except that she had no knowledge of how to open one. And even that paled into insignificance as she considered whether she wanted to open one, not with an Alphiri at its controls and herself trusting that she would be delivered where she wanted to go. She could not forget the expression in the eyes of the one who had turned to glare at her through the Portal, one of the three in the woods near her home who had been waiting there for her to return.

What is it that they want from me?

As though searching for a way to make her feather talismans yield the virtues for which they had been named, Thea touched the eagle feather, the middle one, and stroked it gently. Courage: to face the night alone, or to find a way to call the Alphiri, to have them open the Portal that would take her home. . . .

Her fingers, stroking the feather, suddenly froze as they came into contact with something else, hidden under her tunic—something she had worn ever since she had first set foot in Cheveyo's world, something her own father had placed around her neck.

You'd better wear it.

The Pass. The medallion that had paid for her passage here. The price of the passage home.

Thea spared a thought to wonder why she had almost forgotten about the Pass medallion since she'd stepped out of the Alphiri Portal and into Cheveyo's hands, but the light was fading and she had no time to meditate on the matter. It was a Pass—her father had neglected to mention exactly *how* it worked, but it was supposed to take her home.

She fished it out of her tunic, untangled the chain from around the thong on which the feathers hung, slipped it over her head and held it in the cupped palm of her hand. One side of it was smooth and rounded, like a polished river pebble. The other side bore an engraving, so stylized that she could not really tell what it was supposed to represent, but there in the center of the medallion disk was a symbol she recognized.

Each of the trading polities—the Faele, the Alphiri, the Dwarrowim, and a number of smaller partners—had their own sigil, a symbol of their people, which was used as a seal for their trade agreements and contracts. The humans had one, too—a human form within a circle, adapted from a classical drawing by Leonardo daVinci, one of the best-known creative mages of human history. It was this that was carved on Thea's medallion.

It suddenly seemed obvious what she should do. She touched the relief image with her finger as the last of the sunset began to dim from the western sky. Then she waited.

The Portal approached just as it had done once before, a distant glow of light coming closer, becoming larger, taking shape and form and solidity until it finally rose before her, the gateway home. It halted, shimmering, a few paces away from the Road, as though its presence would not be sanctioned on that holy ground. The Portal's Guardian took a step out of the gateway. Thea wondered briefly if it could have been the same Alphiri who had brought her here, perhaps even the one who had been so furious at having lost his prize in the woods behind Thea's home. She never could tell them apart; they all looked alike to her, aloof and soulless and coldly beautiful.

"Galathea Winthrop, we come as agreed," the Alphiri Guardian said. "The bargain is concluded—are you ready to depart?"

Thea took one last look around her, at the mesas now brooding in shadows, at the high desert sky with a scattering of glittering stars, and then stepped carefully over the edge of the

Road into the tumbled rocks beside it. She did not turn, did not see, but knew as surely as if she had watched it happen that behind her the Road had vanished as if it had never been, gone as soon as her feet had left it.

She wondered if the Alphiri had even known it was there.

"I am ready," she said, closing her hand around the Pass. "Take me home."

MOON OF THE GREEN CORN

1.

It had been cold dark February when Thea and her father had boarded the airplane to New Mexico, bound for Cheveyo's country, but the air was scented with late summer as the Alphiri Portal deposited Thea near her home and winked out of existence behind her. Dark green leaves of the big-leaf maple trees and the fernlike fronds of cedars nodded in the slight breeze as she made her way from the woods. A squirrel chittered at her from a cedar branch, and something unseen, a bird or a small animal, rustled in the underbrush before falling silent.

A raven, sitting on a log sprouting a thicket of new growth, stayed put for a long time as Thea approached, keeping its beady eyes on her. Then it cawed loudly in a manner Thea could swear had been dripping with resentment, as though the bird had something against her personally, and took flight.

Thea suddenly remembered the raven that had escaped the Alphiri lying in wait for her in the woods, the ones into whose clutches she had sent Corey the Trickster, and followed the raven with her eyes until it disappeared into the trees. She felt uncomfortable, awkward, could not seem to shake the unpleasant sensation of being watched—could not wipe the image of the fury on the face of the thwarted Alphiri. She knew that she had played by the rules, that the bargain had been closed, perfectly concluded with every nuance of the contract fulfilled. That didn't help. She saw glowing Alphiri eyes peering greedily at her from every shadow.

Her family was out in the backyard. Thea could hear the gabble of voices as she approached, and a whiff of barbecue smoke drifted toward her. They were too busy at first to notice her as she rounded the corner of the house, and she stood for a moment observing them, realizing with a sudden pang just how much she had missed them all.

It was full summer, and all Thea's brothers

were at home at the same time. Anthony, the old-est and the one most conscious of his dignity, was lounging back in a green plastic Adirondack chair with his long legs stretched out in front of him and crossed at the ankles. He looked on with benign indifference at Doug and Eddie sit-ting cross-legged on the grass, devouring hot dogs and baked potatoes dripping with butter. Ben was reading by himself in a corner, as usual, his round glasses perched on the end of his nose. And Charlie was poking fun at Frankie, who appeared to be trying to turn a pinecone into a lizard. He had only partly succeeded, because the pinecone had four legs and a long swishing tail but no head (and hence no eyes) and was there-fore capable of escaping Frankie's clutches but not of seeing where it was going. The lizard-cone was skittering all over the lawn, bouncing off people's feet and lawn furniture, with Frankie chasing after it in hot pursuit.

Thea's father, sporting a long green chef's apron, was manning the barbecue itself, ignoring the ruckus until the fleeing cone skidded against his own bare foot. It must still have had prickly edges, because he jerked his foot away quickly, making a small gesture with his free hand in the cone's direction. Its feet instantly disappeared, its tail flicked frantically a couple of times before vanishing in midair, and the pinecone was finally still on the ground, inanimate once more.

"Frankie, *try* and control your . . . ," Paul Winthrop began, and then looked up and saw Thea standing there.

He threw down the barbecue fork and ran toward his prodigal daughter, wiping his hands on the apron.

"Thea! Oh, my God! They said they would let me know when you— They were going to call me— When did you get here? How did I not sense anything?"

Thea had to wait to reply, swept into his fierce bear hug. By that time her mother had arrived, and had to have her own chance at a hug, laughing and crying all at once. Thea got the distinct and uncomfortable impression that there was a great deal of relief mixed into the simple joy at her homecoming, as though Ysabeau had had her doubts that Thea would *ever* return.

Her brothers had clustered around her, too, chattering excitedly, with Eddie pawing at her with greasy, buttery fingers and great affection. All of them except Anthony, who had remained in his chair, content to smile languidly and wave in Thea's direction as though he were visiting royalty.

"What *are* you wearing?" Eddie said through a mouthful of baked potato.

"I . . . ," Thea began, fending him off, but she was given no chance to reply.

"I saved a coyote claw for you!" Frankie said happily. "They shot one up in the hills. I saw it when they brought it down, and I asked if I could have a claw for you."

"Thank you," Thea said with a grimace. She had an unexpected and wholly unwelcome vision of trying to explain to Corey just what she was doing with the knucklebone of his kin.

"Bobbo disappeared for a week or so after you left," Doug said, suddenly reminded of that event as a stately black-and-white cat appeared from the bushes at the far side of the lawn and sat twitching its tail and narrowing its emerald green eyes in Thea's direction. "Mom was really worried. I think he just missed you and tried to go looking . . ."

In the middle of the melee the back door opened to reveal Thea's Aunt Zoë, closely followed by two freshly baked apple pies floating serenely in midair.

"Welcome home!" Zoë called out, flicking out a hand and expertly sending the pies to a resting place on the picnic table before hurrying over to the chattering throng around Thea.

"Are you hungry?" Ysabeau said. "I think the burgers are just about ready."

"If you put them out first," said Doug laconically, glancing back at the barbecue where something was beginning to smoke ominously.

Paul Winthrop shot a quick look over in that direction, and uttered a sharp monosyllable. The smoking stopped.

"Come on over here and tell us everything," Eddie said, having finally swallowed the last of his potato and wiping his mouth with the back of his hand, leaving both far greasier than either had been before. "Where *were* you, anyway? All Dad would say was that you were in a kind of school camp. It's all very mysterious."

"You missed such a great summer!" Frankie said. He was clutching his pinecone, and Thea was careful to avoid any close contact with the object—being Frankie, he might try again just to show off, and this time give it nothing but a set of sharp teeth.

"Later," Ysabeau said. "Doug, you'd better

get another hot dog. I think somebody stepped on yours."

"That was me," Eddie said brightly.

Doug cuffed him, but not hard, since he would get another hot dog out of the deal.

They milled back to the barbecue, everyone talking at once. Zoë had slipped an arm around Thea's waist and now she leaned down and planted a quick kiss on Thea's hair.

"Tell your brothers nothing until you've talked to your folks," she whispered into Thea's ear, and then lifted her face, wearing a broad smile of genuine delight. "I knew you were back," she said confidently out loud. "The sun was singing."

"Oh, Zoë," Ysabeau said with an indulgent smile.

"What was its voice like?" Thea asked, looking up.

"Rich and gold," Zoë said complacently. "And strong. And gentle."

Thea smiled, remembering the voice in which Tawaha had spoken to her back in the First World.

"Oh, yes," she said with feeling.

Both her parents looked up sharply— exchanging a swift glance with each other—but neither chose to pick up on it, not here in front of Thea's brothers.

Luckily Frankie had a few exploits he simply could not wait to tell Thea about.

"I figured it out!" he said happily as Thea was being plied with picnic food: Paul flipping a hamburger onto a paper plate, Ysabeau adding potatoes and salad, Zoë fussing with her apple pies. "I figured *everything* out, and wait till I get back to school and show them how it's done!"

"Don't take the pinecone with you," Eddie said.

"Yeah, they'd never believe you," leered Doug.

"It was an accident," Frankie said hotly. "I'd like to see *you* do better!"

"There will be," Paul said calmly, "no further messing around with pinecones. Thank you."

Frankie turned back to Thea. "But I have to show you," he said. "I have it in my room. The thing—you know, the *thing*—the thing that you . . ." He remembered belatedly what the "thing" he was talking about had meant to Thea herself, and paused for a moment, swallowing. And then decided it didn't matter anymore. "The assignment, remember? The steel ball?"

"Yeah," Thea said carefully.

"I did it—I figured it out! I have to show you later."

"I made a cockatrice," Eddie said smugly.

"Yeah, and got detention for it," Doug said. "The teachers usually don't like critters bent on mischief running loose around the school."

"Well, they might as well keep both of *you* home, then," said Ben mildly, fussing with his glasses.

"Oh, please," said Anthony. "Kids' games."

"You were one, too, once," Ysabeau said. "There was the time that you—"

"Uh. Over and done with." Anthony stood up rather faster than the Adirondack chair allowed and almost lost his balance before gaining his footing. Doug and Eddie looked up at him, smirking. "I think," Anthony said, "I want some lemonade."

"We finished it," Zoë said.

"I'll make some more," Anthony said, starting toward the kitchen.

Ysabeau gave her firstborn a long hard look. "*You?* Volunteering? Who are you and what have you done with my son?"

"No spells," Paul said without lifting his eyes

from the grill. "You always make it too sour when you make it that way. Either squeeze the lemons or do without until someone makes more."

Anthony looked as though he wanted to reply, but then thought better of it and stalked off toward the house with his chin held high in a manner that was almost theatrical.

Behind him, one of the younger brothers giggled.

Thea's absence had been explained away in mundane terms to her brothers. They had all been sent to summer camps over the years. Two of them, Doug and Eddie, had been to one that same year, and assumed that Thea's stories would be identical to their own—hiking, swimming, and such—only more boring because hers would be "girly." Still, she'd been away for a while—and she had been missed.

There were questions, of course, but Thea managed to come up with replies bland enough to nip in the bud any blossoming of dangerous curiosity. There was only one bad moment—when Anthony, having got over his huff and succumbed to the much stronger pull of his curiosity, had asked, in his usual languidly sardonic manner, whether Thea's magical talents had improved any over the summer.

"Well," Thea said after a moment of silence, "I couldn't bring that cone of Frankie's back to life."

"*Frankie* couldn't bring that cone of Frankie's back to life," said Eddie, smirking.

"I could so!" Frankie said, rousing in defense of his new talents. "I showed you before, with the slug."

Thea winced, despite herself. "What did you do to the slug, Frankie?"

Frankie shot her a wounded look, as though he had believed that she would be on his side. "I turned it into a banana," he said.

"Frankie, it was a banana slug to begin with," said Eddie.

"I should have put it under your pillow. And then turned it back into a slug."

Zoë grimaced. "Please," she said plaintively, "I'm eating."

It was a signal for a contest between Frankie and Eddie as to who could think of the most disgusting things, both with and without the aid of magic, to be done with one of the Pacific Northwest's huge yellow banana slugs. Zoë finally heaved a deep sigh and pushed away her plate.

"Come on, Thea," Zoë said at last, getting up and stretching, "I'll help you get unpacked before I go home."

"But I don't . . . ," Thea began, and then caught a conspiratorial glance.

"Anything for the laundry?" Ysabeau said, looking slantwise at her husband and receiving a tiny nod. "The entire bag, if you're anything like the boys. They came home and just poured their luggage into the washer."

"Mom," said Eddie reproachfully.

Frankie snickered; Eddie picked up the abandoned pinecone, which had been lying close to his feet, and threw it at Frankie, who ducked and ran. Anthony leaned back in his chair and closed his eyes, as if the whole thing was juvenile and undignified and beneath him. Paul distracted the others by returning functioning legs to the cone, which chased the two boys.

In the resulting mayhem, Thea, Ysabeau, and Zoë slipped quietly into the house.

Thea's room was much as she had left it. It was a perfectly ordinary room—a single bed, neatly made with a bright quilt on top; a desk still piled with all the things that had been occupying her mind before she had left home; even a few pieces of clothing neatly draped over the chair in the corner. On the wall was the magiposter she had received for her twelfth birthday, in which a landscape went through a cycle of delicately changing seasons. It was summerish now, apparently following the seasons in the world outside; a faint scent of apricots came from it, and there was a distant lazy buzzing of bees in the background. But there were already hints in the corners that another season was coming, with one or two leaves shading into gold as you gazed into the image. It all seemed breathlessly luxurious to Thea now, compared to the house hewn from living rock in which she had been living for the past couple of months. Ysabeau closed the door behind them, and then spelled a magical barrier line across it. Anyone simply eavesdropping would hear a murmur of voices and intermittent laughter. Anyone trying to enter without an invitation to do so would find the room apparently empty.

"Are you all right?" Ysabeau asked, reaching out to brush Thea's cheek gently.

"I'm fine, Mom. I'm better than fine."

Ysabeau sat down rather suddenly on Thea's bed. "I was afraid," she said very simply.

"Did it work?" asked Zoë, more pragmatically. "Don't be silly, Ys, Paul must have known that she'd be okay. He wouldn't have handed his child over to just anyone. I'm not certain of where you went, Thea, but we all know *why*— did it work?"

Thea opened her mouth to speak and time froze. The presence of the two women watching her faded into sudden background as swift thoughts swam through her mind. Grandmother Spider's unequivocal acceptance of Thea's gifts, and of the reasons that they had never shown themselves in her world. Cheveyo's voice: *You pick the battleground.* The memory of that rich golden voice: *Where you are and where light is, I will always be with you.* The ribbon of sunset light: *Who knew you'd be a true weaver. . . .*

She shrugged, and the moment splintered into the present once again.

"No," she said carefully, "not . . . really."

Ysabeau slowly closed her eyes.

"Mom, it's okay," Thea said. "I'm fine. Really I am. With everything. I do have stuff to tell you, but later, when I've . . . sorted it all out."

"With the rest of the world in the state that it's in, I really wanted for this one thing to go right," Ysabeau said plaintively.

"It will," Thea said. She had not really known what she would do next, after she came home, but she knew what she needed: time to settle back into this world, to see how much of Cheveyo's world and of Grandmother Spider's world could be brought here, had a place here. "I'll go to the Academy."

Zoë glanced up, an eloquent eyebrow raised. "So all this summer did for you was to finally convince you that you're 'incurably incompetent'?"

"What?" Ysabeau said, turning to her sister.

"Thea talked to me about this, before she went away, Ys. 'The Last Ditch School for the Incurably Incompetent'—that's what she called the Academy. It smelled awfully like a place where derelicts are sent to die and decay, the last time she said it. As I recall, she felt like you were trying to get rid of her, bury her out of sight, sweep her under the carpet, forget she existed. . . ."

"Thea?" Ysabeau turned to her daughter, trying to understand. "You don't believe that we would ever do anything like that?"

"No," Thea said, her eyes locked on the hands she had folded in her lap.

"Come to think of it, it does have a different taste in the mouth this time around. So—what changed?" Zoë asked quietly. "You?"

"Well . . . maybe it's for the best, after all," Thea said. She lifted her gaze and met her mother's eyes squarely, without flinching, sticking out her chin with a mixture of bravado and defiance. "I can always do something *different*. Something I can be really good at." She suddenly remembered her own mental analogy, back in the First World, awash with images, ideas, information that needed sorting, cataloging, collating. "Computers, maybe," she said, and then smiled with just a touch of sadness. "I'll leave the non-transformation of pinecones to Frankie."

"Oh, Thea," murmured Zoë.

Thea bristled, wanting to demand that Zoë should stop feeling sorry for her—but it was not pity that gleamed in Zoë's eyes as her gaze rested on her niece.

"I'll talk to your father," Ysabeau said faintly.

Thea had thought that she would spend days talking about her time with Cheveyo when she got home, especially to Zoë, with whom she'd always had a special rapport. But as soon as she could, she had tried, surreptitiously, reaching out for the light as she had done with such apparent ease in Cheveyo's world, and had discovered that here in her world, she could still not do anything that could be called magic, anything that she could show to the adults in her family as proof that what she had to tell them was the truth. So she let the days slip by and found herself saying as little as she could get away with, until such time as she could find the answers to the rest of her questions and with them the true path to the abilities she now knew she had. Before she could be sure of that, she was back in the same circumstances that she had been plucked from to go to Cheveyo in the first place. The circumstances in which she had apparently chosen to keep her magic lying low, out of sight. It seemed a good idea to continue doing so until she knew just exactly whose sight she was keeping it out of, and if the other polities—most specifically the Alphiri—wanted something from her, she could think of no better place than the Academy to keep out of their way until she was ready to face them.

Her father had asked, outright, later, and would have been less than he was if he had not realized that her account was riddled with lies of omission.

"Thea," he said, sitting in one of the leather armchairs in his office and leaning earnestly in toward his daughter with his elbows on his knees and the fingers of his hands laced together, "you need to tell me everything—I can't help if you're keeping things back from me."

"What did you expect to happen, Daddy?" Thea asked.

Paul had looked away. It was just for an instant, before his eyes came back to rest on Thea, full of love, full of unqualified support. "Whatever happened," he said, "I need to know."

But it had been enough, that moment, and the old hurt had been back—perhaps he hadn't been expecting his daughter to return as a full-fledged mage, but he had been expecting . . . something. And now he wanted to know what had happened, back in that place where she had gone alone, where he could not have followed. Part of him had wanted to cradle his little girl in his arms and never let her go—but that part of him that did let her go wanted her to bring back something, anything, that would have justified his own decision to send her away in the first place. And she was still not quite meeting those expectations.

But it was his very expectations that somehow made Thea wary, held her back. She told her father about her experience without quite telling him the most important lessons she had learned. Not then. Not yet. Not until she could lay it all at his feet, the whole glittering prize, and see him take it from her hands and see that fierce light of pride shine again in his eyes.

Paul had known when he was defeated, and was canny enough not to pursue the direct approach. Thea's mother had wheedled, next, in the artless way that usually got results simply because her children could not believe that she had expected her transparent intentions to be less than utterly obvious to them. Aunt Zoë had simply waited, and looked as if she would wait for as long as it took, and that was the hardest. All of Thea's life she had regarded Zoë as not so much an aunt as a slightly older and wiser best friend—sometimes, during particularly lonely parts of Thea's growing up, an only friend. Thea hadn't even realized how much she would have valued Zoë's advice until her instincts told her not to ask for it.

School was due to start in the second week of September. There had been a summer-school program at the Wandless Academy for people like Thea who were transferring from other schools, who needed to be brought up to speed on subjects other than Ars Magica—but that was almost over by the time Thea had returned home.

"Will they still take me early?" Thea had asked, wondering if the dormitories would be open before the fall term began.

"Yes, but there would be no point in—"

"Then I'd rather go now," Thea said. "It's only another week or so until school starts. I could do some catch-up work on my own."

"But you could do it here at home, sweetie," Ysabeau had argued.

"I'd rather go," Thea said.

It was a hard thing to explain, but Thea felt something changing in the air around her. The newspapers and the television news were full of apparently random bad news—but Thea's every instinct told her that the randomness was fake, a setup for something even worse that she could not wholly grasp yet. It was all very ominous and full of nameless dread, and the worst of it, perhaps, was that Thea was acutely aware that she was seeing all of this through very different eyes from before. It was hard to figure out what had really changed, her world or herself.

She said some of this, carefully, to Zoë, but for once her aunt was not helpful.

"It's always been a nasty world," Zoë said to Thea. "It smells of putrid things all the time— politicians' promises are always a pile of rotting herring. Have you been listening to late-night talk shows again?"

But Thea was uncomfortably aware that it wasn't just the late-night talk shows. It was everywhere. It was everybody . . . but, in particular, it was everyone who held magic, in whatever way. It was just a nagging feeling, an insistent little whisper at the back of Thea's mind—something like a persistent headache. If she were to believe that little whisper, she already had answers in her possession without being aware yet that they added up to anything whole.

2.

Parting with everyone only a few weeks after her homecoming had been harder than Thea had anticipated. Her mother had cried as though Thea were leaving home for good. As for her brothers, Anthony (thankfully) had not been home for the farewells, so Thea had been spared his barbs; Frankie looked subdued and a little frightened as he hugged her good-bye, as though he was bracing himself to go down the same path; the others sounded vaguely bewildered at yet another sudden departure. It was Ben—gentle, quiet, studious Ben—who had taken her aside and thrust one of his own books into her hands.

"Take that with you," he said. "It will remind you of home if you get lonely."

"What is it?" she asked, glancing down.

"Spell primer," he said, with a tiny twist to his mouth.

"But I'm not allowed . . . you know I can't . . ."

She had tried to thrust the book back at him, but he had folded her hands around it. "It's in Swedish," he said. "You couldn't do any damage if you wanted to. But I just wanted you to remember us. Even Frankie. Now him, I couldn't give this to him. He'd manage to read a sentence backward, turn it into Hungarian, and produce a fire-breathing dragon when he was trying to pull a rabbit out of a hat."

Thea hiccuped, half crying, half laughing, and suddenly hugged him tightly, full of fierce affection.

"They'll just take it away from me at the school," she said, clutching the book with both hands as if someone wanted to snatch it from her right there and then.

"If you tell them about it," Ben said smiling, peering at his little sister with an almost comical air of conspiracy. "You'll be fine. And if you're not, just call me."

Zoë had hugged her, too, and reiterated her promise. "If you're in trouble, I'll know," she whispered. "And I'll come get you."

"You didn't, in the summer," Thea said. She didn't mean it as an accusation—there had been no way Zoë could have possibly kept her promise that summer—and she suddenly heard Cheveyo's trenchant voice: *Don't whine.*

"Well, I will this time," Zoë said sturdily.

It was with those words ringing in her ears that Thea turned her back on them all and slipped into the passenger seat of Paul's car.

Paul drove Thea to the school. Even this gesture was an admission of failure; everyone owned cars in their world, but more as an indicator of social status that as a necessity or an essential means of transport. Cars were used to drive to the theater or even just the grocery store, places where they might be shown off, noticed, admired—not as the only available means of transport. The necessity to drive to a place like any mundane being without an ounce of magic in their blood was particularly galling—but Wandless was that isolated from magic. Not only did it turn its back on Ars Magica in its curriculum, but there was no way to gain access to it other than by humdrum, grounded ways without any sparkle of enchantment to them—no portals, no slipways, no transfigurations, nothing of the sort. No working of magic was permitted inside the grounds of the school.

They boarded the commuter ferry that would take them to the small town on the Olympic Peninsula that was home to the Wandless Academy. Paul seemed to want to talk, but Thea wasn't ready to discuss Cheveyo with her father—not fully, not yet. There, on the ferry, suddenly aware that she would be far away from home for a long time, Thea began to miss her father even before he left her behind. It was a fierce feeling, colored by the absence that had gone before, by the fact that she had barely had time to reconnect with him before she was gone again from her home and her family.

Perhaps perversely, she dealt with the emotions by simply going off by herself to the back of the ferry and standing there, leaning on the railing, watching as the gap of ocean widened between her and home.

She had thought herself alone, but she slowly became aware that there was another person on the ferry's back landing with her, a young man nursing a plastic cup of something that smelled like coffee, his head bare and the sharp wind ruffling his sandy hair, his feet encased in snakeskin cowboy boots with impossibly narrow tips, incongruously dusty for the location they were in. Dusty with earth of a different color . . .

"I've a bone to pick with *you*," the young man said, sounding aggrieved.

She knew that voice. Her eyes snapped to his face, now turned toward her, the expression in his golden eyes half amused and half annoyed.

The last time Thea had seen Corey the Trickster, he had been flapping away on raven wings from a trio of very annoyed Alphiri.

"How did *you* get here?" Thea asked, panicked, looking around for any Alphiri he might have brought with him.

"*You* pushed me," he said. "I've been trying to get back home ever since, but somehow it's been . . . quite difficult. It was as much as I could do, for a long while, just to get back to my shape. And even now . . ." He glanced down at his hands, and Thea realized he was wearing gloves. They appeared innocuous, until she noticed a couple of raven feathers sticking out in the gap between one glove and his sleeve. "I can't get rid of all of them," Corey said. "I didn't plan on turning into that raven, and the shape is remarkably perisistent when you're forced into it."

"Hey," Thea said, "you would have handed *me* over without a qualm, and I can't turn into anything."

"Looks like you can do many other things," Corey said conversationally.

Thea threw a covert frightened glance back toward the other end of the ferry, where her father was.

"Not much I can do," Corey said wolfishly, "not out here, not with raven feathers still sticking to me, but I can still do little things. Don't worry, nobody will come to interrupt. I can't hold it long, but I can hold it long enough."

Thea suddenly lost her temper. "What do you *want*?" she demanded. "Just what *did* they promise you for delivering me?"

"More than enough," Corey said, and there was a glint of greed in his eye. "The offer still stands."

"So they *do* want me," Thea murmured.

Corey threw her a quizzical look. "But you knew that."

She met his gaze squarely. "Why?"

"Why what, child?"

"Why do they want me, Corey? What do they want with me?"

"How should I know?" His eyes had slid off hers and he appeared deeply interested in the contents of his coffee cup, which he lifted to his lips. "But we're not done yet. . . ."

"Unless you've got a posse of Alphiri behind you ready to hand me over to," Thea said, "I think we are. And from here on . . . I am aware of you. And of them."

A metallic door opened and closed somewhere behind them. Corey threw a startled glance in that direction, and a stray black feather suddenly popped up beside his eye.

"Wait a minute," he protested, "I didn't release—"

"Thea?" it was Paul's voice. "Is everything all right?"

Another feather materialized beside Corey's nose, and then the nose itself did a disturbing woggle between being an actual nose and a yellowish beak.

Corey let out a small squawk.

"This isn't over," he said, or tried to say—it was hard to talk with the beak getting in the way. An outraged growl rumbled deep in his throat, and he turned on his heel and sidled out of sight behind a bulkhead just as Paul came up to stand beside his daughter.

"Who was that?" he inquired conversationally. "He wasn't from around here, was he?"

"Nobody," Thea said quickly.

Too quickly. Paul threw her a sharp glance. "Thea, you aren't telling me . . . ," he began firmly, apparently choosing this moment to get everything out in the open.

But Thea was aware that Corey was close by, somewhere—close enough to overhear things and, being Corey, to offer what he heard for sale.

"I will, Dad," she said, letting a swift sideways glance dart back toward the bulkhead that had hidden Corey from her. "But not now. Not now. . . ."

Thea could see mountains marching by on either side of her as they docked into the ferry bay—the Olympic range on the one hand and the Cascades on the other, snowcapped ramparts rearing high into the sky, edging both horizons.

By the time they drove onto the school grounds, the mountains were barely visible, only the distant Olympics gleaming with white ghost light. The campus itself was almost bland, set into its own acreage on the outskirts of town, a handful of redbrick buildings in a parklike setting full of mature trees. It looked exactly like what it was—a school with a history and a reputation.

If only everyone didn't know just exactly what the reputation was.

They had been met by a Mrs. Chen, the teacher in charge of the girls' residence.

"Galathea Winthrop?"

"*Thea,*" Thea murmured mutinously, eyes downcast.

Mrs. Chen's hearing, honed by years of being housemistress in a boarding school, was sharp. "Thea? Okay. Mr. Winthrop, the principal is expecting you both. You can leave her luggage at the girls' hall, and I'll be over there when you're ready, to help settle Thea in."

The meeting with the principal was brief, and then Thea had been excused while he and her father remained closeted together for another quarter of an hour or so. And then Paul was out, shaking the principal's hand at the door of the office.

"Let me know if there is anything we can do to make Galathea's stay here a rewarding one— as is our wish for *all* the students who enter our school. It was a pleasure meeting you, Mr. Winthrop."

They made their way back to the girls' hall and then stood awkwardly for a moment, facing each other. Paul, standing beside the car with his hands by his sides, looked almost trapped.

"Do you have everything?" he asked, his voice strange, distantly polite.

"Yes, Daddy," said Thea, suddenly moved to the diminutive again. She hadn't called him Daddy for a long time. Not since he had left her with the Alphiri guardian of the Portal that would take her to Cheveyo.

Her father gave her a swift hug and turned

away, pouring himself into the driver's seat of the car, turning on the ignition with an almost savage little motion, and driving away with an acceleration that was not quite necessary.

Apparently Mrs. Chen had been watching through the curtains for Paul's departure, for she emerged to stand at Thea's side as the car leaped forward with an angry little motion and then sped, with Paul driving way too fast for the school speed limit, down the curved road and out of sight behind a copse of trees.

"Your things are already in your room," Mrs. Chen said. "Your roommate isn't there just now, so you'll have a chance to do most of your unpacking in peace."

"Roommate?" Thea had not thought further than getting here. She had always had her own room—except for the months in Cheveyo's house, but that had been different.

"Ah, it won't be that bad," said Mrs. Chen. Thea had almost, but not quite, succeeded in concealing her misgivings in the tone of her voice, but the expression on her face, apparently, was quite enough for Mrs. Chen to read between the lines. "You'll like Magpie. You'll see. You two will be good for each other. That's what I do, you know," she said, pushing her short silvery-white hair back behind her ear in a gesture that Thea would quickly begin to find very familiar. "All of us have pieces of spirit—of personality—that we lack. We can't help it, it's the way we are. I'm here to find the best matches. To help our students graduate from here as whole as we can make them."

A heavy silver medallion hung around Mrs. Chen's neck. It looked oddly familiar to Thea, but she had not paid close attention to it earlier. Now something in the way she had described her position in the school made Thea focus closely on the medallion for the first time. What Mrs. Chen had just said had a nuance to it—the words might have been innocuous enough, but somehow they had *sounded* magical, and the medallion confirmed it. It was silver, dark with age and embossed with an insignia Thea suddenly recognized. Her eyes snapped back to Mrs. Chen's face. The woman was smiling, an expression that managed to conceal more than it revealed.

"Mage, First Class," Thea said, nodding at the medallion. "But I don't understand. I thought this place was positively *warded* against magic."

"Mage, First Class, *retired*," Mrs. Chen said with light emphasis on the last word. "You are right, no magic is practiced here. But Thea, in order to know what it is that we do not do here, we have to be aware of what can be done. Many of the teachers here have volunteered to come here after a lifetime of service to the magical world. Some come once their gifts start fading with age—that happens sometimes. Others come because they have renounced their talents, for whatever reason—that happens, too. Most of us at least know what it feels like to practice magic, and some of us even still *do*, outside these grounds, of course. That is more important than you realize, in a place where magic is not permitted."

"My father has a medallion like that," Thea murmured.

"I know," Mrs. Chen said. "We even worked together for a while. But he is still active in the field and I . . . I just decided the time had come to bow out. Magic can be exhausting, you know, very wearing on body and mind. It isn't for the very old."

It would have been very rude to ask, and Thea had been brought up to be polite. But something about Mrs. Chen put Thea in mind of

Grandmother Spider. She did not flow and shift and change as Grandmother Spider did, but Mrs. Chen's white hair framed a smooth, unlined face, with only a hint of laugh lines crinkling the corners of her eyes.

"Older than you think, dear," Mrs. Chen said with a smile, aware of the scrutiny and of what lay beneath it. "I'm *much* older than I'll ever admit to being. Trust me, you're safe here—and you'll enjoy Magpie."

"Magpie?" Thea repeated blankly. Mrs. Chen had said it before, but repetition didn't make it sound any less odd.

"Everyone calls her that," Mrs. Chen said, waving her hand in dismissal. "Her given name is Catherine, but I don't think she's answered to that in years."

There was magic in names. Here, where there was no magic, names did not matter. People could choose their own identity and not have one thrust upon them.

Thea found the concept strangely liberating.

The room she was to share with the girl called Magpie was a mess. One of the beds was obviously in use, although it had been rather sloppily made. The chair beside it and the dresser that belonged on that side of the room were draped with discarded clothes and piled with stuff that glittered or gleamed, giving Thea a sudden insight into what had given Magpie her nickname. The dresser mirror was almost obscured by a quantity of gold-sprayed plastic pearls, the kind used for carnival beads or to adorn Christmas trees. There were four bottles of different-colored glitter ranged on the windowsill, for what purpose Thea could not tell. A prism hung in the window, throwing rainbow light into the room.

The other bed, the one that was to be Thea's, had been obviously used as a repository and only halfheartedly cleared. Debris remained on it: an inside-out T-shirt, a dog-eared book, a sketch pad, and a half dozen colored pencils. A string of the golden plastic pearls was draped across the headboard of Thea's bed, like an offering.

"Having another person in here will be good for Magpie," Mrs. Chen said. "She has a tendency to fill any vacuum she is given access to. That side's yours, the drawers are clear, that closet in the corner is for you. I'll be back when Magpie returns, to do the introductions. There's a leaflet in the drawer, there, that tells you a bit about the rules of residence—laundry days, and all that. It should all be pretty simple and self-explanatory, but shout if you have any questions. Welcome to the Wandless Academy, Thea."

Mrs. Chen knew who Thea was, who she had been expected to be. Her welcome was commendably free of pity or condescension. As far as the people in this school were concerned, no student would ever be made to feel inferior by having arrived here—that attitude had been made very clear to the Winthrops in the principal's office.

Thea knew her choice to come to this school had been the right one. There was something waiting here for her to stumble across and make her own.

She gathered up a few stray items of clothing belonging to her roommate and deposited them back on Magpie's bed, clearing her own space, but she didn't have much to unpack and was almost done by the time the door opened again, maybe an hour later, and a voice said, "You must be Thea."

The voice fit with the cheerful untidiness of the room—it bubbled with laughter just under the surface, like water running over pebbles in the streambed. Thea realized with a wince she could not quite hide that Magpie was going to be one of those annoying people who were always irrepressibly chirpy first thing in the morning.

Magpie showed no sign of having noticed it. She was short, maybe five foot two in her stocking feet, her face surrounded by untidy black hair, her eyes round and dark. She was wearing jeans and a green T-shirt with a scattering of sequins on it, her narrow brown feet thrust into a pair of plain sandals.

"I'm here because I'm useless at ancestral magic," Magpie volunteered.

It seemed that the introduction ritual in this place involved just that: getting the awkwardness out of the way. Wandless Academy had a good academic reputation, but the name spoke eloquently of all that it was not, and people usually arrived here for reasons other than the pursuit of a sterling academic record. It was ironic, because actual wands had not been used in contemporary magic for generations, so even the common, everyday magic of Thea's world was at least technically "wandless." But here in the school, it had been a name deliberately chosen to emphasize its identity.

A nickname, in a way. Just like "Magpie."

Thea had offered the usual comfortable excuse as a response to Magpie's words. "I'm here because I can't do any magic at all."

Magpie had given her a sympathetic look but had not pried. That, too, was in the unspoken rules. One did not ask for what was not freely offered. Thea didn't ask further about "ancestral magic," either—somehow understanding that if Magpie felt so inclined, she would share any relevant information.

"Sorry about the mess," Magpie said with a grin, seamlessly shifting the topic of conversation.

That had been all in the way of introductions. Somehow, here, it was easy to accept.

It was strange at first for Thea, having a roommate. The room at the Wandless Academy's girls' residence was not large, and they had both had to adjust their personal space to fit the circumstances; Thea soon took to picking up anything she could not identify as belonging to her and leaving it on Magpie's bed. It was harder to remember not to leave stuff of her own lying around, particularly if it was shiny or sparkly. It wasn't that Magpie was a thief, but the nick-name was definitely there for a reason. She was fatally attracted by glitter, and if Thea left a pair of earrings on the dresser she would likely find them stuck into the woven blanket that Magpie had draped over her bed's headboard. Not because she had stolen them or particularly wanted them, but because they looked pretty there.

But as a roommate Magpie was soon simply a part of the whole place, her presence almost unnoticed unless Thea happened to be looking for a favorite pair of earrings that were missing again.

The golden moon of August, Sunyi'ta, the Moon of Green Corn, faded quickly as the days fled by, and then it was September, the end of summer, with another moon trembling on the verge of something—not quite round, not quite full, but very quickly it would be. It would hang low in the sky: a bleached white circle, casting cold light. Cheveyo would have called it Senic'ta, the Harvest Moon.

Senic'ta, the moon of September—the moon under whose bright light you were supposed to reap what you had sown. And here was Thea's harvest—with herself ensconced in what she had once called the Last Ditch School for the Incurably Incompetent. This place—the only place free of magic in a world where magic ran free—was this really the only place where someone like Thea could hide, in plain sight, from those who waited to use her for their own ends?

Cheveyo had been a last resort. Thea had been sent to him in order to break a seemingly impregnable barrier, to bring down the wall that stood between her and the gift of magic that ought to have been hers by right. The ruse had succeeded better than anyone could have dreamed—but it had also given Thea a knowledge of danger that nobody had banked on her having. Now she could see the perils that lurked in the illusion of that golden dream held out to her like a shiny bauble to a child.

Whatever it was that she had, the Alphiri wanted. And they were waiting for it. She had thought she had been right not to mention her fears and suspicions when she had returned home, but that had been before she had encountered Corey on the ferry. Thea sometimes found her heart beating very fast, as though terrified, at some thought she had not quite pinned down in her own mind. And it was about the Alphiri, always about the Alphiri. . . .

Back on the red mesa, Thea had asked the single important question: *What do I need to know?*

It was astonishing how alive and vivid Cheveyo's catechism was, here, beyond his world, beyond anything he had ever known. Thea allowed herself a small smile as her hand went to the three feathers that hung around her neck.

Patience, Catori . . .

If there were answers, and if she dared not use magic to seek them, the orb of the full moon rising in the heavens would turn a new page for Thea. Things that might have been hidden under a veneer of magic in the world that she knew could well be exposed when that magic was removed . . . and the only thing left behind would be the stark facts behind the choice she had made long ago.

HARVEST MOON

1.

WITH JUST A HANDFUL of students, the Academy was a quiet and dignified place, its stately buildings shaded by ancient trees. Those students who were present strolled without hurrying, drifting through the woods and court-yards, taking their time. It all changed almost overnight with the beginning of the new school year.

The returning students began to arrive as the merest trickle, a week or so before school officially started, much as Thea herself had done. That trickle turned into a steady flow, and then into a torrent. The windows on the redbrick buildings resembled wide-open eyes, as though the entire school had just been shaken awake from its summer slumbers by the slamming of car doors, the scraping of trunks and suitcases being carried up the stairs, by the shrieks and shouts as friends encountered each other in corridors.

Thea, together with a handful of other new people, lurked self-consciously at the fringes of the student body, in the wake of the first student rush. For Thea this lurking-on-the-fringes thing was nothing new, really—she had done something like this all her life. The pattern, however, was different this time. The fringes had usually been achieved after she had first been cultivated by those eager to gain social cachet by hanging around celebrity—what Thea had once, in a bleak little heart-to-heart with her Aunt Zoë, called Seventhology. It usually lasted just long enough for the groupies to discover that they weren't getting what they thought out of the bargain and begin drifting away. Meanwhile, all sorts of other groups, the kind Thea might have wanted to join and be a part of, passed her by, apparently without so much as being aware of her existence. She had had only a bare handful of people in her life who were what she thought of as friends, and even they hadn't lasted longer than a couple of years apiece.

But there was something at Wandless

Academy that Thea had never had the advantage of before: a roommate like Magpie, who seemed to know everybody and who, in turn, seemed to be on everyone's "To Do" list when it came to rekindling friendship connections for a brand-new school year. Thea was introduced to half of her classmates before classes started and was already accepted as Magpie's sidekick at lunch on the first day of school.

"Hey! Tess! Over here!" Magpie yelled, half rising from her seat beside Thea, and waving vigorously at a dark-haired girl with elegant gold-rimmed eyeglasses who had just walked in with lunch tray balanced in one hand and a bulging book bag in the other. The girl waved awkwardly with the bag, barely managing to avoid dumping the contents of her lunch tray on top of an oblivious student seated at the next table, and started to thread her way to where Magpie had cleared a space for her. Depositing the bag on the floor with an alarming thud, Tess slid the tray expertly onto the table with one hand while swinging her legs over the bench.

"Hey," she said. "New year. New idiots. I've already had to start training people in etiquette."

Magpie giggled. "What did they bring in this time?"

"A bag of Sweet Spells," Tess said. "This one newbie gave a handful to my roommate. She's yet another newbie, and she doesn't know any better, and she offered me one—and I suppose *I* should have known better and recognized them but, hey, my mind was elsewhere, so I had one. At least I scared those two good and proper. Good thing Mrs. Chen was right there."

"You okay?"

"Still have this," Tess said, pushing up a sleeve and showing an angry red rash on her forearm.

"You allergic to candy?" Thea said.

"To magic," Magpie said laconically. "That's why she's here. If she eats anything made with an ingredient of magic, content or process, she might choke to death."

"I thought magic wasn't supposed to work here," Thea said to Magpie.

"It can *work* here, it's just that there are rules against it *being* here. For obvious reasons," Magpie said. "You and I, we're exiles from that world. We don't fit, we don't belong, we can't perform magic. With Tess it's far more serious. The stuff can kill her. This place is more than a haven for magic refugees. It's a sanctuary."

"You mean you can't *leave* this place?" Thea said, turning to Tess.

"Sure I can. My family is pretty good about things," Tess said. "But they *know*. We don't eat anything prepared with magic. My mother makes her own bread, with real flour and real yeast, and she kneads the dough herself. My brother and I couldn't go trick-or-treating at Halloween, because people *will* give out Sweet Spells or Enchantmints, or even just apples with a gigglespell put on them. The first and last time we went—I think we were five or so at the time—my dad was with us, and if he hadn't been there to do first aid I could have died right there."

"Wow," Thea said. "What happens?"

"I can taste the stuff," Tess said, digging her spoon into her mashed potatoes. "Not like this— these are real potatoes, and they've been pre- pared and cooked by hand. No magical shortcuts."

"If they'd used a spell to make it come out creamy . . . ?"

"My throat would close right up," Tess said. "I can't breathe. And then I get the rash. You new?"

"My roommate, Thea Winthrop. She's a magidim, like me," Magpie said, making belated introductions. "Thea, this is Tess Dane—we came up through middle school together. We were roommates for a semester before Mrs. Chen decided to split us up."

"Hi," Tess said, spooning potatoes into her mouth, and then paused, doing a double take. "Wait a minute. Winthrop? Why is that name so familiar?"

"My given name is *Gala*thea. Galathea Winthrop. I used to be famous," Thea said abruptly. "You might have read about me in newspaper archives somewhere."

An expression of understanding crossed Tess's face, and perhaps an echo of sympathy. For a moment Thea heard it whispered, far away, the inglorious echo of her childhood: *Oh, Thea . . .* But in the spirit of Wandless Academy and the unspoken rule of no prying that seemed to apply here, Tess merely nodded at Thea.

"Welcome to the madhouse," she said with a small smile, and turned back to her mashed potatoes.

They finished lunch in companionable silence, and then Magpie fished in her back pocket, com-

ing up with a tarnished broken boxchain necklace, a silver daisy charm with a sparkling crystal
as its centerpiece, the stub of an old movie ticket,
and finally a crumpled class schedule.

"What's your next class?" she asked Tess,
dragging her finger along her schedule to find her
own. "I've got Dead Languages."

"You're taking Latin?" Thea said.

"I had to take something." Magpie shrugged.
"Languages I'm good at."

"I've got computer studies," Thea said.

"With Twitterpat?" Tess said, looking up.
"Me too. Me and Terry both."

"Twitterpat?" Thea repeated with a grin.
According to her own class schedule, the com-
puter science teacher's name was Patrick
Wittering.

"Pat Witter. Patwitter. Twitterpat," Tess said
helpfully. "Just watch his hands."

"Okay," said Thea, still grinning. "Who's
Terry?"

"Her brother," Magpie said. "I have no idea
why anybody would want to futz around with
those infernal machines."

"For the same reason that you took Latin,"
Tess said. "One has to take something. And at

least it's marginally *useful*, huh, Thea?"

"Maybe she could learn how to program in Latin," Thea said.

Magpie giggled. "You two deserve each other," she said. "Go, torture your machines. Say hi to Terry for me."

Patrick Wittering looked barely older than his students, his long, dishwater-blond hair tied back in a funky ponytail. He wore sandals on bare feet, and Tess, nudging Thea in the ribs, imparted the information that those were his preferred footwear all year round; he just added socks in winter. Perhaps it was the minimal age difference, the simple fact that it wasn't that long ago that he had been behind a school desk himself, but he seemed to have an instant and casual rapport with his classes. If he knew that every single one of his students addressed him as Mr. Wittering in class and referred to him as Twitterpat behind his back, he seemed quite unperturbed by the idea.

Tess snagged three computer stations as they arrived for class; Thea took up one, and the other was claimed by Tess's brother, who turned out to be her twin. They had the same huge hazel eyes in long oval faces, and they even wore their hair more or less the same, with Tess's only marginally longer than her brother's.

"Terry, this is Thea. Galathea Winthrop," Tess had said by way of introduction, laying a light emphasis on the surname. It was that unspoken subtext in the Academy—the introduction that gave one's identity and one's reason for being at the school, all in as economical a fashion as possible.

Terry's eyes had sparked with recognition—it was obvious that he knew Thea's name—but he did no more than grunt and nod.

"Some of you I know from last year, back in middle school," Twitterpat said, starting the class. He did have a tendency to talk with his hands, just as Tess had said. As he spoke, his fingers were curling as if making spell gestures, though obviously he was doing nothing of the sort. For some reason Thea found herself thinking about Mrs. Chen's words: *In order to know what it is that we do not do here, we have to be aware of what can be done.* Twitterpat looked as if he too might have known the taste of magic sometime in his life . . . known it well. He was still speaking. "Others have just joined us. Before we can learn more, we should figure out just how much we already know. So. You've got a somewhat jumbled set of arbitrary data in front of you. Let me see you organize it using the computer."

Terry grunted and tapped a set of keys on the keyboard. A grid appeared on the screen of his monitor; he typed furiously for a few moments and then leaned back, arms crossed, eyes flickering across the screen. Things seemed to be happening there, but from her angle Thea could not quite see what.

"What *is* he doing?" she whispered to Tess.

"Oh, leave him alone," Tess retorted. "He thinks he's beyond all of this. He thinks he should be doing college-level stuff."

"Can he?" Thea said, impressed despite herself. She tapped her own data into her computer, looking at what tools had been left for her to use. There had been two computers in Thea's home when she was very young, one Paul's, one Ysabeau's; both Anthony and Ben had eventually added their own. Thea could play a mean game of computer solitaire, and she had used it for writing assignments and, under parental control, research on Terranet, but that was as far as she had gone—this assignment was a new thing for her.

"He's a self-confessed *genius*," Tess said, giving her brother a teasing glare. "He was only top of his class all during middle school. He's probably going to stay in this class only long enough to impress Twitterpat, and then he'll be off on some road to glory all by himself. Brothers. Always thinking they're a superior class of being."

"I know," Thea said, sighing. "I have six of them."

Tess shot her a sympathetic look. "You poor thing."

"That's very good, Terry," Twitterpat said. He had come up while the girls had been whispering and was scanning Terry's monitor closely. His hands came fluttering up to his face, and he beat a contemplative tattoo on his cheeks with his fingertips.

Terry grunted.

"Let me see. . . ." Twitterpat leaned over Terry's shoulder and touched a few keys. A few things blinked, rearranged themselves; the grid redrew itself around the new array. "Very good, very good indeed. What about you, Tess?"

"Working on it," Tess said, bending her head over her keyboard.

Twitterpat nodded and smiled, dropped his

hands, then lifted one and let it drift briefly in Thea's direction, recalled it to his side. "New this year?"

"Yes, sir."

"Have you had much background?"

"No, sir," Thea said. "My father has a computer, for e-mail and storing stuff on, and Mom does, too . . . but we weren't allowed to use them much."

"I see." The hands danced again, as though he were typing in midair, retrieving information. "You are . . . Galathea."

"Thea," Thea corrected him. "Sir."

"Of course. Well, carry on. *Very* good, Terry."

Twitterpat walked off and then stood, watching another student's screen over his shoulder.

Terry leaned back in his chair, arms crossed, staring at his screen.

"He can't be *done* already," Thea muttered.

"Oh, he's always done," Tess said.

Terry flashed her a smug smile, and then flicked his eyes back to his screen.

"Does he talk?" Thea said a little sharply.

Terry turned and stared at her, and Tess flicked her hair back with one hand, tapping the keyboard with the other.

"Only when he has something essential to say," Tess said. "He kind of . . . got turned off talking at an early age. You know how I can't put anything magic-made into my mouth?"

"Yeah?"

"Well, he's kind of allergic to magic, too. Except with him, it's speech—he can't utter a word with a magical shading without choking on it. Literally. He can't *talk* about spells, let alone speak one. His tongue swells and his throat closes and he turns a neat shade of sky blue."

"But not *every* word one utters is magic. . . ."

"You want to bet?" Tess said, typing furiously, her hair falling forward to hide her face. "In our family? My mom's older brother is Kevin MacAllan, the head of the Federal Bureau of Magic, and she works in the department—few words spoken in our family are free of magic. It's hard enough to make sure that I don't eat anything with magic in it, but it's far harder to keep a child quiet all the time because a stray word he utters could kill him. That's why we're here— Terry was packed off to Wandless when he was practically in kindergarten. They kept me out in the mainstream a little longer, but it proved just as impractical in the long haul—I've been here since grade school. We go home for the holidays, but he pretty much doesn't say a word all summer because it could kill him to try. It takes him a while, once we get back to the school. He does have a voice, he just needs to remember that it's safe to use it, here."

"This isn't working," Thea said, frowning at her screen.

"Wrong software," Tess said, peering at Thea's computer. "You can do it with that, but it's harder than it should be. Try the other spreadsheet."

"Which?" Thea said.

Tess reached out with a pen and tapped an icon at the bottom of Thea's screen. "That one."

"I don't know that one," Thea said, staring at the screen that came up, pulling down menus to examine their contents.

"Easy," Tess said. "Just pretend you're playing hopscotch."

Thea shot her a startled look and then sat forward, face cupped in the palms of both hands, and stared at her computer. Things seemed to blink and rearrange themselves—on screen or in her mind—and her frown suddenly cleared. "Oh!" she said. "I get it!"

Terry looked over and smiled wolfishly.

"Oh, just ignore him," Tess said instinctively, not even turning to look at her brother.

Twitterpat bade them farewell at the end of class with promises of doing something far more interesting very soon, once he had had a chance to look at their work.

The next class was mathematics, where the twins and Thea were joined by Magpie, who had another protégé in tow—a tall, thin boy with a shock of dark red hair and an expression of lugubrious resignation on his long face.

"This is Ben Broome," Magpie said. "He's new this year, too. I saw him moping by himself just outside Latin on the way over here and he seemed lost, so I steered him in the right direction. His dad's Bernard Broome. The chemist who won that prize last year, for the new fuel, remember? When the Alphiri sold us that great fuel that only worked for six months and then never again? Ben's dad figured out what the matter was and fixed it. They're making a whole new kind of car for it now."

"Hi, Ben," Thea murmured.

Terry uttered something between a greeting and a growl. Tess just smiled.

Mr. Siffer, the mathematics teacher, had iron-gray hair cropped close to his skull, wire-rimmed glasses, and a frown that seemed genetically coded into his face.

"For those new to the school," he barked, "I can't stress this often enough—we teach *real* mathematics here. The science of numbers. None of that mathemagic drivel that you might be used to in all those soft schools you went to. No spell-solving of equations, no cheating, no number demons or fractionators, no transformations—other than those defined by the laws of geometry. Nothing but old-fashioned number crunching. Anyone I catch cheating will regret it. Is that clear?"

The class nodded mutely, as one.

"Good. Then we shall all get along very well. I reiterate, no cheating will be tolerated."

"If most of us could cheat in the way he thinks, we wouldn't be here," Tess muttered. "He has a reputation, you know."

"For what?" Thea said.

"They say he was once a very promising math-emage," Magpie said. "And then he walked past a construction site minding his own business one day and a beam fell from a crane and hit him in the head. He's never been quite sane since. . . ."

"Chattering shall cease," Mr. Siffer said with a cold stare. "Now. We have a lot to do."

"He'll be sweet as brown sugar tomorrow," Ben Broome volunteered in a low whisper.

Magpie looked at him with a raised eyebrow. "Oh?"

"I heard about him. He's been here forever, and there are tales . . . later," he said hurriedly, as Mr. Siffer turned gimlet eyes in his direction.

"Mr. Broomstick, is it?" he inquired silkily.

"Broome, sir," Ben said in a small voice. There were a few titters in the back of the classroom.

"Well, Mr. *Broome*," the teacher said, "one more word out of you—or your cronies over there—and you will all be given detention. Do I make myself clear?"

"Yes, sir."

"I'm afraid he's stuck you with a nickname, all right," Magpie said later, as they left the mathematics classroom, with a few whispered catcalls of "Hey, *Broomstick*" following them out of the room. "Now what's this about him being sane tomorrow?"

"Not sane. Sweet. He won't even remember calling me 'broomstick' tomorrow. Aw, *blow*. He won't remember, but everyone else will." He kicked the toe of his sneaker against the scuffed wall.

"Never mind. *We'll* still call you Ben. It won't be a total clean sweep," Magpie said with a not quite innocent smile.

Tess snorted, and even Terry let out a guffaw. Ben glowered at her, and then realized he was being teased. He grinned back wanly and wrinkled his nose, screwed his eyes shut and froze, holding his breath. The others held theirs for a moment, too, and then Ben unscrewed his face and sniffed, his eyes watering.

"What was that?" Magpie said, her own nose twitching in sympathy.

"Thought I'd sneeze," Ben said. "You know how it ambushes you sometimes just behind your nose, and then you don't. Something's been tickling my nose all morning, and I can't tell you what. And it shouldn't, not here. I can smell magic, but here it should be clean. Back in my father's lab . . ."

"Back in the lab, it was the Alphiri magic you could smell, right?" Thea asked.

Ben shot her a startled look. "That's how it started, yeah," he said. "Then it all fell apart, real fast. Six months after that first whiff I caught, I suddenly couldn't stop sneezing. I was in Ars Magica class at my old school, and the smell made my sinuses want to explode. I was homeschooled one year, because I couldn't go to school anymore. It's been really bad in the past couple of months. My father sometimes puts a block on me for a few hours, but then it's back, and it's worse than ever. And then even that didn't work anymore because my dad would come home from the lab and I'd smell him as soon as he came inside and start sneezing like a maniac."

"So you're allergic to magic, too?" Tess said.

"No, it isn't that," Ben said. "Not really, not quite. It's just that it's getting worse, and they thought putting me here might help desensitize me. I don't know what triggered it, unless it was that one time when Dad was redistilling that damned fuel for the twenty-fifth time, and something went wrong, and it escaped into the lab and I got a whiff of it. But so did he, and a lab assistant, and at least one of the cleaning staff. And *none* of them got it. Just me." He sniffed again. "And I can smell something . . . *something*. . . . I don't know. It isn't really there, maybe it's just a memory of it. . . ."

"You smell what? Magic?" Magpie was fascinated. "You do know most of the teachers would
get the whiff of it—old Siffer himself was a
mathemage, you said so yourself—but none of
them have used it, not for years. Maybe it's just
that: the *memory* of magic."

"If that's it, then I'm doomed," Ben said
morosely. "If just the memory of magic is enough
to set me off, I will never be fit for decent society
again."

"And who'd be decent society?"

The voice was unfamiliar, but came from
within their group—it took Thea a moment to
realize that it was Terry who had spoken.

"Welcome back," Magpie said, smiling.
"Look what you've done, Ben—you got him
talking. Now he'll never shut up again."

"Sorry," Ben said, glancing up at Terry. "Um,
present company excepted. . . ."

"Sometimes magic is so over*rated*," Tess said,
tossing her hair back. "Think of it this way—by
the time Siffer is done with us, if the magic in the
world went away tomorrow we could still figure
out how to calculate the square root of minus
one, and nobody else in the world would be able

to do it—not without mathemagic."

"You *can't* calculate the square root of minus one," Ben said earnestly. "Not even mathemagic . . ."

"Lighten up, Sneezy," Magpie said, cuffing him on the shoulder. "She knows. Well, I've got Environmental Studies after the break. What about you guys?"

It turned out that they had all taken that particular elective. Their teacher was a willowy blond woman with narrow hands, long fingers, and ears so pointed she could almost have passed for Alphiri. Certainly Ben seemed startled by her, and Thea felt a distinct urge to start looking over her shoulder again. The teacher, whose quiet voice ensured silence as everyone strained to hear her, spoke with a soft foreign accent and introduced herself as Signe Lovransdottir.

"Norwegian?" Tess wondered in a whisper.

"Icelandic," Ben hissed back.

"Woodling," Magpie murmured with authority.

A girl sitting in front of Magpie overheard her comment, and whipped her head around.

"*What?* What's she doing out of her tree?"

"What on earth is she doing *here?*" Tess whispered.

But that question was quickly superseded by the things that Signe was saying in that lilting accent.

"A lot of our work will be done outside," she said, her moss-green eyes somehow giving the impression that she was focused on every individual student. "We will be looking at environmental impact studies and reports on many different regions. But we also have at least three national parks within striking distance, as well as threatened areas close enough for us to investigate or even adopt and rehabilitate. All of that provides plenty of opportunity for honest-to-goodness fieldwork, which means you might have to give up the occasional weekend to your academic pursuits. In fact, I thought I'd start the school year off with a field trip. We'll be spending the next week or so studying the temperate rainforest phenomenon, and then later we'll go and investigate a real rainforest—a day-trip to the Hoh forest."

A murmur swept the class.

"Background reading assignment," Signe said. "Section Four, starting on page twenty-eight of your textbook . . ."

After class, Magpie found herself the center of

a small but fascinated audience.

"The Quilcah elders, back at the reservation, claim that the forest was full of them," Magpie was saying. "There was a time that Woodling wives were a prize. They were quiet and hardworking and they gave a man his space because they had to go back to their tree every so often. . . ."

"How often?" someone asked. "Every year? Every week? Every day . . . every hour? *That* would be a bummer."

"They could last for a month without returning, I think," Magpie said.

"And if they didn't?"

"They'd, I don't know, wilt and die," Magpie said. "I was told these stories years ago. I don't remember it all. But in my great-grandfather's time they were everywhere."

"But not anymore," said a bronze-skinned boy with dark hair who looked very much like Magpie. "Even the tribal elders haven't seen many of them in the last forty years, and younger folk barely remember them. A Woodling wife would be something that people would pay to see."

"She smells odd," Ben volunteered. They all

turned to look at him, and he flung out his hands defensively. "I don't mean she *smells*, not like that. I can just . . ."

"He has a nose for magic," Magpie explained.

"Yeah. And she smells . . . she almost doesn't smell of anything. There's just a whiff, like a memory of a scent. Like she once touched the source, but she's been away from it for too long."

"Well, she can't be a true Woodling," Tess said. "You couldn't employ one in any kind of real job. They'd be in and out of their tree, probably at all the most inconvenient times. And unless her tree was close enough, it would be impossible—she couldn't get to it fast enough to survive."

"But what are they? Something like a dryad?"

"I guess that's one of their names," Magpie said. "My people have always called them Woodlings. There are different kinds, you know—cedar Woodlings were common around here, they're dark, and they sometimes look too much like us to tell who they really are."

"So what would Signe be?" someone asked.

"Hard to tell. Remember, most of us have never even *seen* one. But I'd say something graceful and silvery and light—willow, maybe, or silver birch or aspen. . . ."

"Remember the Woodling wives?" Thea said. "Did they have children? Could she be half-Woodling, or maybe even less, with just enough of the blood to get Ben's nose twitching but not enough to need a personal tree?"

"Could be she's a foreign Woodling, too, with that name and that hair," Magpie said. "Even Faele get exiled sometimes."

"But if she was exiled, then what happens when she needs to get back to her tree?"

"I'd have to ask my grandmother," Magpie said. "I think the exiles were given a twig and a leaf of their tree, and that was all they would have of their home, all they could ever have again . . . but I think I'm mixing it up in my head now."

"Woodlings are Faele?" Thea asked sharply.

"They're related, I think," Magpie said, glancing at her. "Why?"

"Not important. I thought . . . she might be Alphiri, that's all," Thea said, keeping her voice carefully neutral. She could not possibly have explained the sudden unraveling of tension deep inside her, something utterly impossible to put in rational terms, the sense of having just been saved from an enemy who had breached the defenses of her fortress. The idea of an Alphiri inside the school had, for a moment, chilled her with a cold and gripping fear.

Magpie gave her a long appraising look, but didn't pursue it further.

The discussion petered out, and Tess sighed, perusing her class schedule.

"First day, and I've already got more homework than I know what to do with," she complained mildly.

"And cheating," Terry said, his voice an almost perfect imitation of Mr. Siffer's peevish tones, "will not be tolerated." He grinned and the smile transformed his face, making him seem almost mischievous.

Thea found herself grinning back.

It was going to be a good year.

2.

The work piled up ever higher; the first week of high school disappeared in a flurry of new classes, classmates, and teachers. There were highlights—like that first field trip they took, during which Magpie kept half her attention on her work and the other half on trying to see if Signe ever disappeared from sight while a particular kind of tree was nearby. But Signe avoided classification, and all that happened was that Magpie managed to get herself messily involved with a couple of huge slugs she had been too distracted to notice, so she was nicknamed "Slugpie" for the rest of the trip.

But soon the days began to shake down into routine, enlivened by Mr. Siffer's arbitrary decisions as to what was covered by the syllabus on any given day and the increasingly complex problems posed by Twitterpat in the computer lab, where the students were starting to write programming code.

For most of the students in Twitterpat's class, intensive computer study was a fairly new thing. Computers had been used in business for nearly half a century, coming into use about the same time the Alphiri had made their presence known to humans. Personal computers in homes, however, had not become commonplace until the year that Thea herself was born, when the discovery that they were inert to spells and magic made magic-users across the world suddenly scramble to own one, in order to safely store otherwise potentially dangerous material.

In ordinary schools such as the one Thea and most of the students in Twitterpat's class had attended before they had come to the Academy, computer science was still considered to be very much an area of study that was of more use to those few people who were born non-mages. In circles in which Thea's own family moved, it was considered to be perfectly adequate to be able to use just enough of a computer's capability for it to be immediately useful, and although there were mages overseeing certain aspects of computer software, those that involved spell storage, the code for these programs themselves was written by and large by people who were not magic-users. It was almost considered beneath a mage to know precisely how his or her computer functioned. If there was trouble, one called a technician—until then, it was considered perfectly acceptable to be only just as knowledgeable about the home computer as was necessary to keep it running.

The Academy offered a choice of foreign languages, from French and Japanese to Alphiri; for a moment Thea had been terrified that there would be an actual Alphiri teacher in charge of that particular course, but in fact it was taught by a Miss Eden, a tiny woman with snow-white hair and eyes like black beads who, apparently, had lived in the Alphiri cities for a couple of

years before she returned home to the human
world. Rumor in the school had it that was what
had turned her hair white in the first place. There
was certainly enough strangeness about her to
believe that. Thea wasn't taking the class, but
anything Alphiri had taken on a patina of dread
for her and she avoided the whole issue. None of
her particular group had chosen to take that
option, either, but every now and then some of
the students who were taking the Alphiri class
would show off their new mastery of the language by breaking into its liquid syllables with
each other, and it always made Thea's hackles
rise when she heard it spiking through the white
noise of conversations in the school cafeteria.

"You'd think that it wouldn't be allowed,"
she muttered, stabbing her chicken viciously
with her fork.

"What are you talking about?" asked Ben
Broome, looking up.

"*That lingo,*" Thea said, pointing with her
fork. "Alphiri prattle. You'd think that it would
be forbidden here."

"But the Alphiri aren't magic," Ben said.
"Not really. They're just . . . a different people.
You might as well say that we shouldn't learn

French or German."

"They are, too," Thea said stubbornly.

"If you're that strict about it," said Magpie, "we couldn't have Signe as a teacher. But she isn't *magic*, not herself. She's just . . . foreign."

Aside from its obvious lack of Ars Magica classes and perhaps a stricter emphasis in academic credentials than Thea was used to, school was school. But sharing her life with Magpie had been a different experience for Thea. For the first week or so Thea kept waking to Magpie's gentle snores, but she had finally got used to having another person asleep in the room with her, and having a roommate soon ceased to be a novelty.

Magpie's occasional nocturnal excursions were less easy to sleep through. She was a self-appointed healer of wounded creatures, and every now and then she'd bring a patient into her room to nurse back to health. The first time it had been some small nestlings in a cardboard box in her closet; Thea had lain awake for almost an hour trying to locate the source of the chirping, before Magpie, who had been out, had returned and confessed.

"You can't tell anybody, I'm not supposed to

have them in here. Mrs. Chen would take the poor things away and it'd be the end of them," Magpie said.

"Don't be silly, Mag, she's got ears, same as me," Thea said. "If she comes in here and they don't shut up, I don't have to say anything."

"They know when to be quiet," Magpie said.

"What are they, anyway?"

"Baby blue jays," Magpie said. "I found them on the ground; they were nearly dead."

"Baby birds *die*, Mag."

"Not when I've got anything to do with it," Magpie declared.

Thea looked at her with a sudden speculative glance. "Healing touch?"

"Nah," Magpie said, but she had hesitated, just barely. "They just . . . live, when I get hold of them."

"You'd better not let *me* anywhere near them," Thea said. "I kill potted plants, never mind animals."

Magpie cuffed her on the shoulder. "Oh, *really*."

"I'm serious, you just try me," Thea said. "If you let me *look* at them, they might die of shock right then. It's best if I . . . don't know they're there."

It was a statement of complicity, and Magpie understood it as such. She flashed Thea a grateful smile, and no more was said about the baby jays. But they were followed by other things: maimed squirrels, a rabbit with a broken paw that Magpie splinted with matchsticks, a young raccoon that Magpie rocked to sleep in her arms and which nuzzled at her with its pointed little snout like an affectionate cat.

The familiar rustling of Magpie sneaking in yet another patient woke Thea from a light sleep one night in late September. The room was dark except for a wash of moonlight through the window; the curtains were open to a sky that was crystal clear with the first cool touch of autumn.

"What is it now?" Thea whispered a little crossly in the general direction of a moving shadow tucking something small and squeaking into a cardboard box in the corner of her closet. A mouse maybe. Or a bat.

"Shhh. Go back to sleep," Magpie commanded.

But the moonlight was in Thea's eyes, and she propped her head on her hand, staring out at the sky.

"Senic'ta," she murmured. "Achievement and success. Harvest Moon . . ."

Magpie straightened. "What was that?"

Thea shifted her weight to turn and look at her roommate. "What was what?"

"I haven't met many people outside the reservation who know that the full moon has a name," Magpie said carefully.

"I learned," Thea said, "from a tribal elder." She sat up, reached for the top drawer of the dresser beside her bed, and rummaged in the moonlit shadows inside. Her fingers found the three feathers of her necklace and closed around them. She hesitated, then hauled out the necklace. "I never wear it where people can see . . . but he gave me this."

Magpie padded across the room, her bare feet making almost no sound on the carpeted floor. She perched cross-legged on the edge of Thea's bed, reaching for the necklace, and fingered the feathers curiously.

"There's ancestral magic in this," Magpie said. "These things stand for something. They can be used by those who know how. I thought you were supposed to be a magidim, that you couldn't touch this stuff—isn't that why you are here?"

But Thea answered with a question of her own. "If *you* are supposed to be such a magidim, how come you can sense that it's ancestral magic at all?"

"I went through the rites," Magpie said. "I went through *all* of them. I was even sent out on a guardian spirit quest, and lived in the wilderness by myself for a week waiting for my guardian to call my name—but neither animal nor tree did, or perhaps they all did and I was deafened by the cries. Either way, when I came back, they told me that magic ran through my fingers, that I could not hold it, that I had no guardian, that I would never be a medicine woman."

"Is that what you wanted?" Thea asked softly.

"All the women of my family have been," Magpie said, her voice small and sad. She fingered the feathers, paying out the leather thong of the necklace between her hands. "Raven—for wisdom, I presume. Eagle . . . for pride?" she questioned.

"For courage, Cheveyo said."

"Cheveyo." Magpie rolled the word on her tongue, tasting it.

"The Southwest," Thea said helpfully.

"What tribe?"

"Anasazi."

Magpie sat up and shot her a look full of astonishment. "The People of the Light? The Old Ones who vanished? Where on earth did you find one of them? I thought they were all dead."

"It wasn't a place," Thea said carefully. "My father . . . I had a Pass. I went . . . I went *back*."

In the shadows, Magpie's jaw dropped. "You time-tripped? Your father must have more influence than you can possibly know—do you have any idea how expensive those Passes are?"

"I'm a Double Seventh," Thea said, letting her head fall back into the pillow and staring at the ceiling. "I guess they thought it was worth any price to try and wake whatever it is that was asleep inside me."

"And you agreed to go? Just like that? I would have been terrified."

"When my father left me there," Thea said, "I was."

"But you went anyway," Magpie said, stroking the eagle's feather that she held across her palm. *Eagle, for courage.*

"There wasn't really a choice. And anyway, after . . ."

"Did it work?" Magpie asked softly.

"It showed me a different sky," Thea said after a few moments of silence. "There are many worlds, not just this one. And there are many choices within those worlds. It brought me here, in a way. Before I went to Cheveyo, I hated the very idea of coming to this school. . . ."

"Few people *want* to come here," Magpie said.

"Yeah, but with me it was always more than one magidim child of a magical family," said Thea. "The way I saw it, if I came here I wasn't just a black sheep, I was *the* black sheep, the one who could never be redeemed."

"And after?"

"After . . . that last day, back on the mesa, Cheveyo gave me that third feather, the turkey feather as a reward for learning what patience I could. He told me to go home and pick my own battlegrounds for the battles I'd have to fight. After that, coming here didn't seem like a defeat anymore. It was more like I had picked my battlefield."

"Without magic? In a world that depends on it?"

"I spent a very brief while in a world that

flowed with it," Thea said slowly, "and there . . . I was different. Things were different. Light was different. It let itself be plucked from the sky like ribbons, and it could be woven together like a braid."

There was awe in Magpie's face and a little envy. "I wish I could have seen it."

She handed the necklace back without another word. They would keep each other's secrets.

The new patient in Magpie's animal hospital turned out to be a mouse, a tiny, timid creature that barely stirred in its nest of shredded paper in the cardboard box. It had been there only a few days before Signe announced another field trip and Magpie had to scramble to make arrangements for its care while she was away. It was a full weekend this time, with the class divided into teams mapping out the ecological profile of a river mouth, a place where freshwater met salt and where creatures shaped by two sets of very different circumstances met and mingled. By the time the class returned to the school, it was fairly late on Sunday night. The mood should have been relaxed and laid back. Instead, the place was ablaze with lights. Students hung out of residence windows, calling to one another, and the administration building was lit up like a Christmas tree.

"Something happened," Signe said in her soft accent as she shepherded her charges off the school bus. "Please gather your things and go directly back to your rooms. No sense in adding to the commotion."

"What's going on?" Magpie demanded of the first person she met in her residence hall.

"Nothing is in the news again," the girl said. "And this time, I think people are dead."

"If people are dead, that isn't nothing," Magpie said reasonably.

But Tess was frowning. "Not nothing, Mag, *Nothing*. That's what they called it at home. The 'Nothing.' I didn't really know what they meant, not then—but Terry and I tend to avoid magic where we can, and I wasn't really paying attention. I do know that it's a . . . it's . . . they don't know what it is. It's just a Nothing, a black shadow, and people see different things when they look at it—it's like looking at clouds and seeing shapes in them."

"But what is it? Where did it come from?" Magpie asked.

"Nobody knows. And it's just there, like a blot, not actually doing anything but just hanging there in the background like it is waiting for something."

Thea was remembering little comments dropped in passing by the adults in her family—what she had taken to be dismissive responses of "Oh, nothing!" when she asked if anything was wrong. But she had been out of circulation for some time, in a place where she had not been able to access the mainstream news or Terranet. Her parents had been talking in hushed worried tones about unspecified events—what Thea had always lumped together under a general heading of "Bad Stuff"—for a long time, even before she'd left for Cheveyo's world. At first she had been too wrapped up in her own self-pity to notice or to care, and after she had returned home, her time had been taken up by preparations to come to the Academy and she had not paid much attention. Now, however, she could not fail to focus on the matter. As Aunt Zoë might have said, the very air she breathed smelled excited and afraid.

"A magical thing?" Thea said, frowning, aware that she should have known far more about the subject than she did. "Or something physical?"

"No, it isn't actually physical—the way I think I heard my mother describe it is that it's more like the coming of a migraine, a black shadow coming over your vision."

"Your mother has *seen* it?" Thea said. "Is she in any danger, then?"

Tess turned suddenly panicked eyes on her. "I don't know," she whispered. "I wish I *had* been paying attention, now. All that I'm sure of is that it's just *there*, waiting. . . ."

"Where's 'there'?" Magpie asked. "Don't look at me like that; I spent most of the summer at the rez and they don't really pay attention to outside news, at least not in my family. Then I came here, and you know what *this* place is like with anything to do with magic. I have absolutely no idea what you're talking about."

"We'll all know soon enough," Thea said grimly. "If people are dead because of this thing, that's news. So far, it seems, it's been just an inexplicable shadow, lurking in the background, and only a handful of people could see it, sense it, whatever. Now, if it's turned physical . . ."

But no details were forthcoming, and finally Mrs. Chen came over to the residence hall to make them all turn their lights off and go to bed. Tess asked her outright what the matter was, but Mrs. Chen merely looked grave.

"You will know if it is necessary for you to know," she said.

"But people *died*," Tess persisted. "Are . . . people in danger?"

"Are *we* in danger?" another girl asked.

"Here, in this place, you may be in less danger than anyone else you know," Mrs. Chen said. And then she closed her hand tightly about the medallion she wore around her neck, pressed her narrow lips together until her mouth was little more than a thin line, and said no more.

"It's something to do with magic, then," Magpie whispered to Thea after lights out, as they both lay wide awake in their beds. "And the people who died must be mages. What do you think it means?"

"I don't know," Thea whispered. But she had placed her feather necklace under her pillow and her fingers stroked the eagle feather that Cheveyo had given her. Raven, for wisdom. Eagle, for courage.

A turkey feather for patience.

Thea had an awful sense of something huge that

stood in her path, not yet visible, brooding just beyond the next bend. And it was Cheveyo's voice that kept coming back to haunt her in the darkness of her room, there in the Last Ditch School.

When there is a battle to be fought, it is you who can choose the place of the battlefield.

HUNTERS MOON

1.

THE TRANSFORMATION of the Academy from a sanctuary into a place where isolation had bred a predictable surge of sudden interest bordering on fascination was almost frighteningly fast.

The school subscribed to several newspapers and magazines, and there was little that could be done to prevent access by those eager to know more about the doings of the Nothing. But the media was very circumspect about the story—surprisingly circumspect, in fact. Although newspapers carried the names of several people who had had fatal encounters with the Nothing, very little was said about the nature of their demise, although magical circumstances were strongly implied.

Teachers took pains to return the school to its

normal everyday pursuits in the days and weeks that followed that night of excitement when news of the Nothing stirred the school's quiet halls into a frenzy. But that was almost impossible to do. Scared students phoned home to check on their families and found out more information, a lot of it conflicting and unsubstantiated, which promptly flew into a flock of rumors buzzing like angry hornets around a ruined nest. Teachers wouldn't answer direct questions, but every now and again they'd let something slip and that, too, was grist for the rumor mill.

In Thea's own little circle of friends, it was the twins who reacted the worst. Terry physically could not talk to his family about the phenomenon in any meaningful way. Even the suspicion that the Nothing was a magical entity or was being fought in magical ways would be enough to steer the conversation into waters dangerous to his health. He could not even talk to his own sister about the matter. He was constantly scribbling little notes to Tess, so *she* could phone their parents and make sure everything was all right. The weight of those expectations, in turn, made Tess herself terribly anxious, especially as nobody at home was either able or willing to give her the full scoop—and she knew for a fact that her own mother had seen and felt the Nothing.

And the newspaper reports, although they never said so unequivocally, hinted strongly and darkly that anyone who had direct experience with the Nothing was in grave danger, in ways far too gory, apparently, to be revealed to the general public.

Thea's contribution had been to phone her Aunt Zoë. Her father had government connections every bit as good as Terry and Tess's parents, and her mother was no slouch when it came to Ars Magica, but for some reason Thea shied from talking to them about magic while she was at school. Besides, she had always trusted her aunt's forthright honesty.

But Zoë was of less help than Thea might have wished.

"Darling child, I would tell you more if I could, I swear," Zoë had said. "But not even your father will talk about it in any kind of detail. I do know of those deaths, and I do know that the . . . the *thing* . . . has been unsuccessfully attacked by magical means, and that this is where the deaths come in. So you're perfectly right, it has something to do with magic. But just what . . ."

"Do the Alphiri have anything to do with it?" Thea had asked. Somehow, she had begun to associate all dark dangerous things with the wielders of the Trade Codex. She could not figure out how the Alphiri would benefit from something like this directly, but she was sure that, if there was a way, they could be trusted to find it.

"The Alphiri?" Zoë asked, astonished. "There have been rumors . . . but . . . why would you think that?"

"I don't know. I just keep having visions of them coming in at the last moment with a vial of antidote and asking a high price for it," Thea said.

She could almost see Zoë's eyebrow arch on the other end of the line. "Well, *that* smells nicely conspiratorial," she said.

"What *does* a conspiracy smell like?" Thea asked, diverted.

"Like milk just beginning to turn," Zoë said. "Thea, what on *earth* have they been telling you up there? You sound like you've been gazing into a dozen crystal balls at once and getting decidedly mixed messages."

"You might say I have," Thea said. "Nobody says *anything*, really, which is far worse than just telling us what they know—because I'm sure that what we imagine is bigger and blacker than even the Nothing can possibly be."

"Don't be so certain," Zoë murmured.

"Have *you* actually seen it?" Thea asked, suddenly aware of a small cold touch of fear.

"Smelled it," Zoë said. "Felt it. Like a stench of carrion. Like the weight of night. Like that smoky last gasp of a just-extinguished candle. No, I haven't seen it. But it's been present. There can be few with any kind of magical talent who aren't aware of its presence."

The conversation left Thea feeling frustrated and unsettled. She shared whatever information she could winnow out of it with her friends, and saw Tess blanch at the images that Zoë had invoked. Tess had started chewing on her fingernails until she drew blood. But there appeared to be little any of them could do, except wait.

And then their teachers started to disappear.

The first one to go was Magpie's Latin teacher. His name was Guy Hadden, but his class knew him as Master Gaius—a man with a hooked nose and raptorlike glittering eyes who wouldn't have looked too out of place in the Roman Senate. His facility with languages in general—he spoke twenty-seven of them fluently—and classical Latin in particular was a legend in the school, where he had been teaching for nearly a quarter of a century. He vanished without warning one day, and was replaced by a young substitute who couldn't say when Master Gaius would be back but that he had left instructions for his class to memorize (and pay attention to the correct accent while doing so) an entire batch of poems by obscure early Roman poets, and that there would be a test on it before the end of the year.

"I've never heard of any of these guys," one of Magpie's classmates had muttered. "I wouldn't be surprised if he made the whole heap up himself."

It had been an attempt to introduce laughter, as if that could be raised as a weapon against the Nothing. But whatever relief it had brought didn't last.

One of the English lit teachers was the next to disappear. Mrs. Entwhiler's claim to fame was that she could quote almost the entire body of William Shakespeare's work by heart, and expected her charges to aspire to the same level of accomplishment. There were those in her class with less than perfect memories, who actually breathed a sigh of relief at their reprieve before they admitted to being worried about their teacher's whereabouts.

She was closely followed by Keiko Yamaguchi, who taught Japanese.

And then, unexpectedly and somehow far more frighteningly, by Twitterpat.

"I have to take a short leave of absence," he told his class, his expressive hands weaving a dance in the air before him. "I know that you have had a number of your teachers leave you in the past couple of weeks, and that there have been some fierce rumors flying around. Some of you may already have realized that most of the teachers in question have been language experts—linguists—and the possible link this might have to Ars Magica and its own connection to the power of the word. Well, you may or may not take comfort in the fact that I am not a language teacher."

"Yes, sir, you are," Tess said unexpectedly. "Computers have a language, too."

Twitterpat ducked his head, his hands fluttering around his ears like crazed butterflies. "That may indeed be so, if you choose to look at it that way," he admitted.

"Have they gone to fight the Nothing?" another student asked, her hand at her throat.

Twitterpat looked over at her, and half smiled. "We cannot discuss that. As for myself, I can only say that I have . . . personal concerns I need to attend to, and that I hope and expect to be back with you very shortly. In the meantime, I have prepared some work sheets for you to complete. There will not be a substitute teacher for this class, only a supervisory presence to ensure that you are in fact doing the required tasks during class and not spending the time discussing my absence from it among yourselves. You will be working on your own, and I know I can trust you to achieve these tasks by yourselves. You start tomorrow."

After Twitterpat's departure, the teacher disappearances ceased for a little while, but the mood at the school was getting darker and more frightening by the day.

Perhaps triggered by the absence of Twitterpat, who had quickly become one of her favorite teachers, or by the work that he had set them to do, Thea's mental filing system suddenly decided to access a memory she first thought had no real connection with the situation at hand. Indeed, the early moments of the dream that came to her were infused by a sense of comfort, almost of delight, because it took her back to the summer, and to that strange night she had spent with Grandmother Spider under the First World stars.

In the dream, Grandmother Spider had been in spider form when she had instructed Thea to make for the sparse piney woods on a ridge of high ground that rose on the horizon, a black shape against the cartwheels of light in the sky.

"Over there," the spider said. "Can you see? On the rock face?"

Thea narrowed her eyes. The light in this place was disturbing, as bright almost as day, as if a full moon rode in the sky. "Where? You mean . . . is that a painting?"

There was a crude drawing on a sheer wall of rock straight ahead, a vast shape, barely formed—much like the cave paintings Thea had seen in books, back in her own world, except this one was about twenty times the size of any-thing she had ever seen before. It depicted, in vague outline, a deerlike creature, its body one vast bulbous oval. It was supported by four legs, rendered in broad strokes, making them look like pillars. A short powerful neck sketched out in dark heavy strokes ended in another oval, a huge head bent down to the ground, as though the animal was either grazing or in the act of bowing to something. Feathered lines of what Thea supposed were meant to be antlers radiated from the front of the head. Although it was drawn in profile, it—somewhat disconcertingly—also bore two large dark circles, eyes, as if the beast was capable of looking through its own solid form and substance.

"What is it?" Thea said, staring in fascination. There was something about the drawing, a raw power, despite its almost childish simplicity.

"Big Elk," Grandmother Spider said. "You'd better put me down again. I think I should probably be a little larger when he comes. He may not mean to hurt anybody, but sometimes he stands on you without knowing what he does. . . ."

"What do I need to know?" Thea said softly, obeying.

Grandmother Spider, now a woman again, gave her an approving look.

"The perfect question," she said. "Cheveyo would be proud of you. But it's Big Elk you should talk to. And listen—here he comes. . . ."

There was indeed a crashing of undergrowth, the sound of something immense moving with no regard to what stood in its path.

Thea stood her ground; this time it was Grandmother Spider who took the few steps back, melting into the shadows, becoming merely a voice and a presence.

"I bring you a guest," she said, just as the animal she had named Big Elk stepped into the light.

Thea almost quaked. Big Elk stood almost twice as tall as she did. His legs were pillars of muscle and sinew, his head enormous, with a hint of white breath, like steam coming out of the nostrils, and eyes that glowed milkily in the starlight. Just as in the painting, they both seemed to be able to focus at once on an object to the side of the great head.

Thea had thought nothing could take her by surprise again, but the last thing she had expected this behemoth to do was speak, in a voice full of rich resonance and deep wisdom.

"Welcome," it said.

"Thank you," Thea said politely.

"Show her," Grandmother Spider said.

The stag folded its magnificent front legs, kneeling in front of Thea. "Come," it said, its voice trust and awe and serenity. "Climb on my back, child, and we shall see what we shall see tonight."

There seemed no way to do what Big Elk asked without injuring its dignity in some fundamental way. Thea almost felt as though she should apologize as she stepped as lightly as she could onto one folded foreleg, grasped the base of a huge antler with one hand, and vaulted onto the animal's neck, her feet dangling to either side just behind its ears. It rose to all four feet again, and Thea felt as if the earth itself had risen up beneath her.

Thea turned frantically to look at Grandmother Spider, seeking reassurance, but all she saw was the shadow of a smile under the trees, and words that came into her mind, gentle, like a caress: *Trust him.*

"Hold on," Big Elk said, and leaped.

Thea cried out, at first with panic, but that vanished in the blink of an eye. The fear of falling off evaporated almost instantly—whatever this animal wanted to carry on its back, it would make sure that it stayed there. It would not, *could* not, be ridden unless it wished it so—and if it wished it so then the rider might as well sit back and relax.

It did not seem to Thea that they moved very fast—she would almost have called their pace a stately walk—but tree-shaped shadows passed by them in a blur, and Big Elk's feet struck sparks where they met the ground.

"The Old One," Big Elk said in that rich, resonant voice, "does not often come with visitors like you."

"I am . . . a student," Thea said. "I was sent here . . . to learn."

"Ah," said Big Elk. "One who seeks wisdom. Many have tried to win their way here, but most of them fail. It is your kind who make it this far."

"Are we still in the First World?" Thea said, glancing up. The skies were darker than they had been in Grandmother Spider's chaotic sphere, the stars, although more brilliant and far larger than they had any right to be, were still; things looked rather more like what she was used to and not Grandmother Spider's fascinating universe.

"In a way," Big Elk said. "It is *a* First World,

my First World, not *the* First World where the
Old One dwells and everything began. I, too,
began there—until I became what I am and was
given this place for my own."

"What are you?" Thea said, her voice rather
small.

"Every living thing," Big Elk said gently, "has
a beginning, a source, the thing that it is like, the
thing that it sprang from. I am the father of every
elk that ever was, ever will be. I am the spirit of
the elk tribe."

"There are others like you? For other living
things?"

"Many," he said. "Big Bear. Big Wolf. Big
Eagle. Big Owl. Big Catfish. There are even shad-
owy worlds shared by such growing dreaming
things like Big Oak, Big Cedar, Big Pine—ah, but
I have walked in that forest, and it is beautiful.
We are that of which all else of our ilk springs."

"So you're an Elk God," Thea said.

"Not a God. I am Elk Spirit, rather. My kin do
not pray to me."

"Is there a Big Human—someone like you, for
someone like me?"

"Humans," said Big Elk, "are different from
other kindred. My folk does not dream of futures

or remember distant pasts. They know what they are and they live their lives that way. It is a simpler way of life. With your kindred, it is . . . difficult. You might say that every one of you has a Big Human. Or that you sprang from a line different from ours. Or you come from the Old Ones themselves. It is hard to tell if the Old One you came with wears your shape because *you* wear it, or whether you wear that shape because she does. With humans, it is hard to tell. When they call upon that Big Spirit that should be the image of them all, every mind has a different picture. . . . Perhaps that is the trouble, you put in too much detail and what you get is specific, not general."

Thea thought back to the drawing on the rock wall, almost childlike, rendered in only the barest minimum of strokes necessary to create an impression of an elk. "I think I understand," she murmured.

"We are," said Big Elk, "of the spirit realm. And communication with the spirit realm requires an all-inclusive figure. They could have drawn an image of a perfect elk back there on the stone wall—but that would have been only *one* elk, the specific one whose image was captured there on the wall. What is there now calls to me, the spirit of all the elk, something that connects all of us, like a shining strand of time. When they need me, they will come, my kind. When I can help them, I will. If there is a place with clear water or better pasture or safer shelter with fewer hunters to take them—I will lead them there. I can, because I am all the elk. They can see me, there in the dawn light, enough to follow me when I call them."

"But they can't see any of the others," Thea said. "The other ancestral spirits. For other creatures."

"The others are not of their world," Big Elk said.

"But elk share the earth with bears and eagles and foxes," Thea said. "At least in *my* world they do."

"Yes," said Big Elk. "And all of these things they will notice living around them. But if Big Fox comes to his brethren, the elk will not see that guardian spirit—and if I come to my folk, the foxes will never see me. All that the elk and the fox tribes will see on the earth is what they themselves do upon it. And they answer to none but the spirit of their own kind. They do what they must. That is the rule of all life."

"Curious," Thea said softly.

One of the great stag's ears turned marginally in her direction. It was an unspoken invitation to continue.

"The stars," Thea said. "They send their spirits to walk the worlds—they make, I don't know, small incarnations of themselves—they make themselves small to talk to their folk. You—your kind, the spirit ancestors of what lives on those worlds—you make yourself big, large enough to hold every soul of your kindred within your own."

"Yes," Big Elk said. "That is the way of it. The living worlds both need us and call us, and in order to meet that call, that need, we do what is necessary and we teach those who need to know how to invoke us."

"And us?" Thea asked. "My people?"

"There are so many more of you than there were when the world was young," Big Elk said. "And although you have gone a long way from what you once were, few of you are now able to see the things that your ancestors knew and understood. It seems to me that your numbers grew, but your faith remained finite—and now it's spread so thin that sometimes it's hard to believe in the things your rational mind tells you are impossible."

"But I believe in you," Thea said softly, running a hand down the corded muscle of the great stag's neck.

Big Elk tossed his head, lifting the side of his face into the caress. "That is why I am here," he said. "Even the Old One could not have called me to you if you did not have the ability to believe in my existence, to see me when I set foot in that sacred wood. And that is why *you* are here—because you are capable of that faith—and why so many of your kindred never can be."

Beneath them the world turned, bright and dark, starlight reflecting on water, swallowed by dark forests, a primeval world wrought to be home to a primeval spirit. For no particular reason, Thea found herself close to tears.

"Thank you," she said, although she had no real idea what she was thanking Big Elk for.

"You are welcome," he said, sparks from his hooves still arcing upward to extinguish themselves in the night air. "And while this is nothing to do with me or with my kindred, and therefore I can do nothing to help you, I can give you a warning, freely and without price."

The hair rose on the nape of Thea's neck, as though the air was suddenly electrified. "Warning? Of what?"

"Be wary," Big Elk said, "because you are marked. And there are those who will come for you if they can, if you give them the least nod, if they believe in any way that they have offered a price and it has been accepted."

"Are you talking about the Alphiri?" Thea said, suddenly afraid.

Big Elk lifted his head fractionally, and Thea followed the direction of his gaze. She had been too enthralled by this ride, too enchanted by what was happening to her, and far too over-whelmed by her surroundings to notice that any-thing might be amiss—she didn't know what any of the rules were, never mind when they were being broken. But now, with her attention focused on one particular thing, she realized that something *was* in fact wrong. The sky was just as brilliant and beautiful here as she knew it ought to have been—all but one patch of it, a growing emptiness, spreading like a stain and extinguish-ing stars as it grew. Thea felt it tug at her senses; she could not decide whether she felt a banked malevolence or a supreme indifference to anything that stood in its way, or whether those two things could exist in the same terrifying entity, soulless and dangerous and utterly pitiless.

"The Alphiri brought *that*," Big Elk said.

"What is it?" Thea whispered, staring, her mouth dry.

"Nothing," Big Elk said. "An emptiness, a hunger that cannot be sated, a wanting that will not be denied."

"In *this* world?"

"In all worlds. It comes where they go." He tossed his head. "But have no fear. Here, tonight, with me, it cannot harm you."

Thea found herself torn between a wish to hug the great animal and the distinct urge to bow down before it. She compromised by scratching it behind the ears, something the elk accepted without a word and even gave some indication that it enjoyed.

"We'd better get back," she said reluctantly after a while.

"Yes," Big Elk said, and came to a stop, right beside the great rock painting on the cliff face in the wood. As if they had never left the place at all.

He knelt again for her to dismount, as he had

done before, and this time Thea gave free rein to instinct and kissed the great head right between the eyes before she swung herself off his back and came to stand beside him. "Thank you," she said again. "For everything."

He rose, towering above her, and reared for a moment onto his hind legs, outlined heraldically against the diffuse light in the night sky.

"Go well," he said, "and remember what I told you."

And then he was gone, vanished, disintegrating into the bright air as if he had been no more than mist and shadows.

There was a rustle, and another shadow stepped out from under the scattered pines.

"He carried you," Grandmother Spider said.

He warned me. . . .

Thea woke suddenly, sitting bolt upright in her bed. For a moment she was completely disoriented, and then she became aware that what had woken her was not the impossible presence of Big Elk in her bedroom but a quiet rustling noise by Magpie's closet. It took her a moment to calm her panicked heartbeat and realize that what had startled her awake was no more than one of Magpie's usual nighttime excursions.

"It's just me," Magpie whispered, cradling something in her arms half-wrapped in a trailing bit of what had once been a decent blanket, before it was chewed, clawed, pecked, and shredded into near oblivion by a succession of clawed and beaked convalescents.

"I wish you would call a halt to that for a while," Thea hissed back, knuckling her eyes with one hand. "You just don't know *what* is out there, and I hate the idea of your being out alone at night. What have you got there . . . ?"

The new patient appeared a little larger than Magpie's most recent acquisitions, the size of a small adult raccoon or a comfortably tubby full-grown cat.

Except that it was neither.

Through the shreds of blanket, Thea suddenly saw a familiar pattern of black-and-white fur. The last pieces of her dream vanished as she swung her legs out of bed, both bare feet on the floor, suddenly and vividly awake and ready to run.

"That's a *skunk*!" she hissed.

"He won't hurt you," Magpie said, giving up the attempt at concealment and setting the animal on the floor between the two beds.

"I'm not worried about it *hurting* me," Thea

said. "That's it, Mag, I don't mind the blue jays or the squirrels, but I don't want to think about living in this room if that creature decides it doesn't like you."

"But he's hurt," Magpie said. "He won't do anything I don't want him to do."

"I know you have the healing touch with the critters, but not that one, Magpie. I'm serious. None of them should be in here in the first place, else you wouldn't have to smuggle them in like this in the middle of the night. And I haven't said anything, and I don't plan to. But one accident with *that* animal and I won't have to say a word. They'll smell a rat."

"A skunk," said Magpie with a grin.

"I'm not joking! Get that thing out of here!"

"But what am I supposed to do with him? I have to keep an eye on him, or else he might . . ."

"No, Magpie. Not that one. Don't you have anywhere else you can stash that thing? Somewhere . . . outside, preferably . . . ?"

"There's the garden shed," Magpie said unwillingly, as though an important secret had been wrung out of her.

"But that's locked," Thea said.

"So?" Magpie asked, grinning mischievously,

her teeth a sudden flash of white in the shadows. "But in any event, it doesn't matter. The big front doors of the shed are locked. The back door isn't, and the window is always open."

"*Magpie.*"

"What?"

"You mean you could have used that place all this time instead of bringing Animal Hospital up here?" Thea said. She tried to be cross, but the laughter was already bubbling up to the surface.

"It's halfway across the campus," Magpie complained. "How was I supposed to keep an eye on them over there?"

The skunk stirred, lifting its head. Thea stifled a small scream.

Magpie flung up her hands in defeat.

"All right! All right! I'll take him to the garden shed!" She gathered up the creature again, rewrapping it as best she could in the blanket, and then stood uncertainly in the middle of the room, her arms full of skunk, staring at the door handle in a calculating way. Sneaking the skunk *in* had been easy enough—the door opened inward into the room, and a jiggle of the handle and a light push with her foot had done the trick. But now she needed to open the door with her hands full of what might be a problem. . . .

Thea growled deep in her throat. She got up from the bed and pulled on a pair of jeans and a T-shirt from the top of a pile of dirty clothes beside her bed.

"Wait a minute, I'll come and help you. You'll have the entire residence up in arms in a moment if you aren't careful."

"Thanks!" Magpie said chirpily, hugging the skunk closer to her. It seemed, improbably, to be snuggling.

"Why do I do this?" Thea said, rolling her eyes, as she hopped toward the door on one sneakered foot while easing on the sneaker's mate, a flashlight tucked under her arm. "*What* was Mrs. Chen thinking? Come on, skunk mama. Let's get this over with. We both need to stay awake for classes tomorrow."

She opened the door and peered out into the corridor. It was deserted, not surprisingly— Thea's bedside clock said it was nearly half past midnight.

"All clear," she whispered, and motioned Magpie forward.

Their room was on the second floor, and Thea stole a moment to wonder just how Magpie had managed to sneak so many animals up and down the open stairwell without being observed. She climbed down the center of the stairs with her creature in her arms, without hugging walls or seeking concealment in shadows, as though it was a perfectly natural thing for her to be on the stairs at midnight carrying a skunk wrapped in a tattered blanket.

"Are you sure that you have no trailing magic somewhere?" Thea asked when they reached the main hall.

"No, why?" Magpie said, apparently genuinely astonished by the question.

"Just because you don't seem to be . . . Wait a minute, the front door is locked. . . ."

"It's always locked at ten thirty," Magpie said.

Thea blinked. "Then how do you . . . ?"

"The back door . . . ," Magpie began, and Thea rolled her eyes.

"Back doors are never locked in this place, it seems. Okay, which door?"

Magpie pointed with her foot, and Thea led the way. They found themselves in a laundry area, with a small bank of washers and dryers . . . and a narrow, glass-paned back door that let out into a paved yard.

As Magpie had said, the door was unlocked. It swung open soundlessly, letting in a wash of cold air.

Thea shivered. "I should have thought about a sweatshirt," she said. "It's definitely October out there. Okay, it's completely deserted. Go."

She switched on her flashlight, letting the light play out from between her fingers. The girls slipped out of the residence, closing the door carefully behind them, and scuttled out of the paved area, across a stretch of lawn and into the friendly shadows of a nearby copse of trees. Somewhere near them an owl hooted, and Thea shivered.

"I feel like I'm being watched," she whispered.

"You are," Magpie said. Thea turned her head sharply to meet the beady gaze of the skunk, still quiet but definitely wide awake and contemplating possible mischief. Thea took an involuntary step backward.

"The sooner you settle that thing down somewhere, the happier I'll be," Thea said. "Let's just get to the shed!"

Again, just as Magpie had said, they found the garden shed's back door closed but not locked.

The shed had only one small and very filthy window that let in almost no light at all, and they could not risk showing any and exposing themselves to detection, so Thea wedged the flashlight between two shovels, facing the wall, almost but not quite touching it. A bare halo of light escaped, just enough for them to identify shadowed gardening implements by their shapes and locations.

In the back of the shed an old wheelbarrow with no front wheel sat propped on a cinder block. It held an assortment of things impossible to identify in the murk, but it definitely looked as though it hadn't been touched for a while. There was a sense of cobwebs and abandonment about it.

"That will do," Magpie said. "Can you help me clear a space?"

"I'm going to regret this in the morning," Thea said, grimacing as she reached out and scrabbled with bare hands amongst cleaning cloths stiff with dirt, assorted rake handles, balls of string, sections of watering hose, and two or three old brooms.

There was just enough room in the back of the wheelbarrow for the skunk, wrapped in his blanket, to curl up. Magpie piled the junk in the wheelbarrow artistically about her patient in a concealing dome, and then stepped back and surveyed her handiwork critically, her hands on her hips.

"That'll do until tomorrow," she said at length. "I'll have to come back with some newspapers or an old sheet or something to make it softer and more comfortable, but he'll be all right tonight." She reached out to pet the skunk on the head. It didn't move.

Thea was wiping her hands ineffectually on her jeans, which were now dark with dust and pale with fluffs of cobweb stuck to them where she'd peeled them off her fingers. She had the uncomfortable feeling that she was crawling with cross and dispossessed spiders.

"Are you done?" she asked. "We'd better get back before anybody misses us."

"They aren't doing bed checks," Magpie said.

"Yet," Thea said darkly.

Magpie suddenly shivered. "Did you have to remind me?" she murmured. "I feel perfectly safe . . . as long as I don't think about it."

She gave her patient a last reassuring pat and followed Thea out into the night with a sigh.

It was a cold night. They could almost see the white cloud of their breath as they hurried back through the trees, the muted light of the flashlight bouncing on the ground. Goose bumps almost large enough to cast their own shadows stood out on Thea's arms, and her teeth were chattering.

"We'll get pneumonia," she complained softly to Magpie.

"I've *never* had pneumonia, and I've been doing this for years," Magpie retorted.

"There's always a first time," Thea said a little waspishly, and then gasped. She held her breath and thumbed off the flashlight just as Magpie blundered into her from behind.

"Hey! What are you . . . ," she began, but Thea silenced her with a gesture. Magpie subsided into silence, and then she, too, gasped as she heard soft voices ahead.

"We can't get past them," Thea hissed. "They're between us and the back door."

"Who is it?" Magpie asked, taking a careful step forward to stand beside Thea.

"I don't know. I can't see anything. Shhh . . . let's go around to the side . . . that way. . . ."

But the acoustics of the night were treacherous. They had barely started to sidle off to the edge of the woods closer to the corner of the residence before Thea came to a sharp halt and flung out an arm to stop Magpie from plowing into two people who stood less than a few paces away. Their voices were very low, but the night had the clarity of early winter to it, and sound carried as if through crystal. It was possible to make out every single word that was being said.

"I still think it will not come here," a female voice said. "For weeks I've watched, and I've seen no sign of it. There isn't enough here to sate its hunger."

"You don't know that—there is enough just in the ranks of the staff," a male voice responded. "They've already called in a number of us. Who is to say there won't be more, and there may well be those in the student body who might be in danger still."

"But without magic . . . ," began the female voice.

"That's Mrs. Chen," Magpie hissed.

"And the principal," Thea whispered back, making sure her own voice was muffled into her T-shirt against Magpie's ear to prevent its own sound from carrying too far.

The principal could be seen to be shaking his head slightly. "You know how hard we have tried to keep this place clean of it," he said. "But remember, we can't know about everything that is brought in as contraband. Who knows what attracts the Nothing to people? We have thrown some of our best mages at it, and at least three of them have paid for it with their lives. The Nothing is impervious to magic. What's more, it *feeds* on it—the more you throw at it, the stronger it becomes—but who knows that it won't come for a hoarded bag of Sweet Spells in some junior's bedroom? And the very worst of it is that I don't know how to guard against that."

"Then why are we still sending mages out?" Mrs. Chen asked. "What possible use is it to have good people lay down their lives only to strengthen the enemy for doing worse things to us?"

The principal shrugged his shoulders, lifted his hands in a gesutre of helplessness. "I don't know," he said. "I am awaiting Patrick Wittering's report within the hour. Perhaps then we will know more."

"How could you send him?" Mrs. Chen said, and Thea heard her voice tremble. It was the first time she had ever seen Mrs. Chen show fear, and she felt its cold breath on her own skin, stirring the hair on the nape of her neck. She shivered, and this time it was nothing to do with the October night.

A hunger that can't be sated . . .

"Everyone else thought they knew what the Nothing was. Everyone else was wrong," the principal said gently. "It's up to him now. We send those soldiers we can into our wars. Sometimes it is all we can do just to fight our battle; it is not given to us to choose where and how they are to be fought."

When there is a battle to be fought, it is you who can choose the place of the battlefield.

The echo of Cheveyo's voice was a startling and thoroughly unexpected addition to the conversation. Thea could not suppress a small gasp.

The principal and Mrs. Chen both turned their heads a fraction. "What was that?"

An owl hooted very close to Thea, suddenly and unexpectedly, making her jump; turning around, she saw Magpie just letting her hands fall from where they had been cupped around her mouth to imitate the owl so perfectly. The girls exchanged almost invisible smiles in the dark.

"It's late," said the principal, relaxing the tense set of his shoulders. "You'd better get back to your charges. I still have some work to do tonight."

"What's going to happen, John?" Mrs. Chen said, lowering her voice even further, almost beyond the hearing range of the two in the woods.

"I don't know," the principal said, his voice startlingly bleak. "A day at a time, Margaret. We will take it a day at a time."

They touched hands lightly, and turned away from each other—the principal toward the main administration block, Mrs. Chen, playing lightly with a bunch of keys on a key ring, back toward the residence.

"We'll never get back so she doesn't see us!" hissed Thea.

"Yes, we will! She's going around by the front—by the time she gets there and unlocks the door, we can be halfway up the stairs! Come on!"

"Halfway up the stairs is right!" panted Thea, as she raced to keep up with Magpie across the open grassy area and into the paved yard at the back of the residence building. "She'll throw the door open and there we'll be, like two skinned rabbits. . . ."

"Not if you stop talking and hurry *up*!" Magpie flung back.

For all her haste she opened the back door very gently, just enough for both of them to slip through, and closed it with the barest click. They skidded out of the laundry area and rounded the edge of the main staircase just as they heard Mrs. Chen's keys in the lock. Thea had no idea that either she or Magpie could move so fast; they tore up the staircase taking two or three stairs at a time, managing to be almost unnaturally silent about it. They only just made it, hearing the front door ease open and shut as they paused at the top of the stairs, peering back the way they had come.

"Is she coming up?" Thea mouthed, her heart beating a tattoo against her chest.

"I don't know. Let's go," Magpie returned. They cast final wary glances down the stairs and half ran, half tiptoed down the corridor to their room. Magpie eased the door open with a practiced touch, they both slipped through and dived into their beds fully clothed, pulling the sheets up over their heads. Thea spared a brief pang of self-pity for the mess her filthy jeans and sneakers were making of her clean bedding, and then held her breath as she waited for the door to be flung open and Mrs. Chen's voice demanding to know just what it was they thought they were doing. But nothing happened. The night remained quiet and undisturbed, and in due course Thea drew a deep breath and realized her heart was no longer beating like a drum.

"Magpie?" she whispered from underneath her sheets. "What do you suppose it all means?"

But there was no response to her words . . . other than a gentle snore. Thea risked poking her head out from underneath the covers and peered over at Magpie's bed.

Unbelievably, Magpie was fast asleep.

2.

The one class the whole group of friends had together the next day was math, and since Mr. Siffer was in a particularly unlovely mood they didn't get much talking done. Thea and Magpie merely hinted at having important information, and it was Tess who finally got a note to everybody to meet at the computer lab later that evening after classes were over for the day. Terry was running some sort of advanced project and had been given the access code for the computer lab by Twitterpat in case he wanted to put in some overtime.

They gathered there after supper, the five of them—Thea, Tess and Terry, Ben, and Magpie.

"Did you know Mrs. Chen's name is Margaret?" Magpie asked mischievously.

"No," said Terry, "but I would guess that isn't the big secret. Spill!"

Magpie glanced at Thea, who shrugged and launched into an abbreviated account of the previous night's adventures.

"Wow," said Ben when she was done. "And I did nothing more interesting than go to sleep last night."

"You think poor Twitterpat and the others are in some sort of real danger?" asked Tess, nibbling on a hangnail.

"I have no idea where they all went, but Mrs. Chen sounded really worried," Magpie said. "And you know how serenely laid-back she always is."

"I was following the newspaper reports all of last week," Ben volunteered, "and there isn't a thing in there that I can put a finger on, but—"

He sneezed, suddenly and violently, and rubbed his nose with the back of his hand.

Magpie threw him a startled look. "You smell something, Ben?"

"Just your skunk," said Tess, grinning. "Honestly, *Mag*. The things you do."

"Maybe we can find out another way," Terry said, whirling around and switching on his computer.

"What are you thinking?" Thea said, as they waited for it to boot up.

"Maybe I can get this thing networked," Terry said.

"It is, with the rest of the class. . . ."

"No, I mean Terranet. The News-Net. Not that there'd be anything drastically different in the mainstream media, but some of the alternatives might have better info. They cracked down on the use of computers in the library as soon as this broke; I tried logging on from there once, but some sort of alarm sounded at the librarian's desk because I was off that machine as fast as she could flip a switch. I thought it was a glitch on one machine, but I tried it three times and every time they blocked me."

"Why would they do that?"

"Because they are denying the Nothing access to this place. Any way they can. If they can keep the school off the radar, then we are all out of the danger zone."

"But we are supposed to be out of the danger zone anyway," Magpie said stubbornly.

"You heard what they said last night," Thea said. "You don't know what triggers it. It could be anything at all. But Terry . . . how come you didn't try it from here?"

"Because although all these computers are networked, they're tied in to Twitterpat's machine as the main Terranet gateway," Terry said.

"Don't you need his password to access that?" Magpie asked.

"Sure, but it isn't his system password, it's the network, and I could probably hack that—it would mean skimming off the IP address from the surface of his machine's memory . . . but I hate doing that—I *like* the man, I don't want to get him or me into any really hot water. It's easy enough to do, from here—I don't need to hack to any deep level. Besides, there's the other thing. I didn't want to be alone when or if I did it."

"Why?"

"Because he could have said something inadvertently . . . or Twitterpat's password is a spoken spell, or something. . . ." Thea paused as Ben sneezed again. "See? Even you smell something."

"I have a cold," Ben said. He ended on a rising note, making his words come out rather more like a question than a statement, as though he was asking himself to believe his own assertion before he could convince anyone else of its truth.

"Wait a minute. It's up. Let me figure out . . ." Terry tapped a few keys, focused on the changing screen.

Magpie and Tess and Ben all hung back, but Thea suddenly sat forward.

"What was that?"

"What?" Terry said, startled out of his fierce concentration.

"Go back a sec," Thea said, pointing at the screen. "That. I thought I saw . . ."

"But that's just my report of the Hoh field trip," Terry said, annoyed and a little bewildered. "What's that got to do with—"

Magpie looked up with a sudden start, her eyes wide. Tess's tongue moistened her lips. Terry's hands were frozen over the keyboard.

Thea felt a whiff of moisture-laden, forest-green air that had no business being in the computer lab.

When there is a battle to be fought, it is you who can choose the place of the battlefield.

"Wait a minute," Thea said. "Let me see that report."

Terry looked up, at a complete loss.

"Just do it," Tess said.

He brought the cursor over the file name, let it hover there for another moment, then shrugged his shoulders, and clicked the mouse to open the file.

The screen changed again, into a word-processing program, and after a moment the Hoh forest trip document appeared on the screen. Terry was not a particularly lush writer at the best of times and this prose was more spare than most, being a dry school report on an official outing, but the words that *were* there suddenly triggered Thea's own memories of the trip. They sparked the images in Thea's mind's eye, and that was the beginning.

The rest followed, falling into place with an air of uncanny inevitability.

Thea's images—the color washed over them,

rushed in and obliterated the mundane benches and the blank computer screens that surrounded the five of them. The filtered light of an ancient forest; glimpses of a gleaming white waterfall or glassy green mountain stream; the many shades of forest green, from moss to fern to cedar fronds; the glimpses of the reddish cedar heart-wood revealed by the peeling bark of old stumps; the twisted grayish burls on the spruce trees; the distant glimpse of blue sky and white clouds that was sometimes allowed to intrude like a strange vision, into this shrouded, mystical place.

Magpie's touch, the touch of the healer's hands that understand what they hold—the harsh ridged bark of old cedars, the feathery brush of fern fronds, the rough texture of moss- and lichen-upholstered big leaf maples.

Ben (who had sneezed one last time and then, miraculously, stopped) came in with the slightly damp green smell of the woods, the fresh rush of air beside a waterfall, the smell of sap on trees and broken branches and trampled moss.

Tess brought a slightly acrid, slightly breeze-fresh taste of the open air and the ancient wood, as well as an ancestral memory of this place being a hunting ground for a people not her own, of feasts long forgotten where elk and bear reared by this forest had offered themselves for the good of the tribe.

Terry provided the soundtrack—the whisper of wind in the treetops, the sound of rushing water, the crack of a twig breaking, the rustle of some small creature in the underbrush.

And they were there, the five of them, standing bewildered and awestruck beside a stream broken into white-water rapids, ancient trees looming over them like pillars in some long-gone but still magnificent cathedral. The computer lab had completely disappeared, as if it had never existed.

They all knew that they had created this place, somehow, together. Just how, none of them had any idea. Not a single one of them was supposed to have the ability to do anything like this—if they had, they would not have been at the Last Ditch School. But they had done it . . . and what was more, they had done it breaking all the rules of magic.

They had done it with a computer.

This was not possible. This was not *doable*. Computers were inert things used to safely store spells. They simply were not magical.

And yet, they were.

Or one of them was. . . .

"What did you do to your computer, Terry?" Tess asked carefully, too afraid to move, standing frozen in the place where this world had set her down.

"Not a thing that I know of," Terry said, staring at the woods as though willing himself to believe that they were not there.

"This is supposed to be magic, right?" Ben said in a small voice.

Magpie turned to look at him. "Your guess is as good as ours," she said.

"But I am not sneezing," he pointed out. He took a step back, craning his head to gaze at the tops of the huge trees, and then winced, looking down. He lifted his foot with a gesture of distaste. "And hold back on the hyperreality, would you? I know you had trouble with one on the last field trip, Magpie, but I could have done without the slug. . . ."

Thea fought the urge to giggle out loud, suddenly remembering her brothers and the banana slug conversation from the afternoon of her homecoming. Aunt Zoë had been moved to comment somewhat acidly at the time, as they had abandoned the menfolk in the backyard, that whenever you got the Winthrop brothers together their average age appeared to drop to about twelve.

"All right," Tess said, yanking Thea back into the present. *"What just happened?"*

Magpie suddenly turned and smiled at Thea. "I think *you* know," she said.

Thea was about to deny all knowledge, and then Cheveyo was there in her mind, smiling, and behind him Grandmother Spider and Big Elk.

There are many worlds, and you have yet to find your own.

"I suppose," Thea said slowly, "it's my fault. . . ."

"Where *are* we?" Tess said, staring at the crowns of the towering trees.

"Hoh forest, of course," Magpie said. "That's what the report said."

"What report?"

"Yours, Terry. The one on your computer. The one Thea used to build this place."

"There's nothing like this in my report," Terry said frankly. "I wrote as little as I could get away with. It's just the facts, no more. There is no imagery in it at all—there is nothing remotely like this. . . ."

"But you do remember it like this?"

"Um, yes," Terry said, "now that you bring it up. But not *quite* this. It's . . . different. Just a bit. Just enough."

"Yeah," Magpie said. "It's Thea-Hoh. Not the real place. It's virtual reality. We aren't there now, not really. . . ."

"Oh, yes we are," Ben said, scuffing slug off his shoe.

"Yes, but not *really*," Magpie insisted. "We're in the computer lab back at the school, aren't we?"

"I have no idea," Thea said softly. "Not about the details of it. But yes, there are different worlds . . . many different worlds . . . and I have walked a number of them. They told me that I had to find the one that truly belonged to me. . . ."

Terry was staring at her strangely. "*Who* told you?"

So Thea told them, very briefly, about her summer in Cheveyo's country and the things she had learned there.

And then she told them the most important thing of all.

"Cheveyo said . . . I could choose the battle-field," she said softly. "What about a world that is not of our own? The Nothing feeds on the magic of our world—we heard them say so. But what if a person completely devoid of magic in that world lured it here instead and forced the real battle to take place far away from the worlds where it is strong? What if I could draw it away and fight it in a place like this?"

"You mean *us*," Magpie said with a watery grin. "We all did this together, somehow."

"Absolutely!" said Ben valiantly. "We're all in it."

"Loviqu'ta," whispered Thea. "Hunters Moon . . ."

They were looking at her, as if she was the only one who knew what she was doing. And in a way, they were frighteningly right.

But Magpie grinned at the phrase, and suddenly the grin was wolfish. "Oh, yes," she said. "Hunters."

"But how is it possible?" said Terry doggedly. "Computers don't do things like this."

"Computers are just tools," Tess said.

"Yeah," agreed Ben enthusiastically. "Maybe you guys could ask Twitterpat when he gets back. I always thought he was kind of cool . . . for a teacher."

"Thea," Terry said, "how do we get back? I still have to find out . . ."

He blinked and his voice died mid-sentence. He was sitting in his computer chair, hands poised over his keyboard.

"Hey," he said. "*Hey*. How'd you do that?"

Thea was trembling and very pale. "I don't know," she said, "but I can. I can sense that I can. I wanted us back and I got us back. Don't ask me how I did it."

He stared at her, his gaze troubled, and then turned to his computer again, closing out of the dangerous field trip report that was still on screen and calling up a Terranet search engine.

"So . . . when were you thinking that we should do this thing? Whatever it is that we're, uh, planning to do?" Ben said.

"We'd better wait until Twitterpat *does* get back," said Tess carefully. "We might be meddling with things we don't— What's the matter, Terry?"

Terry's expression had suddenly set into a mask, a mask that was equal parts fury, pity, and grief.

"I got into the Terranet," he said abruptly. "We can't wait to ask Twitterpat anything."

"Why?" Tess asked. She and Magpie both leaned over the computer, craning their necks at the screen. Thea let out a small keening sound.

Terry stood, dragging both hands through his hair in a motion of pure despair.

"It's right there, in today's Terranet headlines," he said, carefully not looking at any of his friends. "Patrick Wittering is dead."

EMBER MOON

1.

THERE HAD BEEN brave talk and grand plans out there in Thea-Hoh, in the world that they had created—but the news of Twitterpat's death seemed to have smothered those ideas right out of existence. After their return from the virtual world, Thea and the others avoided talking about their experience. In fact, for nearly a full week, they avoided one another. There was a desperate sense that if they ignored what had happened they might convince one another and the world around them that a particular moment in time had never happened at all—and if they could turn back time to *before*, to an instant before they knew that Twitterpat was dead, then he would still be alive.

All the students at the school knew was that

Patrick Wittering had died protecting one of his fellow Academy teachers who had gone to battle the Nothing. They were not told how or where or even who that other teacher was—and all those who had gone from the school remained missing, fueling speculation that more than one of them might be dead. The specter of the Nothing had been invited into what had been the safe haven of the Academy, had become an ever-present terror that lingered invisibly in the corridors and the classrooms and the cafeteria where meals were eaten in cowed silence.

It is impervious to magic. It eats magic. The more you throw at it the stronger it becomes.

When there is a battle to be fought, it is you who can choose the place of the battlefield.

Thea turned these words over and over again in her mind in the days that followed the announcement of Twitterpat's death and her return from the virtual forest she had created with her friends. The principal's interpretation of the Nothing. Cheveyo's parting lesson.

The battle was waiting. The battlefield was obvious.

The virtual world.

The only problem was that she had no idea

what exactly had happened on the night the virtual reality forest had been created. It had just . . . happened—and happened so fast that she had barely had time to stop and think about any of it. And the others, who had shared the astonishing excursion with her, whose presence had seemed to be so essential in creating that other world, did not seem inclined to repeat the experience.

The only other person with whom she had had any discussions at all on the matter was Magpie, in the shared moments of darkness at night before they both drifted into sleep—and these days sleep was less restful than it might have been, full of disturbing dreams and uneasy forebodings. And even these conversations were indirect; they talked around the subject, the reference to a possible plot to vanquish the Nothing referred to only in general terms, playing with ideas, not with actual plans.

"The Quilcah," said Magpie on one of these nights, "have a Whale Hunt. . . ."

"How does *that* help?" The covers rustled in the other bed as Thea turned toward her in the darkness. "Ancestral magic, Magpie?"

"Well, it wouldn't be tradition. Not really.

Only men go on Hunts; women wait on shore with the flensing knives. But maybe some aspects of it can be useful. . . ."

"A Magpie Whale Hunt, out in virtual reality," Thea said. "Like the Thea-Hoh woods. Tell me about it."

"One whale feeds many," Magpie said, her voice very soft. "When it is time, the elders call for a Hunt, and the Hunters will be chosen—many will want to go, but few are called. They are marked, after. They are the Whale Hunters forevermore. And of the small handful who are chosen to go, one is singled out even further. 'The One Who Calls the Whale.' There is a melody, a tune, to which the whale will come."

"I think I know this tune," Thea said, transported back to the red mesas of Cheveyo's country, echoing with the First Song.

"It's always different, for every one who is chosen," Magpie said.

"I know," Thea said gently. "Go on."

"The Whale comes. Many may come, but only one will answer the Call," Magpie said, her voice dropping into cadences of chant, of tribal wisdom being passed down the generations. "You will know the one, because that Whale will offer himself to the people—his fat for the winter lamps, his flesh to the living, his bones to the ancestors. And his spirit becomes part of the people, guarding them, helping them, and in time choosing the next Hunter who will go out and call his successor."

"But the Nothing is exactly the opposite. It's not likely to come up to you and roll over belly up and invite you to smite it," Thea said. There was a voice in the back of her mind, Big Elk in the night forest, *The Alphiri brought that. A hunger that will not be sated.* . . . "The Nothing will fight back. It always has so far. Unless . . ." She tapped her chin with a thoughtful finger, frowning in concentration. "But . . . what if . . . what if we create a Magpie Whale Hunt?"

"Huh?" said Magpie. "You aren't making any sense."

"We could go back," Thea said softly. "We could shape that world, the whale hunt world. We would be the ones to decide what laws govern it. If we can lure the Nothing there, we can make it go. . . ." Magpie stirred again, and Thea, anticipating an interruption or an objection, spoke faster, almost gabbling. "No, it makes *sense*, Magpie! If we make a world into which the Nothing would come, but leave it only one way out. We can do a whale hunt. We can do what your ancestors have done for generations. We can call the whale, and the whale will respond in the way that the whale always does. It can't help doing that, that's the way things have always been. But if the one door we leave open for the Nothing is to become one with the whale, then once it's there, in the body of the whale . . . it will have to react in the way that the whale would have reacted. It is *supposed* to offer itself. That's the way it's supposed to happen; that's the way we can make it happen."

"Yes, but if we kill the Nothing-whale in our reality over there, does that mean we destroy the Nothing in this world, too?" Magpie asked. "And are you sure that it would come? How on earth do you call something like that and know it will come to you?"

"It comes to magic," Thea said.

"But we don't *have* any," Magpie pointed out helpfully.

"Not here," Thea said. "But maybe in that place—in that *other* place. Mag, I've walked in a different world and there were things I could do there that just don't happen when I'm back in this world. Maybe it's the same with this. Maybe we can create a place where we can do what we need to do, and it will work."

"And if we do get it there, and it's stuck there, and *we* get stuck there with it . . . ?" Magpie asked.

Thea had no answers. The conversation sank into silence, and the silence vanished into sleep, and the dreams came again—the dreams that haunted Thea because she could never quite remember them when she woke. She recalled the dreams she had had back in Cheveyo's house— visions of the Faele and their gifts and the Alphiri and their offers of trade. Some of her recent dreams were very similar in nature to those ear- lier ones; others seemed to be about the Nothing and the way it was spreading across the worlds, as Big Elk had said. Thea thought of Grandmother Spider's sky full of living stars and an iron band tightened painfully around her heart at the thought that the Nothing had come there, too, that some of those star souls had been devoured by it, perhaps were gone forever. Here, in the less rarefied air of a world where her magic was dormant, dreams of any nature appeared less willing to reveal themselves to her or to stay in her memory for long after she woke. They merely lodged in the back of her mind, like thistles, uncomfortable and prickly.

But while she waited for some sort of sign telling her what she needed to do next, her decisions seemed to make themselves, after all.

Twitterpat's classes were, for all intents and purposes, suspended after the news of his death, but his students were given tacit approval to complete the assignments that he had left behind—it was a sort of homage, one that the students offered without incentive and one that the school accepted without comment. The supervisory presence that Twitterpat had promised was there, in the shape of one teacher or another—hardly ever the same one, as though the teachers had chosen to give their time to this project as their own homage to one of their colleagues, but somehow by unspoken pact not one of them chose to sit at Twitterpat's own desk. Usually the presiding teacher, whose attendance was almost unnecessary in terms of keeping the students quiet and working, would wander in quietly at the beginning of a period, find an empty station or bring out a chair and place it in a convenient corner, and read a book for the duration of the class to the quiet accompaniment of pens scratching on paper and the clatter of keyboards.

It was during one of these classes that Thea, distracted by her inner tumult, allowed her mind to wander back to Cheveyo and his house on the mesa. Outside the classroom window it was a gray and dismal November day, the window-panes weeping rain and low clouds caught and shredded by the branches of wet cedars almost black in the dim light. But Thea could open a window in her mind and transport herself back to the liquid heat of the desert summer, Tawaha's light, hot and heavy on her head and shoulders like a cloak. The red mesas reflected the sun-shine, gave it color and weight, poured it back into the dusty scree of the sage-scented plains.

Without quite being aware of what she was doing, Thea found herself in a new document in her word-processing software, typing out frag-ments of sentences, words that evoked Cheveyo to her.

Red mesas. House in the rock. Sunlight hot, heavy with red and gold.

The cursor blinked at her at the end of the last word.

Thea stared at it for a moment, mesmerized,

her hand hovering above her keyboard.

A breath of hot dry air stirred the loose hair around her face.

All I have to do is press ENTER.

She looked around, blinking, as though waking from a dream. Two stations away from her, Tess was bent over her keyboard, typing furiously. A little farther away, Terry sat with his hands laced behind the back of his head, staring at his screen, his expression curiously blank. Other students wrote or tapped away or stared at their work with focused concentration. The presiding teacher appeared engrossed in a thick book, marking passages with a yellow highlighter pen.

Nobody was paying any attention at all to Thea.

All I have to do is press ENTER. *And I will be there.*

Ah, but will I be here?

What would happen if she simply . . . disappeared?

She couldn't take the chance. But something had crystallized in the back of her mind, a conviction, a decision, a firm intent. None of the others, not even Magpie, appeared to want to try to achieve that alternate reality, the virtual world, again; they had avoided even talking about it. Very well. She would try it herself. Try it first, with the familiar. With Cheveyo, the mesas, perhaps the Road. Perhaps the Barefoot Road could take her to the next place that she needed to be.

Not now.

Maybe tonight.

She mentioned her intentions to nobody, determined to pursue her own experiment, more certain than ever of what she needed to do. When she was called to the telephone after classes that day, it was almost as if she were continuing a familiar conversation, already well begun, when she heard her aunt's voice on the other end of the line.

"Thea," Zoë said, and her voice had an edge of urgency to it, "what is going on?"

"What do you mean?"

"I *told* you I can tell when you're in trouble. I can smell it from here. I can smell the smoke. It's like you've lit a torch, you're bright with danger, I know you're up to something and I already know nobody is going to like whatever that is. What are you doing?"

An edge of an old dream suddenly sliced into Zoë's words. Thea could hear the echo again, the distant words of the Faele clustered around her cradle. *She will be able to conquer nothing.* . . .

Conquer nothing. Conquer . . . *Nothing.*

It all seemed so simple now, so clear.

"I know what to do now," she said. "The Faele told me so, back in the *cradle*, Aunt Zoë. That's what all this has been about—me and magic and everything I've learned."

"What Faele? Thea, there were no Faele gifts at your birth. Your father made sure of that."

"But I dreamed about them. I *remember* them. I don't know how I remember them, but I do—and they did give me gifts. Like they always do. And one of them said I could conquer nothing. I thought that meant that I couldn't actually *do* anything, but don't you see? They meant the Nothing, that thing, that enemy that cannot be conquered by magic. The only person who can conquer it is someone *without* magic. Someone who is known to be without magic. Someone like . . . me."

"Don't be silly, Thea," Zoë said, her voice sharp with fear. "Call your parents. Call them right now, right after you put the phone down. Promise me. Promise me you will not do anything stupid. I wish I could just use a Portal and come snatch you right now, but the school is warded against that. Thea, are you there? Are you listening to me? Stay put. Don't do anything. *Anything.* People have died getting in the way of this thing. Are you listening to me? *Thea!*"

"It's okay, Aunt Zoë," Thea said gently. "This is what they made me for."

She could hear her aunt crying out her name as she replaced the receiver in the cradle, knowing that she was running out of time. Zoë would phone her parents, her teachers, anybody she could think of—anything to try to stop whatever Thea had planned. She had maybe an hour. Maybe less.

Magpie was not in their room when Thea returned there, as if in the grip of dream or compulsion, to retrieve her necklace of three feathers—the light-and-dark-barred turkey feather that granted her patience, the black raven feather that would give her wisdom, the black-and-white eagle's feather that carried the courage she needed now as never before. Despite the way the phone lines must have been heating up in her wake, in the school itself it was as if a clear passage had opened for Thea—she got her necklace, left the room, left the residence hall, crossed the grounds, and entered the building where the computer lab was—all without crossing paths with a single person. There was a sense of movement and purpose all around her, the school full of living, breathing beings, students and teachers going about their own business, but Thea moved as if alone in the universe, invisible to others, the others invisible to her.

The computer lab was locked and deserted. Thea punched in the security code, slipped through a crack in the door, heard it snick shut and rearm behind her, then made her way to where a single computer appeared to be on, its screensaver something that could have been a fireworks display, or the night sky full of shooting stars over the First World where Grandmother Spider lived. It cleared as Thea approached and slipped into the chair before it. On the screen, already open, was the document with the handful of desert phrases she had scribbled down earlier today.

She hadn't known she had saved it. In fact, she could have sworn that she had not. She could have sworn, in fact, that the computer had not been left on in the first place.

The cursor blinked, as it had done earlier, right after the last word, inviting her to ENTER.

Her left hand reached up to wrap itself around her feather necklace.

Her right index finger brushed the ENTER key, very lightly.

The dreary gray light, which had been barely strong enough to pass through the rain-slicked windowpanes, suddenly became brighter, stronger, sharper, more golden, more solid. The world dissolved around Thea . . .

. . . and fell back into shape, like a computer photograph being resolved pixel by pixel on a slow connection, coming into sharper and sharper focus until the gray Pacific Northwest November was gone and she was in a different place, a place now ruled by what Cheveyo would have called Matay'ta, the Ember Moon, the time for coming to terms with one's own self and spirit.

"And have you finally chosen to do that?" Cheveyo's voice asked, as if conjured by Thea's thoughts.

"Are you here? Are you real?" she blurted, turning.

He stood a few paces behind her, a wry smile

on his face leaning on his staff and shaking his head. *Always questions, Catori . . .*

"One thing," he commented serenely, "has not changed."

"It *is* you," Thea said.

"Of course it is. It isn't quite the same place where you left me, but I find I recognize it quite well. You are to be commended. Your powers of observation are acute."

"Does that mean that I've chosen my world? *This* world?"

"You had better ask someone else that," Cheveyo said, making a gracious gesture to his left.

Grandmother Spider stepped out of a shadow, smiling.

"Once upon a time, many years from now, in the web of a dreamcatcher," she said. "Hello, my granddaughter, well met again. Your world, you will find, is one that touches many. You can live in a world where you can be anything you want—and if ever you are trapped in a world where that is impossible, all you have to do is step up to the border where those two meet—the place where you can stand in both worlds at once, and use all the power granted in the one world in whatever other place it is needed."

"So can I do this?" Thea whispered. "Can I go out and fight the Nothing?"

"You can do," Cheveyo said, "whatever needs to be done, Catori. Have you chosen the battlefield?"

"Yes," Thea said, and in her mind an ocean stirred.

The same image of the empty sea trembled suddenly on a tiny dreamcatcher cradled in Grandmother Spider's palm.

"This path," Grandmother Spider said gently, "holds pain, my child. It holds achievement, but also betrayal. You are using the nature of the world to fill your own needs. The need is great, but can you live with asking another to pay the price for it?"

"I think," Thea whispered, "that this is what I was born to do; this is why I stepped out of my own world and watched it from the sidelines. I am the last weapon in my kind's war of survival, the only weapon there is, the only one for which there is no defense or counterblow—because nobody knows it exists. . . ."

"You are beginning to understand the reasons behind your choices," Grandmother Spider said.

"It will be hard, my child. It will be harder than you can believe."

The dreamcatcher ocean stirred, and a single small boat that had not been there a moment before suddenly bobbed upon its surface. And then Thea was in it, and the desert had gone— vanished as though it had never existed.

She found herself sitting in a wooden craft carved with stylized depictions of whales, a single oar laid beside her feet, bobbing and drifting on a pewter-gray ocean with walls of clammy sea-fog surrounding her, almost close enough to touch.

It was cold, bitingly cold, and she shivered violently. She seemed to be utterly alone here in the place where she was supposed to call on Magpie's sacrificial whale, and see it come and allow itself to be taken by her harpoon (Oar? What oar? It had changed into something wickedly sharp that glimmered with an edge and a deadly point even in the blunt and suffused half-light of this strange place).

But first she was supposed to call it.

Her music came to her very faintly, as though sent by Cheveyo as his gift from the red hills behind his house where she had first heard it—

the creation song that Grandmother Spider had said was Thea's own melody, her own version of the First Song. She began humming it, softly at first, but then louder and louder; strands of it separated and fell away, swallowed by the mist, vanishing into the depths of the ocean, weaving together the web of worlds that Thea needed.

The world of Cheveyo's wisdom, her own reality, where her aunt was probably even now marshalling the authorities of Thea's life against her.

The world of Magpie's ancestors and their legends, and the power of an ancient bargain.

The world where, she suddenly realized, she could not feel or see the presence of the Nothing at all—the world of innocence, of a primeval purity, and one where the Alphiri had probably never been . . . and where, therefore, the Nothing had had no access.

Until now. Until Thea Winthrop chose to defile it.

There was a sharp pain that crept into her song at that realization. She had not, even now, even at this breaking point, been sure that she could do this—that she could call, that the Nothing would come. But now she knew that it would. It was a new world, a pristine world, and anything that had the Alphiri associated with it would not be able to resist conquering a new and untapped market.

There were tears in Thea's eyes and in her voice as her fingers wove the melody into a strand of the dull gray fog and then twined both into a short piece of cloud-colored ribbon. She could do this, here, in this world, her world, the world she had called into being. She had been right. This had been the right choice, the right thing to do.

She had not bargained on the guilt . . . or, worse, on the solitude, the loneliness.

In a sense she had been alone all her days, with few true friends, as though her entire life had been training her for this moment. She had been alone so long that she had not thought it would matter to her anymore. But that was before she had come to the Academy . . . before she had met Magpie, Tess, Terry, and Ben. The ones who had made a world with her. She suddenly missed them all, missed them fiercely, missed them with a sinking feeling of having isolated herself from a source of strength without which she would find it impossible to carry out her plans.

Somewhere, far away from the mist-shrouded ocean on which she waited, Thea hummed an echo of the same song of power in defiance of the evil that threatened her own world, heard herself call the Nothing to her, challenge its mindless powers of destruction, focus all of it back on herself—the easy target, back in that other world, the child believed to be without magic, dabbling with things she did not understand, reaching for a power too far beyond her reach. An inconsequential insect, a gnat, an annoyance. It would be the work of a moment to sweep her aside, to swallow her whole, to roll over her with a heavy weight and obliterate her as if she had never been.

And it would have done exactly that, if Thea had had a spark of magic in her home world, where the "real" Thea was.

Instead, the Nothing bore down on her, focusing its full malevolence onto the lone voice of this thin and reedy magical challenge—and passed through her like she was not there, like she was a wraith. No, like she was a Portal—she was the gate through which it roared in the full knowledge that no magical barrier or power could stand before it, and Thea almost buckled with the sheer weight and force of its darkness. But she stood her ground, and it was past her, and then gone. And there was a part of her that recoiled at its passing. But another part, that which had remained in her world and had stood as bait for the thing that she hunted, watched the Nothing leave that world, and slammed the gate-that-was-herself shut behind it, barring all return.

For a moment she thought she glimpsed a pair of glowing eyes, fierce with fury—golden eyes, *Alphiri* eyes—but she could not be sure. It might just have been her own fears taking shape.

Her world was clean. There was no trace remaining of the Nothing's dark shadow. Everything she knew and loved was safe.

But now the Nothing was *here*, in this world of mist and water that she had brought into existence to trap it. Here with her, and lured under false pretenses—lured with the promise of feeding on magic, on new magic from an untapped world—and Thea suddenly knew what her aunt had meant when the two of them had spoken of the Nothing for the first time on the telephone before Twitterpat's death. . . . Was it really only days ago? *Like that smoky last gasp of a just-*

extinguished candle, Zoë had said. *Like the weight of night. Like a stench of carrion.* There was a smell of carrion in the air around Thea now, a smell of something long-dead, decomposing, bones showing through melting flesh.

And here, because here her magic was strong, the Nothing was strong, too. It had an enemy to face.

Or was it an enemy?

A hunger that cannot be sated.

It feeds on magic.

The Alphiri bring it. . . .

Thea had been thinking about the Nothing, and these were things she had been told about it, or had overheard recently. But there was suddenly something else there, a memory of long ago—she had been a child, curious as always, and lurking by a half-open door to the living room where her parents had been having a party. Before being whisked back to bed, Thea had heard snatches of conversation that had meant nothing to her then, which had since been buried under all the other information about the Alphiri she had gathered in the process of growing up in her world. Now those snatches of conversation returned to her and began to make sense.

"The Alphiri don't have an ounce of a native creativity. . . . They buy, they tweak or repackage, they sell. . . . They have nothing at all that we would call magic. . . ."

Her father's voice. He had known the answers all the time.

If the Alphiri could create their own dreams, they would never have needed the rigid framework of the Trade Codex, where everything could be bought. If the Alphiri could create their own dreams, they might begin to build their souls. But they were empty, they were beautiful vessels into which things could be poured and from which those same things, subtly changed, could be poured out—for a price—but they were empty, and that was what they were really after in all of their bargains, the small print in every bargain they made. That was why they contacted other cultures, other nations, other races. They were desperately searching for something— something that was essential, something without which any race, even one as long-lived and proficient at trade as their own, would stagnate, and then begin to die with no hope of rebirth and no legacy. Good bargains were not made for long memories.

They were looking for their souls. For the spirit of their race.

And for this, they had made a tool. A monster. Something that bled worlds dry of the things that the Alphiri might want, might find too expensive to buy or impossible to bargain for. And they had been doing this for a long time, in many places, to many living things in their time. What was it that Grandmother Spider had called them? *World-eaters*.

The Nothing was out there to gather anything that could further this quest. It was just the bad luck of the human polity that the Alphiri wanted its magic, its dreams—and that humans were fragile enough not to be able to survive having their essence sucked out of them by this lethal instrument of the Alphiri.

Here in this empty new world Thea had made, there was nothing else for the Nothing to focus on . . . except herself. Herself and perhaps the whale that was the embodiment of the bargain Magpie's people had made with the sea and its creatures.

But there was no whale. The still surface of the ocean was undisturbed, calm, almost oily, smooth like silk, rolling with deep heavy waves, rocking her craft gently where Thea sat in the mist humming the First Song and drawing to her the enemy of her world, of her people.

And the Nothing gathered itself against her.

The mist suddenly stirred, and the ocean surface rippled as though something had touched it and passed on. Without halting her calling tune, Thea turned her head a little, watching. But it was not the whale she was waiting for. Not yet.

When the bow of another small boat emerged from the wall of sea fog, Thea could only smile.

2.

In the back, Terry and Tess plied a pair of sturdy oars; Ben sat in the middle, clutching a harpoon that was a twin to her own; in the front, right up in the point of the bow carved in the likeness of a whale, sat Magpie, a vividly colored woven blanket around her shoulders, something bright bound on her forehead like a star, long dangling earrings in her ears, catching even the light that was not there in that muted gray murk and glowing like a spark of sacred fire.

Like the ribbon of fire that Thea had once stolen from the sun. *Where you are and where light is, I will always be with you*, Tawaha had promised. And there was light, here, now. Not the vivid hot light of the desert, but it was day—and somewhere, up above the mists, the sun was up. Tawaha. Even here, in this strange place, Tawaha.

But first, there was that other boat, the friends she had wanted to be at her side.

"What took you so long?" Thea murmured, breaking off her humming.

"You've stirred a hornet's nest in your wake," Terry said. "*You* try doing something on the quiet that would bring everyone down on you like a ton of bricks if they knew what you were up to. And besides . . . you left us a pretty thin trail to follow."

"How did you find me?"

"Once the uproar began and the marines were called in to get you, we figured out what you'd done," Tess said. "And we went straight for the computer lab. If you think we took a long time, you try figuring out what 'Magpie Hunt' means without any clues."

"You had clues," Thea said. "You had Magpie herself."

"She came *after* we found the computer," Ben said.

There were things to be done, but Thea was fascinated despite herself. "I left a trail? On the computer?"

"Something like that," Tess said. "You'd better be careful where you leave your base computer, if you do this again."

"Or leave someone behind to watch your back," Ben said reproachfully. "Why did you go alone?"

"Because . . . it was something I needed to do, something that was left for me to do, and none of you seemed to want any part of it," Thea said. "But, Magpie . . . ," she continued, "this is an empty ocean. Perhaps I didn't do it the right way. There is only the ocean, and me, and the Nothing."

"The whales will come," Magpie said, smiling.

"Ancestral magic?" asked Thea, after a moment.

"Yes. I think so. At last. This is for me to do," Magpie said, and her voice was as luminous as the star she had bound on her brow.

"Then call it. Call the whale," Thea said.

And Magpie sat up and closed her eyes and lifted her voice in a long keening cry that pierced the mist like a knife and traveled out over the empty ocean.

Which was suddenly not empty anymore.

Thea could not suppress a small gasp as a huge gray body rolled in the dark waters beside her, almost close enough to touch, and rocked her tiny boat in the wake of its passing.

"It's here," Ben said, curling his hand tightly around his harpoon.

The fog had retreated, and the ocean opened up before them. A ways away, far enough for them not to be swamped by it, close enough to see its form and shape and to call it by its spirit name, a whale's sleek dark shape breached the water and then fell back with a spray of white foam.

But there were more than one. A second whale breached. A third. A splash off to the side in the fog that might have been yet another.

Thea's eyes danced from one huge shape to the next, uncertain. "Which one is it, Magpie?" she asked urgently. *"Which one?"*

"It will tell you," Magpie said. She had broken off her cry as the whales came and now sat watching them, her eyes very bright.

Beyond the pod of spirit-whales, revealed at last by the retreating mists, a dense dark cloud was forming, heavy with its scent of rot and corruption. Thea gagged at the memory of its presence inside her, but reached for it, hooked a strand of it with the index finger of her right hand, holding her breath. When the foremost whale breached again, Thea reached for it with the other hand, across the distance and empty ocean that separated her from the whale, and somehow touched its warm skin, feeling its life cling to her fingers much like strands of sunset light once did back in the desert. She brought her hands together, laced her fingers together into a lattice, wove the warmth and the darkness together: the whale's gift of life with the essence of death that was the Nothing.

"Be One," she murmured, tangling life and death, watching the Nothing shudder and shred, watching the Whale suddenly twist and fall back into the water with a gracelessness foreign to its kind.

A keening cry of outrage, of betrayal, of anger and sorrow and pain, ripped the air. Thea did not know, could not tell, whether it came from the Nothing or the whale. Or perhaps from both.

The surface of the ocean trembled, and was still.

"It's gone," Ben said, scanning the quiet sea, holding his harpoon at attention. The fog was lifting; somewhere far above them there was a hint of brightening, as though sunshine was trying to fight its way through the shroud of cloud. "They are all gone."

"What did you *do*?" Tess asked.

"How did you do that?" Terry said in the same breath.

"It will come back," Magpie murmured, her eyes closed, her hands together. "It will come to the call. That is its nature."

The waters surged beneath them as something huge and angry passed right below both boats, and then surged again as it circled around once more. They glimpsed a ridged back, a dorsal fin breaking the surface, and then it was gone again.

Magpie began her keening song again, very softly, as if singing a child to sleep.

"The Whale's nature," Ben said, and they had all started thinking of the whale as the Whale, as the opposite to the Nothing, as that in which the Nothing was now confined. "How was it changed by the Nothing? Did you even succeed, Thea?"

"Oh, yes," Thea said, feeling suddenly tired, as though a weight had been laid on her shoulders that made her stagger with the load.

The need is great, but can you live with asking another to pay the price for it?

Grandmother Spider's gentle voice came back to Thea, and she all but wept for pity. She had taken the Whale's gentle nature and sense of noble sacrifice and had made them into tools of destruction—it was the only way, but it was betrayal, it was a twisting of everything that was genuine and true.

What if the Whale refused the burden she had laid upon it?

Ahead of them, the waters broke again. The Whale—there was only one now, the One Whale, the rest of the pod might have been pure illusion for all they knew—was swimming away from them, quite fast.

"Follow," Thea said, picking up her harpoon, which had turned back into an oar.

The twins bent to their own oars. The two small coracles skimmed the surface of the ocean, following a sort of wake left by the dorsal fin of the whale that was slicing through the waters before them. It led them for a way, sometimes vanishing for an instant to come up behind them or below them, rocking them dangerously, threatening to upset them, but always it returned to the front, swam ahead a little way, circled, thrashed the water with fin and fluke, fought with itself and the black rider that Thea had saddled its soul with, raced away, challenging them to follow.

Two things were warring in the body of the Whale—the spirit that had come to the ancestral call, ready to offer itself, and that malignant "other," the dark foreign matter that had been implanted into it, wanting to deliver only death, not life—never life. It ran from the Hunters, from itself, from the Hunters again, and kept returning, being called to the music it had already accepted as its fate. It struggled and fought until finally something broke and it stopped, floating, exhausted, right in front of the two boats. Thea could see its eye from where she sat, and there was something in it that was infinitely old and wise and sad.

I came when you called, as I have always done. Why? Why have you done this to me? It is not the ancient bargain between our kinds. It is not clean.

Thea's breath caught in sorrow that she should have to kill a thing like this. *I am sorry. I am so sorry. I needed a strength that was a great and ancient good, and more powerful than my enemy. I needed the strength and the power of that bargain of which you speak. I needed the ancestral magic to cross with the newest magic of all. Either, by itself, is not enough. Together, they were. Barely. But they were enough. I am in your debt, Ancient One.*

A different voice then, a scream of hate and fury. *I WILL NOT! I WILL NOT BE BOUND! I WILL NOT BE BOUND BY THIS!*

For a moment Thea could smell the carrion stench again, and the world darkened, like the falling of night, the air thick around her. She felt bile rise at the back of her throat; it was suddenly hard to breathe. The Nothing may have started out being a sending of the Alphiri, but here and now, it was a beast in its own right, a monster that knew itself, that roared with a rage all its own at being bound.

I AM AIR AND DARKNESS! I AM POWER! I AM THE SEEKER, SENT OUT TO FIND! I AM THE HUNGER! I WILL NOT BE BOUND BY THIS!

And then it was suddenly gone, chopped in mid-shriek, as if suddenly gagged—there was still a sense of outrage, of frenzy, but it was an impotent rage, locked behind bars of something stronger than steel.

The voice that spoke again was that of the Whale, pure, untainted.

I come, as I have always come. I understand. It was necessary. I bring the victory of life—and that is what I have always done, after all.

There was a light in the Whale's eye, a shimmer that played around its great head, and the trace of darkness that was the Nothing was gathered and locked away in a safe place, from which it could never escape. It was a great load, but the Whale would bear it. It had chosen to honor the old bargain.

Take me. Take me now. . . .

They both heard it, felt it, Thea and Ben, holding on to their harpoons—and they acted as one.

The harpoons quivered in the Whale's great body, looking far too flimsy to do any damage— but then, through the mist, the ocean broke on a gray pebbly shore, and the ocean took the Whale and floated the great body forward, toward land. The boats followed, crunching onto the pebbles as the Whale was borne in and beached gently in the shallows.

The first pale fingers of the sun had finally pierced the sea fog completely, turning it from dull, dark gray into a pale shimmering silver-white veil of cloud and then shredding even that until glints of sunlight began to sparkle on the waves lapping at the shore. The air smelled clean, salty, fresh with light and morning.

Where you are and where light is . . .

"What now?" Ben whispered, looking at the Whale's lifeless body with tears of pity standing in his eyes. "I hated killing it. I feel as though I have an innocent's death on my hands."

"You were one of the Hunt," Magpie said, and her own face was etched with sorrow, but also with a fierce pride. "This was not death, but the seed of resurrection. Look."

A small band of women picked their way across the beach, keening quietly as they walked, carrying sharp flensing blades in their hands.

"We can leave it to them now," Magpie said. "Our part of the bargain is done."

"Did we do it?" asked Ben. "Did we really kill the Nothing? Can it have been that simple?"

"Who said it was simple?" Thea said. She felt like crying, and yet some of that pride that Magpie wore so brightly was shining in her own face.

"Isn't it time we got back?" asked Tess. "How long were we here? They're probably looking for all of us by now, they'll tear the school down brick by brick if they have to. . . ."

"Home," Thea said.

As the beach and the body of the sacrificed Whale and the gleam of sunlight on the ocean began to fade around them, Ben flung out a hand and pointed into the shadows of the fir forest that marched almost down to the edge of the water.

"Look!"

It was almost too late, but Thea thought she glimpsed what he had seen: a small knot of shadowy shapes, drifting away through the trees, released into freedom. One of them, with graying hair tied into a straggly ponytail, might even have been Twitterpat's ghost.

The Nothing was gone. The spirits of the people it had taken were free.

And then the five were back in the computer lab, all of them, sitting before a computer, scrolling gently down a document open on its monitor. Thea glimpsed the word WHALE, and then suddenly, there was a noise at the door of the classroom, and she grabbed for the mouse, dragged the cursor up to the menu bar, and clicked on DELETE.

DO YOU WANT TO SAVE CHANGES TO DOCUMENT? the computer dialog box asked politely.

"No!" murmured Thea, clicking on the right button.

The screen blinked, the document winked out of existence, all record of a now-vanished virtual world erased, just as the door opened to allow a handful of frantic adults inside, led by Thea's Aunt Zoë.

"That should be erased off the hard disk," Thea whispered as she turned, catching Terry's eye.

"Leave it to me," he said.

"What is going on here?" demanded the principal, only half a step behind Zoë.

"We're just finishing our assignments," Tess said, with fingers firmly crossed behind her back.

"You all seem very eager to do so," the principal said suspiciously. "Working after hours. Show me."

"I've just shut down, sir, but I'd be happy to," Terry said smoothly, swinging to another station and flicking the ON switch. The computer began whirring into life. "I'm the only one who's finished," he added. "My sister was stuck, and Thea was nearly done with hers in class this afternoon, and we came to try and get some work done while it was quiet. Twi . . . I mean, Mr. Wittering gave us all access codes, before he . . . went away."

"You don't take computer science," said another of the adults, a teacher who had watched over Twitterpat's quiet class several times since his death, staring at Magpie and Ben.

"I hate computers," Magpie said, and smiled.

"I was just keeping my friends company," Ben said. And sneezed unexpectedly, shaking his head to clear his watering eyes.

"Thea," Zoë said, her voice shaking very slightly, "are you all right?"

"I'm fine," Thea said, presenting an expression of angelic sweetness and innocence to meet her aunt's frightened eyes.

"All right," the principal said sharply. "We are *all* done here for the night. You will all pack up, please, and leave the classroom at once. And we will discuss this again tomorrow. As for the code, after-hours access to this place ends as of right now. I will see about changing the security code tonight. Out, all of you. Back to your rooms, please, now. Thea Winthrop, your aunt wants to speak with you. You may use Mr. Wittering's office, Miss Cox, if you wish."

"Thea . . . ," Zoë began, as soon as they were alone.

"You can't tell anyone, Aunt Zoë. Not *anyone*."

"Tell them what? Thea, *what* are you up to? You scared the living daylights out of me on the phone. You were babbling about the Faele and something about doing what you were 'made' to do. . . ."

"It's Matay'ta," Thea said, offering a luminous smile to her aunt.

"It's *what*?"

"The moon, it's Matay'ta—it's the moon of finding yourself, understanding yourself. And I think I have, Aunt Zoë. I think I finally have. Magic is where you find it."

LONG NIGHTS MOON

1.

"**Y**OUR AUNT IS YANKING you home early because of a family emergency?" Magpie said later that night from the shadows of her pillow. "What's the emergency?"

"I am," Thea said. The moon in the sky had changed: It was Raqu'ta, the Long Nights Moon, the moon of gaining wisdom, of coming of age. Thea knew there were many things she had yet to understand, but she also knew that she had crossed some invisible line, had emerged from what had been a chrysalis. She was not yet sure what form she had taken, but she could feel the change stirring her blood.

"Oh," Magpie said. "Figures." There was a small, painful pause, and then her voice dropped into an even lower whisper. "Are you coming back here?"

"Of course I am. I already told Aunt Zoë she couldn't tell anybody about what happened. And since nobody knows, I am still a magical 'blank slate.' I belong here."

"But did you tell *her* what happened?"

"Yes, but she still doesn't quite believe it."

"I still don't know what you did, exactly," Magpie said.

"What *we* did. You were with me, that first time, all of you. And the second time, you followed me on your own. And without you, Magpie, it would all have been a waste. When *I* called, the Nothing came, but it took you to call the Whale. And it took all of us to Hunt it."

"But what," Magpie whispered, "did we *do*, exactly . . . ?"

Thea was about to reply when she heard the door to their room snick open quietly, and a thin ribbon of light briefly snaked into the dark room before the door was shut again just as quietly.

"Are you guys awake?" hissed a familiar voice.

"Tess?" Thea said, sitting up in bed.

"Guilty," Tess said, padding over and perching on the end of Thea's bed. "Are you really leaving tomorrow?"

Thea sighed. "Yes, I am. My aunt is taking me home."

"I'm not surprised. After what you did, they'll want to do all sorts of tests—"

"Tess," Thea said urgently, "nobody must know about this. Not now. Not yet, anyway. Terry understands. When I said that the transcript of the Whale Hunt had to be erased from the hard drive of the computer—we don't want anyone finding any trace of it."

"He's already done that," Tess said. "But I'm confused. What happened? What happens next?"

"Tess, what *was* the Nothing?"

"It was a . . . It was . . . It . . . How should *I* know?" Tess whispered. "The best mages in the world were trying to figure it out, and nobody seemed to understand it. You should ask your folks!"

"Where did it come from? What exactly did it want? Why was it aimed at magic . . . at our people?" Thea continued, undeterred.

Tess was staring at Thea, her eyes only a glitter in the soft light coming into the room through the uncurtained window. "You sound like you know," she said. "What are you saying?"

"Somehow, we dealt with this huge and

dreadful danger that was threatening the entire magical community," Thea said. "But we did it. *We* did it. A bunch of kids from a school for magical discards. And we did it in a way that is considered to be impossible. And it was the only way that it could have been done. The only way to challenge that thing and win was to take it into a place where it did not expect to be challenged, did not expect to lose. When others tried, they used magic, and they *died* for it. Right?"

"I guess," Tess said slowly.

"But I heard you," Magpie said slowly. "I *heard* you, Thea. You spoke to the Whale. You spoke of 'the newest magic.' What did you mean? The computers?"

"Yes, the computers," Thea said. "The only thing that was considered to be totally outside the magical realm—they're inert, they aren't supposed to respond to magic at all. And yet we used one to create something that nobody can deny was a pure enchantment. We opened the road into another world—"

"No, *you* did that," Tess said.

"Thea, I really do hate computers," Magpie said. "I have never understood them, I never wanted to understand them—"

"And Terry and I are supposed to be allergic," Tess murmured. "To *real* magic, anyway."

"But this was real magic," Magpie said. "Just not something that anybody's seen before. They'll have a heap of questions for us before they're done—I saw the look on the principal's face. He doesn't know what we were up to, but he knows we were up to *something*, and he didn't like it."

"What? We were just doing the assignments we were told to do," Tess said, her voice full of aggrieved innocence. "They cannot prove a thing. Wait a minute. Now I'm doing a Thea. Just why, exactly, is this supposed to be such a huge secret? You've just made an enormous breakthrough—computers can be magical, after all—what are you trying to hide?"

"Me," Thea said, her voice very thin. "I think all of this might have been . . . Well, they told me I had chosen not to do magic in this world, my world, the one into which I was born. . . ."

"Who told you that?" Tess said.

"Long story," Magpie said.

"You can tell her tomorrow, Magpie," Thea said. "The point is, the Alphiri knew the magic was there. They came for me before, you know. They knew they were looking for something, but they didn't know what. They never do anything for nothing, so they might simply have decided to play their hand, and see what would happen."

"The *Alphiri*?" Tess said, astonished. "But what did the Alphiri have to do with . . . Wait a minute. . . . You mean to tell me that you think that the Alphiri brought the Nothing here?"

"All I know is that the Alphiri are waiting for me to suddenly turn into . . . into that Double Seventh that I was supposed to be from the cradle and never was," Thea said. "It was magic they were after in our world, and they always went for the strongest bargain that could be made—and if I could be triggered into being everything that they had been led to believe I could be, they wanted that. I have no way of knowing what they want to do with me. But whatever it is, I don't trust it. I don't trust *them*."

"But the Nothing was drawn to magic, and then destroyed the strongest magic that was turned against it," Tess said. "What kind of bargain was that? What could possibly be gained by destroying the very thing you say they wanted? And besides . . . this wasn't aimed at *you*, Thea. It ate up whatever . . . *whoever* . . . was in its path."

"They came to my parents when I was this

tall," Thea said, measuring an improbable toddler-height from the floor with her hand, palm down. "They wanted things, then. But . . . I didn't do what they wanted, what they expected, what they bargained for. And in the meantime . . . there was other magic to be gathered."

"So if you had done what the Alphiri wanted and revealed that you had the magic after all, wouldn't the Nothing have destroyed *you*? Besides, if you did have such magic, what did they think you were doing here in this school?"

"That's always part of the bargain," Thea said mournfully. "That vow of, 'I'll have it, or nobody else will.' And if there's a bargain, you can bet on it that there's an Alphiri somewhere nearby. And anyway . . . we have no idea what the Nothing did with the people it took. Did you see, when we were leaving? On the shore?"

"The ghosts," Magpie whispered.

"Are they still alive? Can they come back?" Tess asked. "Do you think . . . ?"

"I don't know if that Portal leads in both directions," said Thea. "I have no idea what really happened, or where they were taken, but I do think they were prisoners, and now they are free. Who knows? One day they might all find their way back here? But the point is, Tess, *I* did exactly what they wanted me to do. I don't know if it's what they expected, or if they can put a use to it, but they woke it, somehow, or I chose to let it wake up. And they wanted me all along. They offered to buy me from my parents, years ago, when I was still a baby. They were apparently rather taken aback when my dad told them that our people don't sell their children. But Tess . . . my family doesn't know about it yet, about what happened here, to me, to all of us, and I don't want them to. I don't want anyone to know about any of what happened here yesterday. Not until I am more sure of what happens next. Promise me you won't tell. Please."

"Of course," Magpie said sturdily.

Tess hesitated. "But my family will ask . . . ," she began.

"You and Terry at least have an excellent excuse," Thea said. "You guys simply can't talk about it. It is magic, after all."

"This is true," Tess said. "Terry won't be able to open his yap without choking on it."

"And you won't tell?"

"My lips are sealed," Tess said theatrically, kissing her fingers.

"What about Ben?" Magpie whispered.

"He can't stop sneezing long enough to get a word in edgewise," Thea said, her teeth a white gleam in the dark.

"Yeah," Magpie said slowly, as if something had just become clear in her mind. "He *did* say he could smell something, way back, and he couldn't tell what it was. Maybe it was a hint of Alphiri magic, Thea, the little bit that hung around you."

"But that's just it," Thea said. "The Alphiri aren't magic. They don't *have* magic. That's what this whole thing is . . ."

"Ben won't talk," Tess said. "I'll have a word with him in the morning. And besides, he feels awfully guilty about that Whale."

"I feel bad about that, too," Thea said. "But you can let him off that particular hook. The Whale, at least, was a life freely offered."

"He knows that," Magpie said gently.

"You'd better get back to your room," Thea said.

"I guess," said Tess. "Will you pop in and say good-bye before you leave?"

"Sure," Thea said. Tess murmured an almost inaudible good night and sneaked out of the room as carefully and quietly as she had come in.

"So you heard him, too?" Thea said to the darkness after a moment. "The Whale?"

"Yes," Magpie whispered. "Him . . . and that other. Whatever it was that you did, Thea, that dreadful thing was a good enemy to take a stand against. I don't know that you could have done anything different."

"It was you," Thea said. "You and that ancestral magic you held in for so long."

"Thank you for that," Magpie said. "If it never happens again . . . thank you. Maybe in this world I'm just as much of a magidim as always—but now at least I know, I *know* that I can. . . ."

"You've been given the choice, same as me—you can stand in both worlds, that of the Whale Hunt and this one, too, and you can bring the magic back here from the other place. If you want to."

"If I ever get back," Magpie said. "If you're right and it's a computer thing, then maybe I'll never return. But just that once . . ."

"Maybe it is a computer thing," Thea said. "I just haven't figured it all out yet. But I'm pretty sure about one thing—the five of us, we're in.

Whatever it is that we've stumbled into, we did it together, and I know that without you there in the Hunt, I would have failed. I think we will always have the ability to step across that line. It's like . . . You know how you sometimes just smell a smell and the entire memory it evokes is with you?"

"Yeah," Magpie said.

"Well, I think it's like that. That first time . . . every one of us brought something in, something special to ourselves. Terry the words, the *sound*—although he never did say it out loud, but his were the words that started it. Me with the pictures that the words brought up in my head. You with the textures that belonged in there. Ben with the smells, Tess with the taste. You see what I'm getting at? It needed all five senses for the first experience, but all any one of us has to do is remember one aspect of it—*our* aspect, the sense we brought in—and the rest will come. We're all in this."

"But I hate computers," Magpie said again.

"But from here on," Thea said, "all you have to do is type in a set of directions."

"I'll miss you," Magpie said unexpectedly.

"I'll be back," Thea said. "Besides, you'll have

my bed to use to shelter a pregnant cat, or something. Just promise me, no skunks."

The sound of shared laughter floated them into sleep.

2.

There was a short and pointed but inconclusive interrogation by the principal the next morning, before Zoë was allowed to take Thea away. Afterward, Zoë accompanied Thea back to the residence to get her luggage. Thea glanced up to the window of her room as she stepped away from the front door of the residence and saw Magpie's solemn face pressed to the window. Thea smiled, waved, and then quickly turned away, slipping into the passenger seat just as Zoë slid into the driver's side and began buckling on her seat belt in silence. Still in silence, Zoë turned the key, put the car into gear, pulled away from the redbrick residence hall and out toward the main gate of the campus.

Clad in a pair of jeans and a sheepskin vest over a wine-colored red turtleneck, her hair pulled back into a simple ponytail, Zoë looked more like a fellow Academy student than anybody's maiden aunt. But her hands were curled tightly around the steering wheel as she drove, and her expression was not that of a careless teenager. Instead, rarely for Zoë, she had turned into a somewhat grim-faced adult.

"Thanks, Aunt Zoë," Thea said in a small voice, grateful for the tacit support that Zoë had given her so far but suddenly unsure of her welcome.

"I don't much like the taste of lies," Zoë said abruptly. "Are you going to tell me what really happened?"

"It's a long story," Thea said.

"We have a few long boring hours in the car ahead of us," Zoë said. "You can start whenever you're ready."

Zoë had always been Thea's ally, her friend, her confidante and co-conspirator. But Thea had told Zoë nothing of her experiences with Cheveyo, and now it was hard to know where to begin. Put into words, it sounded improbable. She made a couple of stumbling false starts, but once she hit her stride the whole story came tumbling out—Cheveyo, Grandmother Spider, choices made in several different worlds, the Alphiri and the Faele, the crossing over into a strange new virtual world—all of it.

Zoë did not interrupt. When Thea lapsed into silence, Zoë stayed quiet until Thea picked up the thread of the story and continued.

When Thea was finally done, she sank into silence and sat with her hands folded tightly in her lap and her eyes downcast. Zoë finally let out her breath in a deep sigh.

"You do know this is way beyond me?" she said. "There will have to be a higher authority brought in. It's just too big to let lie."

"But I know I can trust you," Thea said. "I don't know who else I can trust."

Zoë was shaking her head lightly, as though trying to clear it.

"If it was not you telling me this, and if I didn't know, somehow, deep inside me, that you were telling the truth—this would be the tallest tale I'd ever heard. Computers . . . ?" She continued shaking her head. "This could make a *lot* of waves. Everyone thinks computers are so safe, such secure repositories for Ars Magica stuff. But now, if this is true, it's anybody's game again. You should have told the principal at least some of this, Thea."

"Would he have let me back into the school?" Thea asked pragmatically.

"What was that?" Zoë turned her head fractionally to stare at her niece.

"The Academy is supposed to be warded against stuff like this. Against people like me. The only reason I was there in the first place is because I *couldn't*. And now . . ."

"You're afraid he won't take you back?" Zoë questioned. "You're *that* fond of the place?"

"It isn't that," Thea said painfully. "Well, I have friends there now, but it's just that, as long as I'm there, I'm safe. I'm safe, because the only reason I could possibly be there is that I can't do any magic. So as long as I am there, I am not what the Alphiri want. And as long as they think that, they won't come after me."

Zoë was shaking her head again. "It's that part," she said, "that I cannot believe. Thea, there were *no* Faele at your cradle bringing gifts." She paused for a moment. "That I know of," she said at length, almost as an afterthought. Zöe had, in fact, asked—and while Paul had been emphatic that no Faele had been near baby Thea, Ysabeau had done no more than shake her head and then refuse to meet Zoë's eyes in a way that was now haunting her younger sister. "And if that part isn't true . . ." Zoë gnawed on her lower lip in frustration. "How do you know the Alphiri are really pursuing you? What on earth would they want with you?"

"They can smell profit," Thea said. "Somewhere."

"No," Zoë said with the ghost of a smile, the first that Thea had seen on her face since her aunt had arrived at the Academy, "that would be me. And profit can smell nasty enough, trust me, and leave an aftertaste to match. I don't think the Alphiri sense it in that way. But anyway . . . let's just get on home. I'll be far happier when you're protected in your own house."

"But my parents . . . ," Thea began uneasily.

"Thea, I already phoned them," Zoë said. "They *know*—they know something, anyway, and you won't be able to keep it from them forever. Besides, you need someone to look out for you, and who better to watch your back? But you probably shouldn't tell your brothers too much, whatever the temptation."

Thea held on for a moment to a delicious thought: the expression on Anthony's face if she told the truth, the sense of deep satisfaction that she would finally cease to be inferior to the ham-fisted Frankie. . . . But Zoë was right, of course, and Thea let it go. "And the school?"

"You may be right, that might be the safest place for you to be for now," Zoë said thoughtfully. "But don't make that kind of assumption yourself. There are people you *can* trust whom you should talk to, and they've had far more experience at this than you. *Computers.*" Zoë shook her head again.

"I wish I could show you," Thea said, her eyes sparkling now, excited at last in the presence of someone she trusted absolutely. "But I'm just me, right now. The same magidim that I always was. Until I can get a computer to help me."

Zoë's face wore a strange expression, as if debating something with herself. In the end she heaved a deep sigh and allowed her lips to curl into a small smile.

"There's a laptop," she said, "in the back."

"You mean it?" Thea breathed.

"You wanted to show me. So show me."

Thea unbuckled her seat belt and swiveled to reach behind her on the back seat, bringing out a leather laptop case. She extracted the computer, balancing it on her knees, and toggled the ON switch.

"Seat belt," Zoë said conversationally, without taking her eyes off the road.

"What's the password?" Thea asked, confronted with a dialogue box as she fumbled with her seat belt.

Zoë grinned. "*Believe,*" she said. "I never knew how appropriate it would turn out to be."

The dialogue box winked off as Thea typed in the password, and Zoë's software icons popped onto the screen. Thea selected the word processor, and began typing something with her right hand, using the left to steady the computer in her lap.

Nothing seemed to happen, not even when Thea stopped typing and simply sat quietly in the passenger seat, her eyes resting on the line of fir trees that marched beside the road, a half page of text on the screen in front of her. Zoë let the silence continue for a while, but finally her curiosity got the better of her.

"Well?" she said.

Thea had not written much—just enough to bring her to what Grandmother Spider had called the boundary between her worlds. Now, as Zoë spoke, she stepped across it—reached out with one hand into that other place, where she *could*, and picked up a strand of color from the gray sky, a thin string of dark green from the trees, a ribbon of bright yellow from the car that they had been following for some miles now. They hung from the fingers of her right hand for a moment, the colors of her world, and Thea realized that her heart was beating fast, that she was close to tears.

This was the first time she had done something like this *here*, in the world where she was born, in front of someone she loved.

She wove the strands into a ribbon of light, cradled the shimmering thing in the palm of her hand, held it out to her aunt.

Zoë's eyes were luminous. "All my life," she whispered, "in my mind, in my soul, I have known that light and color were something you could touch, you could feel. I've never ever seen it done . . . until now. Thea, do you have any idea how utterly impossible any of this is?"

Thea unraveled the light ribbon, reluctantly, releasing the strands to the places from which she had taken them. For a long moment she hesitated over the words on the screen, but then she sighed, erased what she had written, closed out the program.

She was just Thea again. And light was light,

untouchable, outside of her.

"Maybe being impossible is what it means, in the end," Thea said.

"Hmm?" said Zoë, her head inclined. "What do you mean?"

"Aunt Zoë . . . the other Double Seventh children, the ones that came before . . . what were their gifts?"

"I don't remember the specifics, quite honestly," murmured Zoë. "Throughout history it's always been something pretty powerful. But it's always been something much like their parents' gifts were, only much more intense. But you . . . you seem to be breaking new ground, if that's what you mean." She reached out and ruffled Thea's hair. "So—you're the Double Seventh at last, in fact as well as in name," she said. "However weird the road that got you there."

"They still can't tell anybody . . . ," Thea began, and then trailed off, staring out of the window into the distance somewhere.

"But they would know," Zöe said softly, casting a swift and understanding sideways glance.

"Dad would know," Thea said. She wasn't even aware herself of the way her chin lifted a little at those words, finally having something to bring to her father that would make him truly proud of her. Zöe noticed and could not suppress a small sigh. "I can finally tell Dad," Thea continued, oblivious of her aunt's reaction. "He'll know. Even if the rest of the world still thinks I'll never be more than a magidim."

"Only until you get a hold of one of *those*," Zoë said with a grin, glancing at the computer in Thea's lap.

Thea followed the glance, and her fingers stroked the computer lightly.

"I think I know just what to ask my parents to give me for Christmas," she said quietly, and smiled.

Read on for a sneak peak at

WORLDWEAVERS: SPELLSPAM

1.

The first hint of serious trouble came, as trouble always does, unlooked for, stealthily, catching everyone by surprise. It was the day that LaTasha Jackson suddenly turned into an Anatomy teacher's aid.

Thea was engrossed in a book about the social customs of chimpanzees when a bloodcurdling scream rent the air from the north corner of the library, where the computers slated for student use were situated. Thea jumped, dropping her book on the desk with a thump and losing her place, pushing her chair back on its castors to peer around the edges of her cubicle.

Dozens of other heads were popping out from other cubicles, watching in appalled horror as something ghastly leaped back from a computer screen, overturning a chair and sending it flying, and raced down the length of the library and out through the double doors at the far end.

The only reason Thea even remotely recognized this apparition was LaTasha's trademark hairstyle, dozens of tiny braids finished off with trade beads in garish shades of pink and mustard yellow. The face beneath those braids, however, was something else indeed.

She looks like she's been skinned! was the first thought that came swimming into Thea's astonished mind. And then she shuddered as she realized that this was precisely what LaTasha was. *Skinned.* Or at least looking like a reasonably good imitation of it. *But there was no blood,* Thea thought, frowning. *Surely there should have been . . . but no . . . there was just . . .*

That was it, in a nutshell. Instead of LaTasha's skin, which typically was the color of coffee lightened with a touch of cream, her face was a complicated mass of red muscle, striated bands coming down from her temples to wrap around her mouth, neat folds across her nose and cupping her chin, round orbs around her alarmingly protruding eyeballs, with startling and somewhat unnerving glimpses of stark bone structure underneath it all. Her hands, held out in front of her, looked the same way—a naked, tangled mass of tendon and sinew. But no blood. It was like her skin had just gone see-through, somehow, revealing the building blocks of the body that lay beneath.

There was a swelling of noise in the library as students surged out of their chairs, clustered in tight little knots, the librarian on duty frantically whispering something into a telephone, her hand cupped protectively around the mouthpiece.

For some reason it was only Thea who backed away from the pandemonium and edged almost furtively toward the computer LaTasha had been using.

An e-mail was open on the screen, an e-mail that LaTasha should have known better than to open—anything addressed to person@thisaddress.com should have been immediately suspect, at the very least as an advertisement, unwanted junk mail, spam. But what followed was not merely spam:

Having trouble keeping your skin blemish-free? Troubled by zits, lines, old scars? Try our incredible product for 30 days for FREE! We guarantee that we will leave your skin clearer than you could ever have dreamed of. . . .

LaTasha was fourteen years old, and painfully self-conscious of the imperfections of her skin, which was cursed with large pores and periodic zit infestations that made her look like she was coming down with the measles—and that was in addition to an unfortunate scar left behind by her brush with the real measles, which she had had as a toddler. It sat, a small but (to LaTasha) eye-wateringly obvious pit, underneath and to the outside of her left eye.

"It makes my eye droop," she had often complained to friends. "Look, it makes me look like a Saint Bernard puppy, all mournful and woebegone. Who'd want to date *that*? They probably all think I'm going to bore them silly with family tragedies. Like I'd had a twin who was stolen by the Faele or something and never came home. Oh, it's hopeless!"

Perfect skin. The thing had offered perfect skin. That would have been irresistible to someone like LaTasha, who blamed hers for all the injustices in her life—if she could only get perfect skin, she'd be happy, she knew she'd be happy.

Something surfaced briefly in Thea's mind, and then submerged again before she'd had a chance to grab at it. Instead, she sighed and reached out instinctively to clear the screen, as though that e-mail could be used as some sort of evidence against poor LaTasha. Her hand hovered above the red X that would close the e-mail screen; then she hesitated.

The word was *clear*. Not *perfect*.

"Clearer than you could ever have dreamed of," Thea whispered as she hastily clicked on the red X. "Oh, my fur and whiskers . . ."

Clear.

Transparent.

"But that is a spell," Thea muttered to herself, frowning.

She lifted her head to look back across the library, where a couple of staff members were restoring order to the chaos of milling students. The librarian herself, still cradling the telephone receiver, was staring straight back at Thea and at the now-blank computer on the desk beside her. With a sinking feeling that she was still unable to properly articulate, Thea bent her head to hide the sudden color in her cheeks and inched away from the computer desk toward the sanctuary of the stacks.

Everyone knew, of course, that computers

were impervious to magic. Computers were where magic was *stored*, because it could do no harm there, and besides, this was the Wandless Academy, which was both magicless and shielded. There could not have been a spell that broke those two defenses—there could not have possibly been such a spell. And yet, Thea had seen the evidence streak out of the library before her very eyes. And *other* people's eyes. And obviously LaTasha herself had been affected. Thea paused for a moment to consider how *she* would have reacted if she had happened to glance at her hands on the computer keyboard and had seen something that looked more like it belonged on a butcher's block or an anatomy dissection board than the familiar limbs she was used to.

It had to have been a very effective illusion spell . . . and it had been transmitted by computer.

Which, of course, was impossible.

Computers couldn't do magic.

Don't miss the exciting second book in the Worldweavers trilogy!

Praise for the Worldweavers series:

"Entertainingly different, yet engagingly familiar."

— *Locus* magazine

"A fascinating premise." — *Realms of Fantasy* magazine

"Suspenseful and engrossing." —*Kirkus Reviews*